MUD PIES & FAMILY TIES

A LOVEBIRD CAFÉ NOVEL

DYLANN CRUSH

Thanks for picking up this copy of *Mud Pies & Family Ties*! If you'd like to go back to where the series begins, grab your FREE copy of *Lemon Tarts & Stolen Hearts,* the prequel novella for the Lovebird Café series!

For a FREE copy of *Lemon Tarts & Stolen Hearts*, click here! (www.dylanncrush.com/signup)

To the romance authors who have come before me and paved the way for others to do what we love...
thank you!

1

DUSTIN

*W*hoever said there's no such thing as bad publicity must have been misfiring without all of his spark plugs. I sat across the desk from my high-paid Hollywood agent, waiting for him to take a break from the long-winded verbal ass-whupping he'd been delivering for the past ten minutes. I'd never seen him so riled. Spittle flew from his lips. The more worked up he got, the more his cheeks began to match the color of the Bloody Mary sitting on the edge of his desk.

Finally, the onslaught stopped. This was my chance. "Hey Mav, I get that you're a little upset."

"Upset? I was upset when you drove off the set of that television pilot last year. And I was upset when you didn't walk the red carpet at your last premier."

"Okay, okay." I shrugged, wincing as my injured shoulder rose and fell. "What do you want me to do? Call and apologize? Send a bottle of bourbon?"

Mav looked at me, his mouth hanging open like a slack-jawed baboon.

"What? You think I need to send a single malt instead?"

His jaw snapped shut and he waved his hands in front of his face like he couldn't bear the sight of me. "You need to get out of town for a while."

"Don't you think you're over reacting a little?"

"Dustin, you sent America's favorite late night talk show host to the ER." Mav pounded a fist on the edge of his desk, making his drink clatter. "During his broadcast."

"It was an accident." I clenched my teeth. "I've done that stunt a thousand times, ten thousand times. There must have been water on the stage or something."

Mav ran a hand through his stylishly cropped and colored hair as he began to pace. "Where can you go? There's got to be a benefit or fundraiser somewhere I can send you."

Seemed like a good time to mention the email I got yesterday from my high school back home. "I got an invite to a baseball field dedication."

"Where?" Mav stopped in front of me. "Please tell me it's far away."

"Missouri." Even saying it out loud made my heart jack-knife in my chest.

He steepled his fingers under his chin, his thinking pose. "Yes, Missouri. That should work. When can you leave?"

"Wait a sec. You really think I need to get out of LA for a while?" I could understand laying low. But leaving town? "I've got projects in the works. I can't just walk away."

"Yes, you can." Mav nodded, that familiar glint in his eye. The one that meant I was going to do whatever the hell he told me to. "In addition to garnering some good publicity, you need a break."

"My shoulder's fine. I saw the doc this morning and he said two to three weeks max."

Mav shook his head. "You fucked up so bad last night I

haven't even had a chance to tell you. The executive producer for that movie we've been talking about made time for drinks with me yesterday."

"And?" He'd better have good news. We'd been working together for the past ten years and he knew better than to jerk me around.

"And they want you. Bad."

"I knew it." My chest expanded as I took in a satisfying breath. "I told you I had a good feeling about that job."

"You did and you were right. But—"

"Come on." No buts. Buts were bad. Buts could make or break a deal in a flash. "What's the hold up?"

"You're your own worst enemy, my friend. They won't sign on the dotted line until the heat from the late show incident blows over and you're cleared by their doctor."

"Their doctor doesn't know his ass from a hole in the ground. I only need a few weeks to heal. You know that's how I work, how I've always worked."

"Ass from a hole in the ground? That's clever. Are you finished?"

Most of the suits I worked with would have thrown me out already. That's what I liked about Mav. We got each other. He could listen to me rant and rave for twenty minutes then yank me back into reality. Granted, I paid him well to do that, but still—he was Team Dustin all the way. He'd proven that time and again.

"Yeah, I'm done."

"Good. Then shut the hell up and listen. You're going to take that little trip to the baseball field dedication in Arkansas—"

"Missouri."

"Whatever. Fish in a river, feed a goat, get great huge

gulps of that fresh country air. Their doc said he won't even take a look at you for twelve weeks."

"That's bullshit." I slapped my palm on the desk. "My guy said my shoulder would be better in two weeks, three max."

"Yeah, and their doc says twelve." Mav sighed, his telltale sign of being about to enter the part of the conversation where he'd pretend to take my side and then bust my balls in the end. "I know you've got your heart set—"

"Leave my heart out of it, okay? I'm one of the only guys who can do the kind of stunts they're asking for."

"You're right. That's why they're willing to wait until you're good to go."

"What am I going to do for three months?"

"Like I said, breathe in smog-less air, get out on the water, catch up with your high school sweetheart. I don't give a flying fuck what you do, Dustin. Just don't show your face around here until the media's found someone else to crucify and your shoulder's at one-hundred percent."

My breath left my lungs in a huff. "It's not fair. Two weeks, that's all I need—"

"Of all the people I work with, you know the last thing this business would ever be considered is fair." He paused for effect, letting that obvious fact simmer between us. "I might be able to convince him to take a look at you in eight. But you've got to work on that shoulder. Find a PT or someone who can help you get loose. Kiss your mama. Eat some grits. Hell, maybe even get yourself laid."

I wanted to argue, to push back and tell him I'd be back on the lot after Memorial Day, just like we talked about. But it was no use. My future, my fortune, and my career, were at the mercy of public opinion and some fresh-out-of-med school doctor who had no idea he'd just sealed my fate.

"Fine." Mom had been begging me to come home for a visit, but I never seemed to have the time. At least that's what I told her. And what I tried to tell myself. Maybe a quick trip home would make up for the fact I'd stayed away for so long.

Mav grunted, picked up his drink, and pointed toward the door. He wasn't much for small talk, but I couldn't complain about his management skills. He was the only reason I hadn't had to tuck tail and crawl back to Swallow Springs, Missouri, when I'd made the initial trip out to LA. I'd had stars in my eyes and a chip on my shoulder the size of the rusted-out Bronco I'd borrowed from my uncle to make the sixteen-hundred-plus mile drive.

The Bronco didn't make it, but I did. Once I caught Mav's attention, he'd ensured I had my pick of motorcycle stunt jobs. I'd learned early on to shut up and let him take care of the details. That's what I paid him for, and that's what he did best.

So, as much as it irked me to think about sitting around twiddling my thumbs for the next two to three months, I knew he'd make sure it was worth my while in the end. And maybe, just maybe, this was a sign that the time had come to face my past.

LESS THAN FORTY-EIGHT hours later I'd almost completed my sixteen-hundred-mile road trip, and my ass hadn't ached this bad in years. Not since I'd committed to making a living by straddling the seat of anything with two-wheels and an engine.

At least I *had* been making a career on the seat of my motorcycle, until I'd botched that, too. I shifted in the bucket seat behind the wheel of my truck and flipped through the satellite radio stations, trying to find something to take my mind off the sorry situation I'd crashed into. And when I said crashed, I meant literally *crashed*. The mention of my name made my finger pause on the button.

"The internet is exploding with images of last year's Extreme Games winner, Dustin Jarrett's now-immortalized wipeout on the set of Bobby Bordell's late night talk show earlier this week. Rumor has it Bobby's still being treated at Cedars-Sinai Hospital, but should make a full recovery. Bordell was injured when a motorcycle stunt by Jarrett didn't go as planned. If you missed it, we've got the replay on our website at—"

I pushed the off button, silencing the radio. Thank God, Bordell would be okay. The fallout from my TV appearance had been bad—bad enough that Mav had me slinking halfway across the country to hide out at my mom's place. But at least now I knew I hadn't permanently injured America's favorite late night talk show host.

I'd been on the road for close to twenty-eight hours. Would've been less but I had to pull over for a couple of quick catnaps. I'd forgotten how long of a drive it was from Los Angeles to the tiny part of western Missouri where I'd grown up. Apart from having to change a flat outside of Albuquerque, it had been a relatively uneventful trip.

Finally, the eyesore of a water tower that sat on the outskirts of town appeared in the distance. I'd never been so happy to see the ugly pea-green monstrosity as I was right now. It towered over the town of Swallow Springs, Missouri. Sat two-hundred-and-twenty-seven feet off the ground. I knew that for a fact since I'd spent many late summer nights attempting to scale it and leave my temporary mark with a can of spray paint.

Once I reached the center of downtown, the house I grew up in would be another twenty-five minute drive. I'd drained my coffee over an hour ago and hadn't eaten since I'd run through a drive-thru last night. Might be better to fuel up on caffeine and fill my stomach before seeing my mom.

As I drove down Main Street, the bright neon sign of the Lovebird Café caught my eye. My stomach growled. I could almost smell the fresh fried chicken and homemade biscuits I'd enjoyed so many times in the past. Bright hanging baskets filled with pink and white flowers hung from the awning in front, begging me to stop in.

Another half hour wouldn't make much of a difference in my long-overdue return home. My mouth watered in anticipation. Just imagining a platter of blueberry pancakes or one of their famous cinnamon rolls had me pressing on the brake.

By the time I managed to park my truck and the trailer I'd hauled behind it, my belly groaned and griped like I hadn't eaten in ages. I glanced up, running my gaze over the loopy letters advertising the weekly special at the Lovebird Café. Mav was right. Maybe I was due for a little R&R. And I'd start with a giant platter of steak and eggs. Might even add on a Danish or two.

If I had to be back in Swallow Springs, the café was as good as any place to make my first appearance. Odds were no one would even recognize me. And hopefully none of them watched late night TV. I'd been gone fifteen years. Things around here had to have changed in that amount of time.

I was counting on it.

HARMONY

"*M*om, come quick. It's an emergency!"

If I had a dollar—or even a quarter—for every time my son, Liam, summoned me for an "emergency" that turned out to be nothing but an attempt to snag my attention, I wouldn't be waiting tables at the Lovebird Café. I took my time responding. First, I topped off the coffee mugs of the two regulars sitting at the counter, then turned to slide the carafe onto the hot plate.

"What do you think it is this time?" Mr. Blevins, a widowed, retired math teacher from the high school, leaned his elbows onto the counter.

"Who knows?" I shrugged, rounding the counter before heading toward the front door.

My thirteen-year-old son stood on the sidewalk in front of the café. With his fists on his hips, he appeared to be yelling at someone or something across the street. Since we'd moved to Swallow Springs a few weeks ago, he'd done nothing but cause trouble. The move was supposed to provide a safe place for him, far away from the rough crowd he'd gotten involved with out in LA.

"What's going on?" I pushed through the door, causing the overhead bell to jingle. "You'd better not be picking a fight."

"Come quick." Liam grabbed my hand, dragging me around the corner to the back of the parking lot where I'd left the old pick-up truck my cousin Robbie had loaned me.

"I'm in the middle of a shift. You'd better stop right now and tell me what's going on." I planted my feet, not willing to budge until Liam filled me in.

"That douche Rodney—"

"Liam. I won't have you talking like that." Based on everything else that had been going on, his language ought to be the least of my concerns, but I couldn't help but go into auto-correct mom mode.

"He's a dick, Mom."

"Liam." Teeth clenched together, I crossed my arms over my chest. "Language."

"Fine. D-bag Rodney and his friends were chasing something down the sidewalk. Whatever it was ran back here and under the hood. I think they were trying to hurt it." Liam set his palm on the hood of the truck.

My heart warmed. Liam might cause trouble from time to time, but he had a tendency to stand up for anyone and anything weaker than him if he sensed an injustice.

"Looks like you scared the boys away. I'm sure whatever it is will crawl down and run back into the woods. You'd better get going or you're going to be late for school." I pulled him into my side. He gave me a half-hearted hug in return. I counted my blessings every day that he was still willing to hug me, even if it was half-assed.

"But what if it's stuck?"

"It got in there, it can get out, okay?"

"Are you sure?"

Technically I had no idea. Before a few weeks ago my only regular interaction with wildlife was limited to shooing away the nagging seagulls at Ventura Beach. But in the time we'd been in Swallow Springs, we'd already had run-ins with a scraggly rooster and a persistent albino squirrel that regularly raided the birdfeeder I'd managed to hang in the front yard of our temporary living quarters.

"By the time I'm done with my shift, I'm sure it will be long gone." I put an arm over Liam's shoulders. If he got any taller it would be impossible to continue to do that without rising onto my tiptoes. My heart twinged. If his father could see him now… would he be amazed at what a little man our son had turned into? I shook the thought away. Liam's dad had no right to know anything about his son. He'd made a different choice years ago.

"You promise to look before you leave? Just in case?" Liam spun to face me. The look of concern on his face begged for reassurance.

"Yep. Pinky swear." I held out my pinky and he wrapped his little finger around mine, sealing my promise with the gesture we'd used since he was just a kid.

"All right."

"See you at three, okay?" During his limited time at the Swallow Springs Middle School, he'd already been banned from the bus which meant he had to ride into work with me in the mornings then walk the few blocks to school. It also meant I had to stick around to pick him up after, unless I wanted to make another hour-long trip back and forth into town.

"See ya." Liam skulked down the sidewalk, leaving me to wonder if I'd made the right decision by pulling him away from the only place he'd ever known.

"Everything okay?" My boss, Cassie, joined me.

"Yeah. He was defending some sort of animal that might have crawled under the hood of the truck."

"Did he say what it was?"

"No, he didn't get a good look at it. He said those kids were chasing it. Rodney somebody."

"Yeah, he's a troublemaker." Cassie shook her head.

"Do you think I was wrong to bring Liam here? What if he never fits in?"

Cassie put an arm around my shoulder and gave me a squeeze. "He's a good kid. He'll figure it out."

"I hope so."

"You sure you can handle things here for a bit? I've got to go drop off that box lunch delivery." Cassie held the door open as we re-entered the café.

"Yeah, I'll be fine." I'd been at this job for a few weeks, but this was the first time I'd been left alone to wait on customers. We didn't get a huge weekday morning rush, and it was too early for the lunch crowd yet. With only a couple of regulars manning stools at the counter, I'd be fine until Cassie returned.

"All right, then. I'll see you later." Cassie grabbed a huge bag off the counter.

I held the door for her as she passed through. With any luck I wouldn't even see another customer until lunchtime. I poured myself a mug of coffee from the carafe sitting under the massive commercial machine, wishing for an almond milk chai latte instead.

The bell over the door jangled, pulling my attention from the steaming source of caffeine. A guy paused in the entryway of the small diner. Couldn't he tell we had a seat yourself policy?

I grabbed the carafe and a clean mug before pushing

through the swinging half-door into the main room. "You can sit anywhere."

His gaze met mine. Green eyes, somewhere between the bright shade of my malachite crystals and the dusky green of moldavite, seemed to evaluate me. "Is this okay back here?" He pointed to a booth in the corner—the same booth I usually hid in when it was time for my break.

"Yeah, that's fine." I followed him, taking in the breadth of his shoulders and the twisted black ink covering his forearms. "Want coffee?"

"Please."

I set the cup on the table and poured. If I'd learned nothing else during my brief time waiting tables at the Lovebird, it was that everyone wanted coffee and they wanted it as soon as possible. The first time I'd offered a customer a choice of coffee or tea, they'd stared at me like I'd grown another head and asked the question in ancient Greek.

"Thanks." He picked up the mug and lifted it toward his mouth. My gaze followed. As he swallowed, I gulped in a breath. A chunk of his shoulder-length hair fell toward his face. He reached up to tuck it behind his ear. Something about him looked familiar, but I struggled to figure out why. I'd definitely remember seeing someone like him if he'd come into the diner before.

"Um, do you need a menu?" I asked.

"They still make that steak and eggs platter?" He rested a muscled arm along the back of the booth. The twisty ink followed a path from his wrist past his elbow, disappearing into the sleeve of his T-shirt.

"What?"

"Steak and eggs. A T-bone as big as your face with fried eggs on top and a huge side of buttered grits. They still have that on the menu?"

More like a heart attack on a plate. I couldn't get past the way the folks in Swallow Springs loved their country cooking. Cassie made it as fresh and healthy as she could, but still, it was a miracle some of the regulars hadn't collapsed of heart failure decades ago.

"How about a side of fresh fruit or some wilted spinach to go along with it?" If anyone were grading my efforts, I'd get an A+ for trying to introduce some healthier options to the diner crowd.

"No thanks. Just the grease today." He took another sip of coffee while I stood there, totally mesmerized by the way he managed to make taking a sip of coffee look super sexy.

"Harmony?" Mr. Blevins called me from across the room, snapping me out of my trance.

"Be right there." I whipped the pencil out from behind my ear to jot the order down on my notepad. "Anything else?"

"Just keep the coffee coming." He slid his mug toward me, already ready for a refill.

I topped it off before retreating toward the safety of the kitchen, stopping to check on my two favorite customers on the way. "What can I do for you, Mr. Blevins?"

"I told you, hon, just call me Frank. Lou and I wouldn't mind splitting a piece of that coffee cake you've got in the front case over there."

I bit back a grin. They played this game at least twice a week, at least since I'd been in town. "You sure one piece will be big enough to share?"

"Oh, I don't know. What do you think, Lou?" Frank nudged his friend with his elbow. "Maybe we ought to get our own."

I set the coffee down on the counter. "Two pieces coming right up."

"If you insist." Lou leaned across the counter. "Who was that you were talking to over there?"

I looked up, seeking out the stranger in the back booth. "I don't know. You think he's from around here?"

Lou and Frank tilted their heads together, whispering back and forth.

"Well?" I slid a plate in front of each of them, a generous slice of coffee cake on each.

"Looks to me like the Jarrett boy," Frank said, picking up his fork.

"Who?" I refilled their mugs while sneaking another glance at the man who'd taken over my booth.

"Dustin Jarrett. Used to live outside of town," Lou mumbled. "Left to go make movies in Hollywood."

"Hollywood?" I rose to my tiptoes to get a better look. The guy definitely had the looks for the big screen. "Really? Would I have seen him in anything?"

Frank snickered. "You might have seen him on Bobby Bordell's show earlier this week. He was supposed to do a burnout on his bike but lost control and took out the house band and Bobby."

"On a bike?" I asked.

"He does stunts," Lou said. "Motorcycles and such. Haven't seen him around here in years, though."

"Hmm." I shot one more glance at the back corner before heading into the kitchen to drop off the order ticket. That's probably why he looked familiar. Liam had posters of motorcycles hanging on his walls and was always watching stunt videos. I'd have to ask him if he knew of someone with the last name Jarrett.

While I waited for Cassie's new-hire, Ryder, to fry the steak and eggs, I sized up the giant commercial coffee machine. Cassie had shown me a half dozen times how to brew a fresh pot, but it still hadn't clicked. I took a new filter out of the cabinet and reached for the handle of the basket. As I pulled it toward me, brown liquid flowed out of the machine, leaking onto the counter and dripping onto the floor.

"Oh no." I tried to shove the basket into the slot, but it wouldn't go back.

"What are you doing over there?" Ryder asked.

"Nothing. Everything's fine." I tried to fill my voice with confidence, a difficult task as steaming hot coffee raced toward my hand. With a final push, the basket clicked into place. I'd forgotten to check which side was still brewing. Now I had coffee on the floor, the counter, and down the front of my apron.

"Order up." Ryder tapped on the bell. I dabbed at the coffee trailing down my front with a paper towel.

"Got it." I nabbed the plate from under the warming station and snagged the half-full pot of coffee off the burner.

As I approached the table, the man unrolled his silver-ware and slid the paper napkin onto his lap. Somehow that tiny gesture instilled a new measure of confidence in my serving ability.

"Here you go. Steak and eggs and I brought you more coffee, too." I set the plate on the table in front of him before leaning over to fill his mug.

"Did you have an accident in the kitchen?"

"What?" I stood abruptly, causing the stream of coffee to flow away from the cup, slosh onto the table and dribble into his lap.

"Sweet mother of..." His knees bucked up. The platter of steak and eggs flew into the air before it clattered back onto the table. "Aw, shit."

"Oh my gosh, I'm so sorry." As I slammed the pot down

on the table, the carafe cracked. Coffee went everywhere. I grabbed a stack of napkins and swabbed at the spill, wiping up the traces of coffee from the edge of the table then dabbing at the growing wet spot on his thigh.

"I've got it." His hand closed around mine, making me realize I'd just been rubbing my hand over a stranger's groin.

Heat flooded my system. Flames of embarrassment scorched my cheeks as I wrenched my hand away from his. "I'm so sorry. I don't know what happened. I—"

"How about some more napkins?" he asked.

"Absolutely. Right away." I fled to the kitchen where I pulled an entire sleeve of paper towels from the storage cabinet.

By the time I returned to his table, he'd sopped up as much of the coffee mess as he could. I handed him a stack of paper towels and gathered the dripping mess in my hands. His pulse ticked along a vein on his neck. Based on the way his jaw set, clenched and tense, I figured it would be best to leave the man to eat in peace. He held his hand out, flexing his fingers. A patch of angry red skin covered the area between his thumb and pointer finger.

"You've got a burn." I held the soggy towels against my apron. "Let me grab something. I'll be right back."

"It's fine," he called after me, but I'd already raced across the room and pushed through the doors into the kitchen.

I tossed the towels in the trash. My purse was in the office. I always carried a small kit of my oils with me, just in case something like this happened. Armed with my makeshift homeopathic medical kit, I hustled back to the table.

"Here, let me put a little lavender oil on it." Before he could argue with me, I'd uncapped the small bottle and cradled his hand in mine, letting a few precious drops drip onto his hand.

"What the hell is that for?" His brows knit together, drawing my attention to the furrow creasing his forehead.

Once upon a time I might have smoothed the lines away. I couldn't stand to see anyone suffer, no matter how small and insignificant their pain might be. But time and life experience had taught me that not everyone was a willing recipient of my concern. This man looked like he'd experienced his own lessons in the school of hard knocks, and wouldn't be so open to my healing touch.

"Lavender oil. Should help it heal faster."

He gently pulled his hand away. "It's just a little burn."

"Let me know if I can get you anything else." Poised to retreat, I snagged the broken carafe of coffee.

"I think you've done enough." He nodded toward his mug. "Although, if you manage to figure out how to work that machine, maybe you could bring me a refill without a bunch of grounds in it?"

A wave of panic rolled up from my gut, through my chest as I noticed the clumps of dark coffee grounds amid the mess of broken glass and towels. "I'm sorry. I'll bring a fresh pot right away."

"That would be great, thanks."

I waited, not sure if he'd say anything else. When he picked up his knife and fork I considered it a dismissal, and retreated to the safety of the kitchen. Why had I thought this would be a good idea? I'd never waited tables in my life. But things had changed. The life I'd known before had taken a turn, and if I needed to learn how to be the best damn waitress in the world in order to create a safe place for me and my son, I'd figure out a way to do it.

As I dumped the goopy mix of towels, glass and grounds

into the trash, I reconsidered my goals. Maybe becoming the best waitress in the world was too lofty of an aspiration. At the moment I'd settle for becoming the best waitress in the tiny town of Swallow Springs, Missouri. Competition was next to none. I should be able to at least handle that. Or die of embarrassment trying.

Fortified with resolve, I turned my attention to the huge coffee maker. "Let's do this, you shrew."

3

DUSTIN

I slid my wallet out of my back pocket and set it on the table, ready for the check. I knew things would have changed since the last time I'd set foot in Swallow Springs, but at least the steak and eggs at the café had remained the same. We used to come here at least a couple times a week. Mom made such a big deal out of dragging us to town on Sundays. If my sister, Scarlett, and I made it through church without complaining, then Dad would treat us to breakfast at the diner.

Those were the good old days. The days before my life went to shit. I let out a sigh. I'd stuffed my belly, had my fill of caffeine, and given myself a while to acclimate to being back in town. It was time to stop putting off the inevitable. It was time to go home.

I lifted my hand, catching the server's attention.

She nodded. "Be right there."

There was something about that waitress. Sure she was polite and pleasant, but something behind those blue-gray eyes tugged at me. Made me wonder how she ended up waiting tables in a place so far off the beaten path like

Swallow Springs. She had to be one of the worst servers I'd ever had. Having dined in dives around the world that was saying something. At least she hadn't figured out who I was. Though someone would eventually, and then I'd have to deal with how to live down my recent television appearance and explain my absence and return.

Glancing at the red patch of skin on my hand, I flexed my fingers, waiting for pinpricks of pain as the burned skin stretched. Not bad. Maybe her woo-woo oil had worked a little magic. Hell, a tiny coffee scald was the least of my injuries over the years. I winced as I scooted across the bench seat to stand. The rotator cuff I'd pulled when I biffed it on late night TV had me more concerned.

"Here's your check. Was everything okay?" The waitress set it on the table then grabbed my plate.

"Yeah, it was great."

"Except for..." She glanced at my hand.

"I'll be fine. Don't worry about it."

"I'm sorry. You can probably tell I'm kind of new at this." She squinted, glancing down at her feet.

I pulled a few bills out of my wallet and put them on top of the check, making sure I left a reasonable tip. "No offense, but you might want to find another occupation."

Her head whipped up, those blue-gray eyes blazing. "Hey, that's not very nice."

My hands went up, palms out in defense. "Sorry. I guess I call it like I see it. I'm sure you'll figure it out."

She sighed. "No, you're right. I'm not waitress material. I was much better at my real job. But hey, a gal's got to do what a gal's got to do, right?" She reached out, snagging the check and cash, then tucking them in her apron. "If you hear of anyone looking for a licensed massage therapist, be sure to let me know."

I glanced at her hands. They looked soft, the kind I could picture doing all sorts of other things to me, but not giving me a torturous deep tissue workout. But now she had me curious. "What kind of massage do you do?"

She whirled around, giving me a wary once over, letting her gaze skip over me from head to toe. "Not the kind you've probably got in mind."

I chuckled. "No, really. I've got a rotator cuff that's bothering me, and I'm going to need to find someone to work on it while I'm in town."

"Really?" Her eyes narrowed. She appeared to be trying to figure out if she believed me or not.

"Yep. But if you're not up for it—"

She set the tray down on the table next to her and scrawled something on the notebook she'd pulled out of her apron. "Here."

I took the piece of paper she handed me. "Harmony?"

"That's me. I have my massage table, but I don't have a studio space yet. If you're serious about needing some work done on your shoulder, I could come to you."

"All right then, I'll give you a call."

She nodded, picked up the tray, and headed back to the kitchen. Maybe I would give her a call. Although, based on her size and build, I doubted she'd be able to do much. I had so much scar tissue built up that it took a lot of effort to dig in and loosen up my shoulder area. There probably weren't very many options in town—another reason to head back to LA sooner rather than later.

I'd almost made my way to the front door when one of the older men at the counter called out. "You the Jarrett boy?"

Wouldn't do any good to argue that I wasn't a boy any more, but a damn grown man.

"Yes, sir." I turned to face the two men. Half the dining room separated us, but since they were the only customers in the café, that didn't stop the guy in the Swallow Springs VFW hat from yelling to me from across the room. I cringed, waiting for them to make some snide remark about my televised wipeout.

The man I recognized as Mr. Blevins, my high school math teacher, nodded. "We thought that was you. What are you doing back in town, son?"

I hooked my thumbs through my belt loops, my gaze catching on Harmony through the opening from the dining area into the kitchen. She wrestled with the huge coffee machine as I moved closer to the men at the counter. "I came back for the baseball field dedication."

"We never thought we'd see the day when that pipe dream would come together," Mr. Blevins said.

I sighed. "Sounds like Rob wouldn't give up on it." I had nothing but massive respect for Rob Jordan, although we hadn't talked in years. Somehow, carrying the responsibility for the death of Rob's older brother, Jeffy, had put a damper on the childhood friendship we'd shared once upon a time.

"Some folks called him crazy." Mr. Blevins shook his head. "But we're glad he stuck with it. It'll be good for the kids to have a place to practice and finally get some of those night games in."

"Well, I've got to head out. I need to stop by home before I go anywhere else or my mom will never forgive me." I stuck out my hand.

Mr. Blevins took it first, giving it a firm shake. "We'll see you at the ceremony tomorrow."

I shook the other man's hand as well. "Y'all have a good day."

"You too, son," Mr. Blevins said. "It's nice to have you back."

I nodded and shot a glance toward the kitchen. Had Harmony heard the exchange? She wasn't at the coffee machine. Odds were she'd gone to clean up. With a final nod toward the men, I pushed through the door and out onto the sidewalk.

I'd almost made it to my truck when I saw her. She'd managed to pop the hood and stood hunched over the engine of a beat up pick-up truck in the back corner of the empty parking lot. Tempted to pass by and get on with the difficult day ahead, I detoured toward her instead.

"Everything okay?"

Her head jerked up, making contact with the hood of the truck. "Ouch!"

"You all right?" I didn't mean to startle her.

"Yeah, it's nothing." Didn't seem like nothing based on the way her eyes crinkled as she rubbed at her hairline.

I ambled toward the ancient truck. "Are you sure you don't need a hand?"

"I don't know. Something crawled up under the hood this morning. I came out to check on it, and I hear some chirping."

I moved closer. "It would be pretty odd for a bird to nest in there."

"Well, I don't know what it is, but there's something alive and I have to leave in a bit. Should I try to get a mechanic over here to take a look?"

"Probably charge you an arm and a leg."

Her shoulders slumped. "I don't think I have a choice."

"Let me take a look." I peered into the engine. Nothing. I should leave it to someone else. Mom was probably waiting on me, and I didn't want to start this visit off on the wrong foot. But a quick glance at Harmony made me bite my tongue. Instead of telling her to call the auto shop, I knocked on the side of the front panel. A chorus of chirps and squeals came from the engine.

"Is it a flock of birds?" She raised to her toes to peer under the hood.

"Nah. But there's definitely something in there. Let me go get my tools."

"Are you sure you know what you're doing?" Brow furrowed, she put a hand on my arm. "It's not that I don't appreciate your help, but I can't afford to be without transportation."

"Shouldn't take but a few minutes. I promise I won't leave you high and dry. If I can't get it put back together, I'll make sure you get where you need to go. Okay?"

She nodded, although her lack of confidence came through in the way she bit her lower lip. Hell, I'd been taking engines apart and putting them back together since I was a kid. Although, most of the equipment I worked on was a fraction of the size of the ancient truck.

A few minutes later I returned, my toolbox in hand.

"Do you need help?" The words sounded sincere, but the way she wrapped her arms around her waist told me she'd probably rather do battle with the coffee machine than crawl under the hood.

"No, I've got it. I'll come get you if I need you. How does that sound?"

"That sounds good. You know, you never did tell me your name." Her hand stretched toward me. "Maybe we need an official introduction. You already know I'm Harmony."

With the heavy tool chest in one hand and a greasy rag I'd grabbed from the trunk in the other, I hesitated.

"Oh, sorry." Before I had a chance to shove the rag in my pocket, she pulled back. "You've obviously got your hands full."

The way her eyes rolled upward made me smile. I'd mastered the art of awkward interactions years ago and could recognize a kindred spirit. She might be one of the worst servers I'd ever had, but she was trying to be polite. "It's okay. I'm Dustin."

"Nice to meet you, Dustin."

Damn if my ears didn't perk up a bit at the way my name slid off her tongue. "You're not from around here, are you?" Her voice lacked the lazy drawl that was a dead giveaway to being a product of southwestern Missouri.

"No." Her light brown hair caught the glint of sun as she shook her head. "Well, I'll leave you to it. I'll just be inside if you need anything."

"All right." I waited for her to go. She hesitated, like she wanted to say something else. But she didn't. The moment stretched. "Shouldn't take but a little while."

"Thanks." With a final nod, she spun around and headed for the front of the building. I watched her go, appreciating the way her hips swayed from side to side in the short denim skirt she had on under the coffee-stained apron.

As she disappeared around the corner I clucked my tongue, chiding myself for getting distracted by a pair of blue-gray eyes. I didn't come back to town for a fling. I was here to hide out until the publicity storm blew over at home, that was all. And I'd get started just as soon as I figured out what had taken up residence inside the old truck.

4

HARMONY

I muttered to myself as I went about busing tables from the lunch rush. It was taking too long. I hadn't seen a trace of Dustin since I'd left him leaning over the engine. As soon as I got the dishwasher started I was going to head out back and tell him to leave it to the professionals. Robbie or Cassie would know someone who could come take a look at whatever had crawled up under the hood.

"Way to make a first impression. First I dump coffee on the man's crotch, then I practically knock myself into next week on the hood of the truck. Next I'll be falling into his lap or fainting at his feet," I muttered to myself.

"What's that?" His voice vibrated through my core.

I turned around so fast I couldn't see straight. A hand wrapped around my arm, setting me upright. Him. Again.

"You okay?"

"Of course. You just caught me off guard." I backed away. His hand fell from my arm, making me all too aware of the loss of his touch on my skin. What in heaven was wrong with me today?

"You can't be from around here—you spook too easy." The smile he gave me made me forget about my intention. Almost made me forget my own name.

"Sorry. I guess I'm a little sensitive." I smoothed my hands over my apron. "Did you give up? I can just call a mechanic. I'm sure Robbie knows someone."

"Robbie? You mean Rob Jordan?" The smile disappeared. His brow knit together, making him look a lot more serious than he had just moments before.

"Robbie's my cousin. You must have been away for a while."

"What makes you think that?" He cocked a hip, like his jean-clad hips had the ability to issue a challenge.

"Well, if you'd been here recently, you'd know that Robbie and Cassie own this place." I went about my business, scooping dirty plates and mugs into the plastic tub I held at my waist.

"Huh. I knew he built the ball field but I didn't know he had a hand in the café. I have been away a long time."

"That's what Frank said."

"Who's Frank?"

"Mr. Blevins. Said you grew up here but went away to Hollywood to be in the movies. Is it true?" I'd lived a stone's throw from the epicenter of Hollywood, California, most of my life. Why anyone would make the choice to move there went beyond my reasoning abilities. I'd seen my share of hopefuls come for the fame and glory. Then end up waiting tables or holding down two or three jobs just to pay the bills. The irony wasn't lost on me. That someone from Swallow Springs would head to my old stomping grounds seeking fame and fortune while I ended up stuck in rural Missouri waiting tables.

"It's not exactly true." He leaned across the booth to

gather the last few dirty dishes. "I didn't go to Hollywood to be a movie star."

The tub clunked onto the table. "Then why in the world would you want to live there?"

"I'm a stuntman." He slid the dirty plates into the tub before taking the tub from my grip. "Or at least I was. Now, can you show me where to put this so we can get your truck put back together?"

"You don't have to carry that." I made a move to take the tub back but he turned, moving out of reach.

"I got it."

I kept my groan to myself. I didn't need some Hollywood hero thinking he could swoop in and rescue me, even if it only involved a tub of dirty dishes. I'd had enough of that over the years.

"Thanks. You can put it back here." I led him through the swinging doors to the kitchen where Ryder stood scraping the grill clean. "Dirty dishes go by the dishwasher over there."

I waited for him to move, but his feet remained rooted in place.

"Dustin Jarrett." The words slipped from Ryder's mouth. "I thought that was you. You come back home to hide?"

My gaze bounced between the two men. Dustin bristled and the energy in the room shifted. Patsy Cline continued to wail about being crazy, but the dynamic between the two men was the only thing capturing my attention.

"I take it you two know each other?" I tried to defuse the tension.

"That's one way of putting it." Ryder wiped his hands on his apron. "How many times have I seen you do that burnout routine? And you biffed it on TV? Classic."

Dustin shifted his attention to me. "You said this goes

back by the dishwasher?"

I nodded. He covered the distance to the far wall in a few long strides.

"What's going on?" I whispered to Ryder. "Do you know him?"

Ryder wiped the spatula on a kitchen towel. "You could say that. Check out the replay of the Bobby Bordell show. It's all over the internet."

Before I had a chance to find out what he meant by that statement, Dustin was back.

"Do you have a box or something? I figured out what's under your hood, and I need something to put them in." He tilted his head toward the door. "Better get back out there."

Relieved to have a purpose, I sprang into action. "I'm sure I can find something. Cassie had some produce delivered earlier. I bet there's a box left from that."

"Something with a lid would be best. I'll wait for you outside." Dustin slunk away, reminding me of my son's all-too-familiar moves.

"See you later, Evel Knievel." Ryder waited until Dustin disappeared through the door, then tossed the rag and spatula down on the counter. "Damn. I figured that guy didn't have balls big enough to show his face around here again."

"Who is he?" I didn't want to think about how big Dustin's balls might be. But now, thanks to Ryder, I couldn't get the image out of my head.

"Dustin Jarrett." Ryder lifted his cap to tunnel a hand through his hair. Obviously he was thrown. And he was usually the one full of jokes who kept me laughing during my shifts. Seeing him rattled made me wonder exactly what Dustin's connection to Swallow Springs had to do with anything.

"He's a cycle stunt guy, right?"

Ryder nodded. "Yeah. He and Jeff used to be best buds. Until…"

His words trailed off but I knew what went unsaid. The accident. I'd only been about nine or ten when it happened. My cousin Jeff had taken his dad's truck out and got sideswiped by a semi. I'd never forget mom breaking the news. The whole family had driven back to Missouri for the funeral. Robbie blamed himself, but I knew there was more to it than what the adults let on at the time.

"So why's he back?" I located a box on top of a set of steel cabinets. While I jumped, trying to catch the edge of the box to pull it down, Ryder came closer.

"Who knows? Probably came back to hide out. Go check out the video on YouTube. He really botched what should have been an easy stunt, especially for a guy like him." He reached up, easily grabbing the box I'd been trying to reach. "Here you go."

"Thanks."

"His mom still lives on the outer edge of town. And his sister and nephew are here too. Hell, I hope he didn't come back for the field dedication."

The baseball field dedication had been just about all anyone in town had talked about for the past couple of weeks. "Are he and Robbie on good terms?"

"I don't know. I'd steer clear. The only thing I really know about Dustin Jarrett is that he brings trouble with him wherever he goes."

I nodded, clutching the box close to my chest. Trouble was one thing I needed a lot less of in my life. With firm resolve to send Dustin on his way, potential big balls and all, I pushed through the front door, ready to find out what kind of wild animal had tried to move into my borrowed truck.

5

DUSTIN

I could tell Ryder had warned her by her cautious approach. That right there was why I hadn't been home in so long. Why bother when everyone already had their minds made up about me? And with my recent snafu during prime time, it was probably going to be fifty times worse than it might have been if I'd come back when my mom had asked me to. Any one of the million times she'd begged.

"I found the problem." I pressed my palms on the front panel of the truck, waiting for Harmony to reach me.

"Is it birds?" Her eyes crinkled at the edges and a worried frown caused all kinds of creases to form on her forehead. She looked like someone had just forced her to take a bite of something gross.

I bit back a smile and shook my head. "No birds. You've got raccoons."

"What?" Her eyes went wide, and I wanted to laugh at her reaction.

"The mama must have carried her kits over. They can't

be more than a few weeks old." I pointed at one of the tiny squirming creatures nestled against its siblings.

"How? Why? I don't understand why a raccoon would have hid her babies in my truck." She peered into the depths of what remained of her truck's engine compartment.

"Who knows? The good news is I found them, so now we can get them out of there and you can be on your way." I reached for the box and propped it on top of the fan.

"But... what about the mom? If we take her babies away, how will she know where to find them?"

"She won't. Unless you want to sit around here with the babies in a box to see if she'll come back. Your best bet is to find a wildlife rehab place to take them until they're big enough to be on their own."

"Any ideas?"

"Google it? In the meantime, they ought to be fine if you keep them in here." I lifted one of the raccoons out of the engine and placed it in the box. It moved around, bumping into the sides of the box, eyes shut tight.

"They're so little." Her expression softened. She reached into the box to run a hand down the raccoon's back. "I don't know anything about taking care of raccoons."

"It's not that hard. When I was a kid we found a few of them living next to our compost bin. Just get them something to eat and they'll be fine until you can get them to the wildlife place. The feed store up the street ought to have kitten formula. That's all you need for now."

"But..."

I held out one of the raccoons. Its leg twisted at an unnatural angle. Her hands wrapped around the fuzzy little creature before she cradled it against her chest.

"What happened to this little guy?"

"Must have gotten tangled somehow." I didn't know much, but years of being on my own in one of the most cutthroat places in the world had provided me with the talent of reading people. She was a nurturer, I was sure of it. The way she'd tended to my hand coupled with the way she nestled the tiny 'coon against her breast told me she was one of those people I needed to avoid the most—the kind who wanted to heal everyone they met.

"What can we do about it?" Those blue-gray eyes yanked at something deep inside my chest.

"Let me see." I left her standing by the truck mumbling gentle words to the baby raccoon while I rummaged through my tool box. For someone who'd been hurt as many times as me, I'd picked up some basic first aid along the way. I never knew when I'd have to tend to a sprain, a cut, or a break, so I typically had a few supplies on hand.

Harmony had the little guy nestled between her chin and her neck when I returned.

"Let's see if we can splint him. Can you hold him out so I can take a closer look?"

"Do you have any experience with this?" A flicker of concern passed across her face.

"Beyond patching myself up, not really." I gave her a smile that was meant to reassure her. "But I've had plenty of practice at that."

I cut the craft stick to fit the length of the little coon's leg then secured it with a few adhesive bandages.

Harmony waited until I was done, then snuggled the little guy against her chest again. "You think this will work?"

"Better than not doing anything at all."

She nodded. "Thanks."

"There's one more." I set the third baby down in the box. "I'd suggest finding a way to secure the lid. You don't want them crawling all over."

"But what about my truck?" She surveyed the lot. Pieces of her engine spread across the tarp I'd laid down.

"I'll get it back together before I head out."

"Thank you. I appreciate it. Can I pay you for your time?" She set the animal in the box with its siblings before reaching into the front pocket of her apron.

"No. It was my pleasure. Just make sure you take care of them, okay?" I might not do very well relating to people, but I had a soft spot in my heart for anything with feathers or fur. My sister and I used to care for all kinds of critters we found on our family's land when we were kids.

"How about that massage? I'll do the first one for free."

Just hearing her talk about it made my back tighten. "You really don't have to do that."

"I want to. It can be my way of saying thanks for helping me out. Plus, I get the feeling you don't think I'll do a good job, so it can also be a chance to prove myself." Her eyebrows lifted, almost like she wanted to dare me to say no.

I let my head hang while I figured out how to respond. Hell, I didn't have anything to lose. If she wanted to give me a free session, that was her choice. I knew I needed it. "All right. Sounds good."

"Great. Shoot me a text when you want to set it up." She gathered the box in her arms. "I'm off in a bit. I'll just tuck these guys into the storeroom until my shift is over."

I nodded. "Good luck."

"You, too."

Somehow, I knew I was going to need a hell of a lot more good luck than she could muster if I wanted to survive the next few days in Swallow Springs.

AN HOUR AND A HALF LATER, covered in grease from restoring Harmony's engine, and battling to keep my eyes open, I pulled onto the long, gravel road that led toward home. I hadn't set foot on my family's land since I left town nearly fifteen years ago. As I eased the truck to a stop by the huge outbuilding we used as a garage, the front door opened. Mom stepped out onto the porch. She held a hand to her forehead to shield her eyes from the harsh afternoon sun. My gaze swept over her before I climbed out of the cab. Poor woman didn't deserve a son like me. I'd broken her heart when I left.

I took in a deep breath as I covered the distance between us.

"Dustin, oh my stars, it is you." She wrapped her arms around my waist, pulling me close.

"Careful, Mom. I'm all dirty. Sorry I didn't come sooner."

"Shh. I'm just glad you're here now." She swiped at her cheek, brushing a few tears away. "Welcome home."

I pressed a kiss to her temple, wishing I could offer her more than a lame-ass apology. "Thanks. I'm glad to be here."

"Really?" She studied me, making me feel like she could see right through me. What would she find? Could she tell how nervous I was about being back in Swallow Springs? How scared shitless I was about facing the demons I'd left behind so many years ago?

"It'll be good to see everyone." I nodded, trying to convince both of us that I meant it.

"Coffee's on. Let me grab you a mug and we can catch up a bit. Or are you tired? You want to take a rest?"

I would have loved nothing better than to retreat to the trailer I'd hauled all the way from California. But Mom deserved my full attention first. "Coffee would be great. And then maybe a shower?"

She smiled, linking her arm through mine. "I think we can handle that. Will you be staying for a while?"

Her eyes shone with hope. I wasn't going to disappoint her right off the bat. "We'll see. I'm out of commission right now. Can't ride for a while."

"What you do, it's too dangerous." She clucked her tongue. "Your sister told me about that accident. I didn't want to see the pictures." She guided me through the front door and into the kitchen.

Something else to be thankful for. At least my mom hadn't seen the video, even if the rest of America couldn't get over it. Based on what Mav had been telling me, the video of my wipeout had garnered more views than my winning run in the Extreme Games last year. Just goes to show, people sure do love a good fuck-up.

I entered the heart of our home. Mom's kitchen had always been the center of our lives. The smell of fresh baked bread surrounded me. The same cheery yellow curtains hung over the window by the sink. The refrigerator whirred and an old school bluegrass tune floated out of an ancient radio.

"Where's that tablet I sent you?" I scanned the counter tops, looking for the wireless speaker system I'd sent for Christmas last year.

"Oh, that was way too complicated for me. I gave it to Scarlett."

"Mom, that was supposed to make things easier for you." I moved to the sink to wash my hands. She'd always enjoyed listening to the radio while she spent time in the kitchen. My fondest memories involved listening to Johnny Cash while waiting for something to bake in the oven. Of course all that changed after the accident. After my dad walked out on us. After she had to get a full-time job to put food on the table.

"Things are easier when they don't change." She ruffled my hair like she'd done when I was younger, then set a steaming mug of coffee in front of me.

That was Mom. I'd tried to get her to move to California to be close. She preferred to stay in the home where she'd raised her family. At least she didn't have to worry about making payments any more. I'd paid off the mortgage, and the second and third, a few years ago. Now she'd always have a place to call home.

"So when will I get to see Scarlett and the kid?" I leaned back in the oak chair—the same one I used to sit in for supper.

"We didn't know when you'd get here, so she said she'd just plan on coming over for supper tonight. Does Rob know you're back?"

"Nah. I didn't want to tell him since I wasn't sure I'd make it." And since I wasn't sure how Rob would take the news. Years had passed. Some would say it was water under the bridge. But since I still held myself one-hundred percent responsible for the death of Rob's older brother, who once upon a time had been my very best friend, neither that water nor that bridge had budged.

"Tell me everything." Mom sat down next to me. Her hand reached across the table to cover mine.

I rubbed a thumb over her soft skin. It had been so long since I'd touched her. I wanted to savor the moment, pack it up and save it somewhere in the recesses of my mind so I could pull it out whenever I needed to be reminded that someone somewhere still loved me. But then again, wasn't that a mother's job? To love her child no matter what he'd done? No matter how big a fuck-up he was?

"Not much to tell. I work. I ride. That's my life in a nutshell."

"All those movies. All those competitions. Scarlett keeps me posted. I can't bear to watch anything live." She put a hand to her heart. "You scared me enough when you were a kid with those stunts you pulled. How was I to know they'd only get more dangerous over the years?"

"I take precautions. There aren't any guarantees, but I do what I can to make things as safe as possible." At least I tried. Sometimes that didn't work out so well.

"You always were one for taking risks. Why, I remember that time you hauled that old dirt bike to the top of the barn, convinced you could jump all those hay bales if you just had a good start."

I smiled at the memory. I'd been so stupid then. So naive. I'd thought I was invincible. We all thought we were. But we'd been so wrong.

"You know what, Mom? I think I am going to crash for a bit." I needed to make peace with being back in Swallow Springs. And if I was going to be subjected to my sister and nephew in a few short hours, some time alone would help. I pushed back from the table and stood. Although the kitchen hadn't changed, not even down to the salt and pepper shakers on the wooden table, it seemed smaller.

"We'll have plenty of time to catch up. I'm so glad you're home." She stood, wrapping her arms around me. "You want to stay in your old room?"

"Nah. I brought the trailer with me. Figured I'd be more comfortable out there."

"Whatever you need, sweetheart. I'm just so glad you're here."

I leaned into her hug, letting myself feel her strength. Filling up on her faith in me, no matter how misplaced it was.

6

HARMONY

The warm May breeze drifted through the window while Liam balanced the box of baby raccoons on his lap for the half-hour drive home. I'd thought about putting them in the back of the truck but that didn't last long. Liam had been thrilled to find out I'd managed to rescue the critters from under the hood. And even more excited to learn the name of the pseudo hero who'd come to my rescue—Dustin Jarrett.

I knew I'd heard the name before. He was one of those extreme athletes Liam idolized. Liam binge-watched online videos of the stunts Dustin and his colleagues performed and knew all his stats by heart.

"Do you think we'll see him again?" Liam asked.

"I don't know. He didn't fill me in on his plans." Maybe he'd call for that massage, maybe not. I hadn't made peace with the fact that daydreaming about Dustin and that twisty ink of his had distracted me to the point I'd screwed up the giant coffee machine again. I'd barely cleaned it all out and put it back together before Liam showed up.

"But Mom, you think Uncle Robbie knows him? Maybe he can introduce me."

I cringed. Robbie and Dustin did know each other. But how could I explain to my son, who wasn't that much older than Robbie had been at the time of Jeffy's death, that there was too much heartbreak between them? At least that's how it seemed. Dustin appeared to be locked up tighter than a vault, but there was something about him—the energy that surrounded him—that told me the man was in a dark place.

"We'll see, okay? Now let's talk about these guys. What are we going to do with them?" I'd had a chance to call the vet earlier. He told me until I could get them to a rehab center to feed them kitten formula like Dustin had suggested. "Where did you say that wildlife rehab place is?"

Liam glanced at my phone. "The one I found looks like it's around Kansas City."

"Oh, there's got to be somewhere closer than that." With all the woods and nature surrounding us, there had to be somewhere we could take the raccoons that wasn't an hour-and-a-half drive away.

"That's what it says. But we don't have to take them anywhere. I can take care of them."

"Honey, no. It's too much work. I don't even know what baby raccoons need."

"They need to be fed every two to three hours."

"How do you know that?"

He held my phone out. "Says so right here. I think they're probably only a couple of weeks old. Can't we keep them until they can be safe on their own?"

"Where are you going to keep baby raccoons?" Robbie had been kind enough to let us stay at his dad's old place for free. I doubted there would be anywhere suitable to house a family of nocturnal scavengers. "And don't even think about saying they can stay in your room."

"Aw, Mom. Can't you think about it?"

"I'm calling the rehab place as soon as we get home. If that really is the closest one, maybe we can drive up on Sunday afternoon or something." I'd have to work the morning shift. Sunday was the busiest day of the week, and I couldn't afford to go without tips.

Liam stuck out his bottom lip and faced the window. Some moments he seemed like such a grown-up and others I was reminded of just how young he still was.

I was about to try to make peace when the shrill ring of my phone interrupted us.

"It's Reva." He held my phone to me.

"Can you put her on speaker?" I needed to keep my eyes on the road. Driving this stretch of highway made me nervous. Out here in the middle of nowhere, anything could be waiting around the next curve.

Liam rolled his eyes but pressed the speaker button for me.

"Hey, how goes the battle?" I asked. Reva was like the sister I'd never had. We'd met at massage school and hit it off right away. Leaving her behind was one of the worst things about moving to Missouri.

"Swell. I think I'm going to quit though. I can't keep up with the schedule they've got me working at Massage-ology. It's madness."

"Don't leave until you have something else lined up. You can hang in there." A pang of guilt pinched my gut. Part of the reason she was so busy was because I left.

"They expect me to work like a machine. I just did a solid two hours for some B-list actor. An emergency session.

I had to go into Burbank and meet him on the set of his show."

"What happened, did he tweak a muscle or something?" It wasn't unusual to have to travel to an appointment. While most customers came to the studio, quite a few valued privacy and convenience and were willing to pay a little extra to insure both.

"No. His car was being detailed and he didn't have any wheels. I busted my ass, took my table on the bus and spent an hour round-trip on public transportation because his Tesla needed a wax."

I bit my lip to keep from laughing. "I hope he was a big tipper."

"No. He gave me ten bucks. Can you believe it? I'm through with this job. Who was it that wanted you to go on tour with them again? I'm ready to take on a gig like that."

"I thought you said you'd never leave LA." Reva was from a huge family. I couldn't remember how many siblings she had, but it was in the double digits. Her family was tight. They all gathered for Sunday dinner every week at her folks' huge place in Bel-Air. There was no way she'd last out on tour for months at a time.

"My mother would kill me, but it would be worth it to not have to pucker up and kiss ass anymore."

Liam glanced over at me before settling his attention back on the baby raccoons.

"Hey, can I call you back later? Liam and I are about to pull in. We've got a box full of baby raccoons we need to do something with."

"Raccoons? What's going on out there?"

"Long story. I'll fill you in later." I cast a sideways glance at my son. He held one of the raccoons against his chest.

"Sure. But look up that manager's number, will you?"

"Okay."

"And did you say baby raccoons? I thought you lived near a town."

"We do. I mean, kind of. We live about a half hour outside of town."

"So you're in the country?"

"Not really."

Liam gave me some major side eye.

"Okay, so we're kind of in the country. But not like deep woods or anything." I put my hand over the microphone. "If she thinks we live in the middle of nowhere, she'll never come visit."

He shook his head. "What is it you say to me? Always tell the truth?"

"This is different," I whispered.

"Are you still there?" Reva asked.

"Yeah, I'm here." I pulled the truck into the gravel drive and stopped in front of the house.

"How are things looking for starting your own place?" Reva was one of the only people who knew about my dream. With a license in massage therapy and my yoga teaching certificate, I'd confessed to her that my lifelong goal would be to open a wellness studio where I could offer a wide variety of health and healing options.

Fortunately, when we moved to Swallow Springs, my purchasing power rose by about one-hundred-fifty percent. Rent on retail space here went for a fraction of the price it would be out west, even the seediest neighborhoods of Hollywood. If I could just get a handle on our living expenses, I might be able to swing a small studio space. All I needed was enough to get started.

"The city has some reduced retail rent program going that I just found out about. I applied and should know more in a few weeks." The passenger door creaked as Liam climbed out of the truck then turned to grab the box of raccoons. "The perfect place is available, right across the street from the diner downtown. But I don't know if I have the bandwidth to commit to starting a new business while I'm still trying to get us settled."

"You'll figure it out. You always do." Reva's faith in me provided me with the confidence boost I needed. Always had.

"And maybe when I do, you'll want to move to Missouri and come work with me." This wasn't the first time I'd broached the subject, but usually she shot me down with a quick refusal. Based on her willingness to talk about going on the road though, maybe she'd nibble on my offer this time.

"We'll see."

"Mom, come quick. It's an emergency!" Liam rounded the front of the truck to where I still sat in the driver's seat.

"Now what, honey?"

"Snap climbed out of the box. We've got to find him."

I put my hand over the mouthpiece. "Snap? You've named them? Since when?"

"Since on the way home. Snap, Crackle, and Pop."

"You named the raccoons after a cereal?"

He gestured toward the porch where I could see he'd set the box. "Can you come help me?"

"I've got to go." I wasn't sure if Reva could hear me through her laughter. "I'll call you later."

Then I disconnected. There was a famous breakfast treat to be saved.

7

DUSTIN

*K*nock, knock, knock.

I squinted against the afternoon light streaming through a gap in the shades. Rubbing a hand over the scruff on my chin, I stretched.

Knock, knock, knock.

"Coming!" I snagged the shirt I'd left at the foot of the bed and pulled it on. "What's up?" I asked as I pushed open the door.

A gangly kid stood on the metal steps. "Gran says it's time to eat."

"Rodney?" This mix of limbs and angles couldn't be my nephew. Granted, I hadn't seen him in person since he was about four when Scarlett brought him to LA for a quick visit. But no way could this beanpole be Rodney.

"Yeah, hey, Uncle Dustin." He smirked, the same smug look my sister wore when we were kids. No doubt this was her kid.

"Geez, you're all grown up. Let me look at you." I held the door so he could step up into the trailer. The top of his head ended at my nose. "How old are you now?"

"Twelve"—he shuffled his feet together—"almost thirteen. Same age you were when you started riding the circuit, right?"

Sleep fuzzed the edges of my brain. Thirteen. Damn that seemed like a lifetime ago. And it was. "Yeah, about that old."

"Mom says with you back, maybe you can teach me."

I chuckled. "She did, did she?" Over her dead body would his mother let him anywhere near a bike. She'd seen enough broken bones and heard about enough injuries that I was surprised she didn't have poor Rodney packaged in bubble wrap.

"Well, kind of."

"I can't imagine your Mom or your Gran letting me take you anywhere near a bike."

"I bet if you talked to her though—"

"Look, Rodney. I'm not even going to be here very long. A week or two max." I felt for the kid, really I did. His own dad was a major fuck-up and had been out of the picture most of his life. But at least he had Mom looking after him. And as far as I could tell, Scarlett had come a long way from her wild teenage years.

"Yeah, okay." He turned, head down, and ambled toward the steps.

I couldn't play dad to my nephew any more than I could make up for the lost years for my mom. Coming home might have been a mistake. I slid my feet into my flip flops and followed Rodney to the house.

The smell of homemade fried chicken slammed into me about halfway across the front yard. Mom didn't say anything about what she'd planned for dinner, but she must have remembered it was my favorite. The smell grew stronger as I entered the front room.

"Please tell me you made fried chicken," I begged.

"Well look who crawled home." Scarlett hovered in the doorway, one hand on her hip. "I can't believe after all the years we've been asking you to come home for a visit, you finally do when Rob Jordan summons you." A smile teased the corners of her lips upward, but her eyes held no hint of humor.

"I didn't come home for Rob."

Her eyebrows lifted, making her green eyes even bigger. "Maybe it has something to do with you being the top-rated GIF on the internet then?"

Folks used to say they could tell we were related because they'd never seen such big green eyes on a set of siblings before. As I passed her to enter the kitchen, I reached an arm out and slung it around her shoulders, trapping her in a headlock like I used to do when we were kids. She'd been small and scrappy then, easy to outmaneuver. Now, she grabbed hold of my arm and twisted it back, jamming it into my side.

"Aw, shit." My shoulder screamed in pain. I immediately let go of her—a childish prank gone awry. "Watch it."

"You got a big bad boo boo there, Dustin?" She let go. "When are you going to stop taunting death and come home for good?"

"Y'all cut it out. Let's just enjoy being together. Tomorrow's soon enough for questions." Mom set a giant platter of homemade fried chicken on the table, right next to a bowl of creamed corn.

My stomach growled in anticipation. With the exception of the steak and eggs this morning, I'd had nothing but greasy drive-thru food for the past few days. It was all there, spread out in front of me—the chicken, the corn, homemade biscuits, and even collard greens.

"You've outdone yourself, Mom." I kissed her on the top of her head before I slid into my seat at the table, eager to dig in.

"The prodigal son returns," Scarlett muttered under her breath.

Mom shot Scarlett one of her trademark looks and Scarlett's cheeks flushed. Chastised, she turned her attention to the platter of chicken. "Breast, wing, or thigh?"

"One of each." I picked a few pieces off the top of the heap and set them on my plate. "This looks delicious, Mom."

My mother beamed. Her smile erased the worry creases from her forehead, making her look the same as she did the last time we'd shared a meal under this roof.

"There's plenty more where that came from. You take as much as you want."

I stuck my tongue out at Scarlett, a throwback gesture to our youth. Rodney let a snort escape. Mom swiped a hand at my arm. Scarlett glared before breaking into a grin.

"Some things never change." My sister shook her head before biting into a giant piece of chicken.

"Speaking of change," Mom started, "tell me about this baseball field dedication."

I chewed, savoring the taste of Mom's home cooking before I swallowed. "I don't know much more than you. They sent an email invite out to anyone who ever played on the team. Since I'm between jobs right now, I figured it was as good a time as any to come back for a quick visit."

"It's been the talk of the town for the past month or so." Scarlett wiped her chin with her napkin. "Did you check it out on your way into town?"

I pictured the waitress from the café. "No. I did stop by

the Lovebird for steak and eggs though. I heard Rob re-opened it recently."

Ma nodded. "Thank goodness. He and Cassie started it back up again. Everyone was so sad when it shut down. The Lovebird Café has been a staple in this town."

I lifted a glass of sweet tea. "The service wasn't exactly stellar."

"What happened?" Mom asked.

"Got a bit of a coffee bath."

Rodney snickered.

Mom scooped up a spoonful of corn then passed the bowl to me. "I heard they hired a new gal. She's Robbie's cousin from California. Moved here just about a month ago."

"With her stupid son," Rodney added.

"Hey, now." Scarlett cocked her head and glared at him.

"What?" Rodney pushed back from the table. "It's true."

"From what I hear, she's had a rough time of it. Wouldn't kill you to try to be nice to the boy." Always the voice of temperance and reason, Mom nodded to herself. "He's probably having a hard time settling in and making friends, especially with school almost out."

"He can go back to California for all I care. He's always bragging about how great it is there," Rodney said.

"Well, it is pretty great..." I grinned. "But Swallow Springs has one thing that California never will."

"Oh, yeah? What's that?" Rodney asked.

"Y'all." I bit into another heavenly bite of chicken.

"Mom's cooking has gone to your head. I think it's made you loopy." Scarlett nudged my shoulder—the one that hadn't been shredded during the stupid television stunt.

Mom smiled, obviously pleased at the compliment. "There's strawberry-rhubarb pie for dessert."

"You're killing me, Mom." I put a palm on my stomach, already wishing I hadn't eaten so much. "I'm going to gain fifty pounds if I stick around here for too long."

"You keep eating steak and eggs at the café and you sure will." Scarlett waggled her eyebrows at me.

"It would be worth it." I smiled around the table, glad to be among family. Happy to be home. It had been too long.

An hour later, I eased into the swing on the front porch. Dishes had been washed, dried, and put away. The pie had been polished off. I'd had a quick shower, and had just about surrendered to the sheer exhaustion that had been trying to claim me for the past few days.

The screen door squeaked as Scarlett came through.

"How are you doing?" she asked, handing me a beer.

"Thanks. Things are great. My career has never been better, bank account has never been so full...everything's friggin' fantastic."

She settled next to me on the swing. "I'm not going to sell you out to some tabloid. I want to know, how are you really doing? Looks like you've had a pretty rough week."

We might antagonize each other and revert to our preteen selves when we got together, but Scarlett was the one person who I'd confided in over the years. She was the closest thing I had to a best friend, despite our differences. I lifted the beer to my lips and took a deep swig.

"Things were going good, at least until I biffed it in front of millions of people."

"Rodney's been defending your honor at the middle school." She smiled.

"Great. I was hoping that might have passed right over Swallow Springs."

Scarlett clinked her bottle against mine. "Fat chance. You're a celebrity around here. People have kept up with your career, especially your nephew. How bad was it?"

My face heated, thinking about how it had felt to flub a move I'd mastered years ago. "It was awful. I don't know what happened. One minute the bike was burning rubber and the next I'd taken out the entire percussion section."

She bit back a laugh. "Have you watched the replay? It's pretty spectacular."

"Not you, too? Really?"

"I'm sorry."

I waited while Scarlett took a sip of beer. "My rotator cuff got busted up. Mav thinks I need to wait it out, away from the spotlight. I've finally reached a place in my career where I was starting to call my own shots. Now I've gone and fucked it up."

"You might be calling your own shots, but at what price?" Her foot pushed off on the worn floorboard of the porch, sending the swing backward.

"I'm not sure what you mean, Sis."

"Look at you." She gestured to my shoulder. "How many times have you messed up your shoulder? I've been keeping tabs on you. Seems like you can't go more than a month or two between breaking a bone."

"Hazard of the job." I grinned, leaning back against the cushion. "I always bounce back."

She didn't return the smile. "You're not getting any younger."

"You're right. That's why I've got to make my mark now. I'm pushing thirty-two. Now's my time. I can't go out like that. Once I heal up from this"—I ran a light hand over my shoulder—"I'll be stronger than ever."

Scarlett blew a raspberry at me. "You're no good to Mom if you're dead."

"I have absolutely no intention of dying."

"Or stuck in a wheelchair for the rest of your life. Can you imagine? That fall you took after the Extreme Games last year...I read an article that said had you fallen a few degrees the other way, you could have been permanently paralyzed."

I put my hand over hers where it rested on her knee. "But I didn't. I've been doing this a long time. I know how to ride, and I know how to fall."

"What do you think Mom would do if you found yourself in a wheelchair for the rest of your life?" She slid her hand out from under mine. "She'd take care of you. Don't you think she deserves to live a little? She's done nothing but serve everyone else around her. Quit while you're ahead. Don't wait until you have no choice."

I wanted to dismiss her fears. To tell her that I'd be fine. But the truth was, I had been lucky. Yes, I'd broken bones and had a couple of concussions. But I'd managed to avoid any permanent injuries.

She continued to rock us back and forth, her foot pushing off the floorboards when the swing slowed. Mom had spent her life in the service of others, and I'd damn well make sure she didn't end up having to take care of me for the rest of mine.

Maybe Scarlett was right. Maybe it was time to think about the future. Maybe I'd start after I climbed back out of this giant hole I'd dug for myself.

8

HARMONY

I followed the flags directing traffic and parked in the grassy field. Looked like the whole town had turned out for the baseball field dedication. Robbie and Cassie would be pleased. They'd shut down the café so everyone could attend, although I'd be cutting out early to make it back in time for the reception they were hosting after.

Liam climbed out of the truck and slammed the door. He wasn't happy I'd made him come along. I wasn't too thrilled to be there either. Both of us had been up all night, feeding Snap, Crackle, and Pop every two hours. We joined the small crowd of people making their way to the field. Robbie couldn't have asked for a better day. The sun shone high in the sky with not a cloud in sight. A gentle breeze carried the smell of fresh cut grass, and the song of what I'd recently learned was cicadas swelled around us.

I glanced at the people joining us on the trek to the field. A couple of boys I recognized from the middle school walked past. Liam didn't even look at them. I wish he'd make a friend or two, but so far that hadn't happened. He said everyone was a redneck or a bumpkin. I suppose it would take some time for him to accept the fact that we were here to stay.

The long grass turned to gravel as we neared the field. A brand new chain link fence encircled the area. Tall metal posts stretched into the air, holding huge rows of lights. Robbie hadn't spared any expense. I'd heard talk at the café. Some people called him nuts for spending so much money on something so crazy. Others talked about how selfless he was. I'd known him long enough to appreciate this wasn't some crazy idea or selfless act. He blamed himself for his brother's death all those years ago. This field was his way of honoring Jeffy's memory—of making sure he wasn't forgotten.

I took Liam's hand as we climbed onto the bleachers. He held on for a brief moment before pulling away. It wasn't that long ago he'd been climbing all over me and begging for one more hug or kiss. He still blamed me for pulling him away from his friends in LA. I'd tried to explain myself over and over. Hopefully one of these days he'd realize what I'd done was for the best.

As people continued to file into the stands, Robbie stepped onto the pitcher's mound with a microphone in hand.

"Thanks everyone for coming today. Wow. I wasn't expecting such a huge turnout." He tugged on the front of his baseball cap as he scanned the crowd. "As most of you know, I had an older brother. Jeff was the best ball player I've ever known. Some people said he could have gone all the way to the majors."

Heads bobbed up and down throughout the crowd in agreement.

"Unfortunately, his life was cut short, and he never had a chance to find out."

I glanced to where Cassie stood. Robbie's mom had made the trip from California for the dedication. My poor Aunt Karen. She held a tissue to her eyes.

"All my life I've wanted to find a way to honor Jeff's memory. I think he'd be pretty proud of this little set up." Robbie nodded. A few people clapped or whistled, encouraging him to go on.

"So today, I want to dedicate the Jefferson Jordan Junior Baseball Field, where kids can play ball day or night." He pointed to the huge lights.

The crowd cheered. As the mayor stepped out onto the mound to say a few words, I leaned over to Liam.

"I've got to go help with the refreshments. You want to stay here or come with me?"

"Can I just go sit in the truck?"

"No. You need to say hi to Aunt Karen and congratulate Robbie. Then you can come help me pass out cupcakes and lemonade."

"Oh yay." Sarcasm was his new superpower.

"After that I'll run you home to feed the raccoons again before I head to the reception, okay?"

He nodded. I'd take what I could get when it came to Liam.

I walked along the fence line to the place where we'd set up tables earlier in the day. Ryder was already there, unloading cupcakes from the delivery van. I joined him, setting out dozens and dozens of cupcakes. Cassie had spent most of the past few days in the kitchen, baking up a storm so she'd have enough for the event.

Red velvet with cream cheese frosting sat next to dulce de leche cakes with caramel ganache. I'd probably gain ten pounds just by breathing in the heavenly scent of so much sugar.

By the time we finished, the first few people began to wander over. I filled paper cups of lemonade and made sure the cupcake table stayed full. I was just about to start looking for Liam when someone bumped me from behind. The tray of cupcakes I'd been holding sailed from my hand. I watched in slow motion as it tumbled, cupcakes falling left and right, and straight into the crotch of a pair of jeans.

"Ooops." My lips twisted into a grimace. Afraid to meet the gaze of the person I'd just assaulted with frosting, I knelt to the ground instead. Gathering cupcakes one by one, I apologized to the patch of grass directly under my feet. "I am so incredibly sorry."

"This seems to be a habit of yours."

The voice I'd been replaying through my mind for the past twenty-four hours drew my attention. No, please don't let it be him. Not again.

My pleas fell on deaf divine ears. I stood on wobbly legs, my hands full of damaged cupcakes and met his gaze. "It's not."

He took a flimsy paper napkin from the table and attempted to wipe buttercream from his navel. "Really? Because experience is telling me otherwise."

I tossed the grass-covered cupcakes in the trash bin. Grabbing a handful of napkins, I continued to offer an apology. "I mean it. I'm usually pretty good with my hands."

A heat wave rolled up my neck, washing over my cheeks. A quick glance at those magnetic green eyes showed the innocent entendre wasn't lost on him.

"I mean, because I use them a lot. As in massage therapy." *Stop talking, Harmony. Before you dig yourself into a hole so deep you'll need an extension ladder to climb out.*

"So you've said." He tossed a wad of frosting-smeared napkins in the trash. His shirt looked like someone had finger painted on it. Actually, I could almost make out the shape of a heart just under his solar plexus. "I've been thinking, and I'd actually like to take you up on your offer."

"My offer..." I racked my brain, trying to remember what kind of offer I'd made to this dangerously good-looking man I couldn't help but want to lick right now.

"Of a massage. Since you spilled on me yesterday."

"Oh, right. Yes, absolutely. I'd love to rub you down." God, no. Something had happened between my brain and my mouth. Words were coming out so wrong.

One of his eyebrows quirked up. "You have a license, right?"

"Yes. An official one. I actually worked as a massage therapist full time back in California. Your body will be in safe hands." *Make it stop. Someone please, make me stop.*

"Harmony, there you are." Aunt Karen approached. "I haven't had a chance to say hi yet."

Dustin bristled as she came nearer. Being the super sensitive energy maven that I was, at least when I wasn't tossed completely out of my element by a man in sugar-coated jeans, I picked up on the shift right away. As she leaned in to give me a hug he took a few steps back.

"Hi, Aunt Karen. It's so good to see you. I know it means so much to Robbie and Cassie that you were able to make the trip."

"Your mother sends her love. She misses you and Liam something awful. How are you settling in?" She held my hand in hers. Aunt Karen had always been my favorite. When she gave me her attention it was always her full attention. She always made me feel like the most important person in the world.

"We're doing fine. I'm waiting tables at the café while I figure out what I want to do."

Dustin continued to retreat, one step at a time, clearly uncomfortable with my aunt's presence.

"Hey, are you serious about that massage?" I asked, right before he turned away.

"Um, yeah." He pasted a smile on his lips and faced Aunt Karen and me. "Just let me know when you're available."

"You still have my number?"

He fidgeted, tucking his thumb in his pocket then shifting to cross his arms instead. "Yeah, somewhere."

"Wait a sec, I'll give it to you again." I reached into my pocket. No business card. No paper. No pen. "Aunt Karen, do you happen to have a pen on you?"

"Well, I'm sure I do somewhere. Let me check." She opened her purse and began to dig around. Every once in a while she looked up at Dustin like she was trying to figure out who he was.

"You remember Dustin, don't you?" I asked.

"Dustin Jarrett?" Her hand paused in her purse. She peered up at him through her glasses, squinting like she couldn't trust her own eyes.

"Yes, ma'am." Dustin reversed his retreat and came closer. While the two of them sized each other up, I tried to read the situation. If my take on things was accurate, Dustin looked terrified.

"Why, I heard you were living out in my neck of the woods now." Aunt Karen reached out a hand.

Dustin let it linger before brushing his still-frosting-coated hand on the front of his jeans and giving her hand a squeeze. "Mom said you'd moved out west."

"Took me way too long to make that decision. But coming back now, why, the humidity alone is enough to do me in." She smiled, a genuine one, and Dustin's shoulders relaxed.

"I do love the predictable weather out there."

"So how long have you been back in town?" she asked. "Your mother must be thrilled to have you home."

"Yes, ma'am, she is. I just came back recently. Don't plan on staying for very long."

"It's nice that you were able to come today. I'm sure Robbie appreciates it."

Dustin's gaze wandered down to his feet. "I haven't had a chance to check in with him yet."

"Well, be sure you do. He'd love to see you, I'm sure."

"I'll do that."

"Speaking of Robbie, I need to go see if they need help with anything. Will y'all excuse me?" She rubbed a hand along my arm. "I sure am glad you're here, hon. We'll have a chance to catch up before I head home, I hope."

"I'll make sure." I pulled her into a hug, letting the same scent of my mom's perfume settle my nerves.

"Oh, and here's that pen you wanted." She handed it to me then turned to find Robbie in the crowd.

"So my mom was right," Dustin said.

"About what?" I stood on my tiptoes and craned my neck, trying to find Liam in the crowd. He'd be so disappointed he missed a chance to meet Dustin in person.

"She said you moved to town to help Robbie at the café. I seriously hope you're not planning on making a career out of waiting tables." His lips quirked into a grin, obviously in a better mood since my aunt walked away.

Even though he was giving me crap, he was pretty cute when he smiled.

"Here." I scribbled my number onto a napkin. "Give me

a call when you want that massage. I'm a much better massage therapist than waitress, I promise."

He shoved it into his back pocket. "No offense, but that wouldn't take much."

Before I could come up with a good reply, he'd turned and walked away.

9

DUSTIN

"What's going on?" Scarlett gazed up at me from the ground floor of the metal outbuilding we used as a garage.

"Nothing. Figured I'd clear some of this stuff out since I don't need it anymore." I climbed down the ladder to join her.

She ran a hand along a rung on the ladder. "We used to spend so much time out here."

"Those were the days, huh?" I yanked a bandana out of my back pocket to swipe it across my forehead.

"I used to love watching you take a bike apart and put it back together again." She moved toward the workbench on the back wall. "Mom hasn't touched a thing out here since you left."

I swallowed the lump threatening to rise in my throat. "One more reason to get rid of all this. Less for her to worry about."

"It's you she's worried about." Scarlett turned to face me. "I know you say everything's going great and you couldn't be better, but I don't believe you."

"What's not to believe? Besides that unfortunate incident with Bobby Bordell, I'm at the top of my game right now." And I was, too. As soon as I could figure out what turned me into a quivering, nervous mess when I got around the Jordan family, I'd figure out a way to address it and put it behind me.

"Look, there's something haunting you. Mom can see it. I can see it. Why do you think you haven't been back in so long? It's not because you've been too busy."

"Well, you seem to have it all figured out. Why don't you tell me?" I wasn't used to people digging into my business. Being back home had me feeling things and thinking about things I hadn't had to deal with in years. Things I thought I'd forced out of my system a long time ago.

"Um, knock knock." Someone stood in the big open doorway.

Harmony. I'd made an appointment for her to come by today and give me that massage. Seemed like a good idea at the time since my shoulder had been screaming in pain. But now, I wondered if maybe it had been a mistake. I already had enough going on with my sister on my case.

"Come on in," I said.

She entered the huge garage, carting something big with a handle. A portable massage table from the looks of it.

"Who's this?" Scarlett asked as she gave Harmony the once over. "Aren't you Rob's cousin? The one who's waiting tables at the café?"

"Yeah, that's me. Harmony Rogers." She reached a hand out to my sister. "Nice to meet you."

Scarlett took it and the two women stood feet apart, their hands connected.

"I'm Scarlett Jarrett, Dustin's sister." She smiled at me. "His younger sister."

I ignored her as I made my way toward Harmony. She looked different this afternoon, less like a waitress and more like the kind of woman I'd think about asking out on a date. If we'd met under different circumstances. And if my most embarrassing moment hadn't recently been viewed over twelve million times on YouTube. "You sure you want to do this?" I asked.

"Of course. It's the least I can do."

"Least you can do?" Scarlett twisted her head, looking back and forth between us. "Wait a minute, what's going on here?" She wasn't the type to go willingly. Always had to have her nose in my business.

I put an arm around Scarlett's shoulder, turning her to face the door. "I helped Harmony out the other day with some car trouble, and she offered to repay me with a massage." Yeah, that sounded as creepy as I thought it might.

"Really?" Scarlett's nose wrinkled. "That seems kind of—"

"I'm a licensed massage therapist. It's what I did for a living in California." Harmony must have sensed where my sister's warped sense of humor was going. "I'm actually going to be setting up a studio in town."

"Oh yeah?" I asked. "That's great."

"Okay." Scarlett hesitated, reluctant to leave the building. "What should I tell Mom?"

"What do you mean? Why do you have to tell her anything?" I held myself back from actually pushing Scarlett across the threshold of the giant overhead door.

"She might wonder where you are."

"Then tell her I'm in the garage."

"Okay." Finally. Once her toes cleared the doorway I

pushed the button. The door began to lower, casting the cavernous space into semi-darkness.

"I take it you want me to set up in here?" Harmony asked.

"If that's okay with you. I'm staying in my trailer, so it doesn't necessarily lend itself to a makeshift massage studio."

"It's fine. You should see some of the places I've had to work." She bit her bottom lip, drawing my attention to her mouth and making me wonder exactly what kind of working conditions she'd been exposed to in a place like California.

"So what do we do here? How well do you want to get to know me today?" I'd been around enough doctors in my life to not give a flying fuck about who saw what parts of me. But there was something different about being in a pristine, sterile hospital room and baring it all, as opposed to stripping in the oil-stained, gasoline-scented garage where I'd spent many an afternoon staring at the Victoria's Secret catalog.

"Whatever you're most comfortable with. If you want to leave your underwear on, that's fine with me."

"What if I'm not wearing any?"

Unless the low light was playing tricks on me, I swear I saw her take in a deep breath and swallow. "Well then, I guess that takes care of that."

"I'm fine taking it all off."

"Then by all means. I can step outside if you want a minute to get adjusted."

"You're going to have your hands all over me in less than a minute. I don't think it matters if you catch a glimpse before we get started."

As I undid my belt, she turned her back to me. "Suit

yourself. Why don't you start face down and I'll work your back first."

"Perfect." I slid my jeans off and tossed them onto the edge of a workbench. Then pulled my shirt over my head and threw it on top. As I settled on the table, easing my whole body on, ignoring the slight wobble, I pulled the sheet over my lower half as best I could.

"Let's do it." I could barely see through the donut thing where my head rested. She came close and the tips of her Birkenstock sandals appeared. Hot pink. She'd caught me off guard with the woo-woo oil shit. But I was curious enough to see just how good her rubdown would be.

"My hands might be a little cold," she warned. I could hear her squirt something into her palm, then she rubbed her hands together. A moment later her palms slid onto my shoulders. I almost winced; the tightness in my right shoulder was uncomfortable as hell.

"Is the pressure okay?" she asked as she pressed her thumbs under my shoulder blades.

"Perfect," I grunted. I'd had massages by brutes whose only joy came in getting me to scream in pain. No way was I going to tell the woo-woo waitress with the magic hands that she had me on the verge of tears.

"I can go lighter if you'd like." She continued to push into the pressure points that had been bothering me for days.

It hurt like a mother fucker but I'd be damned if she got any kind of reaction out of me. What would that say about me if I could walk away from a fall with a broken pelvis but couldn't handle a sixty-minute massage by a woman who had a unicorn painted on her big toe?

I tried to focus on her toenail. It was a unicorn, wasn't it?

Maybe it was upside down. No, it had to be a unicorn. Either that or a well-hung horse.

"Still okay?"

"Yeah, feels great," I managed to grunt out. "How are you liking Swallow Springs so far?"

"Oh, it's okay. Still getting used to it." She moved to stand at the head of the table. Her stomach pressed into the top of my head as she leaned over me, running her hands over the rigid muscles of my neck.

I breathed in, trying to get used to the feel of being so close to a woman. And not just any woman. A woman who couldn't help but draw a guy's attention. Most of my massage therapists had been guys. They had the strength to dig in, work on my muscles with the kind of deep pressure I needed. The few women I'd made appointments with in the past could have just as easily been members of the Olympic weightlifting team. It had been a long time since I'd had to struggle with not imagining the woman who was running her hands all over me taking it a step further.

Conversation might help. "Does your son like it?"

She walked around to my side, keeping her hand on the base of my neck. "No. He hates it here. I'm hoping once we get more settled, maybe find a place of our own, that he might feel better about it."

"Where are you staying now?" Her fingers swept over my spine as she moved down toward my lower back and began to work her way back up.

"Robbie's letting us stay at his dad's old place. It's fine but kind of a ways out of town."

"And your job at the Lovebird Café? You plan on sticking around there much longer?"

She huffed out a something that might pass as laughter.

"No. My dream is to have a studio space where I can offer massage and teach a few yoga classes."

"Mmm." She'd hit on a particularly sensitive spot on my lower back. Her hands worked just above my glutes, making another part of my anatomy start to take notice. That's all I needed—to get caught with a hard on when I rolled over. I visualized the last successful stunt I'd performed on my bike —the one that won me first place in the Extreme Games. "Have anywhere in mind?"

"Actually, I just signed a rental agreement on the second floor of the building across from the café. The city's offering a reduced rent program right now to try to get some more businesses to come in. First six months are free."

"That sounds like a no-brainer."

"Yeah. But they won't fund a build out. I still have to do that part myself." She shifted, her hands grazing the top of my ass before she dug her thumbs into the base of my outer obliques.

"You've got a cousin who owns a construction company. That shouldn't be too hard to arrange."

Her breath blew over my back on a sigh. Goosebumps popped up along my skin, sending a shiver racing down to my toes. "Thing is, Robbie's already been so generous. He's given me a place to stay, let me borrow his truck. There's no way I'd ask him to give up a paying job to help me out instead."

I squeezed my eyes shut. She'd moved to the middle of my back, getting closer and closer to my sore ribs. I should say something. It wouldn't be a total wuss move to tell her I had an injury. Wasn't she supposed to ask about that before starting anyway? As I pondered whether or not to 'fess up and look like a wimp, her hand reached the ribs on my right. Pain sliced into my side.

"Aw, shit." I rolled over, quick, trying to protect myself. But instead of executing the smooth Bruce Lee type move I'd pictured in my head, I slammed into her, knocking her over and onto the ground. That would have been bad enough, but karma wouldn't let it stop there. Before I could catch myself, I rolled on top of her. The sheet stayed on the table.

"Dustin, honey?" The door cracked open. Mom stood in the open doorway, peering into the depths of the garage. "You in here, sweetheart?"

"In the back. Just a sec." I took a quick inventory of the situation. Me, naked and sporting semi-wood. Harmony, spread eagle underneath me. "I'm so sorry."

"Get off me." She tried to push me aside.

"Just give me a minute." Dammit if the brief contact of my cock on her calves didn't get me ready for action. I reached for the sheet, yanking it off the table and slinging it around my waist.

"What the hell was that?" She got to her feet and brushed off her ass. "Why didn't you tell me it was too much?"

By that time Mom had made her way into the building. "Scarlett said you had a guest out here. I brought y'all some mud pie patties and sweet tea."

It might have been a little dark, but I could make out the flush that crept up Harmony's neck and flooded her cheeks.

I tried to see the situation through my mom's eyes. Had to hand it to her. She walked in on her half-naked son, wrapped in a sheet, arguing with a virtual stranger. Still didn't miss a beat. And here she was offering us refreshments.

"Want a cookie, Harmony?" I asked, not even trying to hide the humor from my voice.

"That's okay."

"I would have made chocolate chip. That's my specialty," Mom said. "But Dustin loves these mud pie patties. They're his favorite."

"Why don't you set everything down on the workbench and I'll bring the dishes in when we're done?" I suggested.

"Sure. Maybe after you and Harmony have had a chance to"—Mom waved a hand in the air—"catch up, the two of you could set a spell with me on the porch."

"Mom, you realize Harmony is here on a job, right?" I asked.

"Oh." Her gaze flitted from the sheet to the bottle of oil on the workbench then back to me again. "What kind of work is it that you do again, dear?"

"She's a massage therapist. My shoulder was killing me and she was kind enough to offer to help me work out some kinks." Damn, I was making it sound even worse.

"Well you two do whatever it is you need to do, then. I need to go check on my cookies." Mom retreated faster than I'd ever seen her go.

Harmony cradled her head in her hands. "This was a mistake. I think maybe I should stop making house calls."

"Hey, for what it's worth, it was good while it lasted." I offered her an apologetic grin.

She folded up the table, tucking the legs in and clasping the sides together.

"You want the sheet?" I held out an edge.

"Why don't I get it from you later?"

If my mother had walked fast, Harmony practically ran, leaving me alone in the dark recesses of the garage, stirred up and still sore as hell.

10

HARMONY

I hauled ass out of Dustin's place as fast as my legs would carry me. Carting a thirty-pound massage table along with me didn't even slow me down. Never in my eight years of working as a massage therapist had I ever been as mortified as I'd been today. Having him fall naked on me was bad enough. But then his mother? Offering cookies? Oh Lord. Not even the seediest set ups in any of my Hollywood gigs had left me feeling so...so...so...flustered.

I tossed the table in the back of the truck, not even bothering to lower the tailgate. With a final glance at the house Dustin grew up in, I fired up the engine and let the tires kick up dust as I floored the gas.

Hopefully he'd only come into town for the dedication and would be well on his way back to California before I had to work my next shift at the diner.

As the truck carried me down the long gravel drive, my heart rate slowed. In situations like this, I'd learned that my best tactic was to focus on my breath. In and out, nice and slow. The aftermath of awkwardness began to fade away. I'd almost reached the road, and almost had my heart rate completely back to normal, when something darted out in front of the truck. I slammed on the brakes, causing the back end to fishtail on the gravel.

Whatever it was, had run into the woods. I must have reached some state of pseudo nirvana because it sure as hell looked like an ostrich. Even being the city gal I was, I figured there couldn't be an ostrich in rural Missouri.

The truck sat at the intersection of the county road that would carry me home. Before I turned, I pulled up Reva's number.

She answered on the first ring. "How did it go with the sexy stunt man?"

"I never said he was sexy." I pressed the speaker button then turned the wheel and pulled onto the road.

"You didn't have to. I could tell by the way you talked about him. Plus, I looked him up online. What a hottie."

Groaning, I let out a breath. "It didn't go well. He had an injury he didn't tell me about. I touched his ribs and he flew off the table, taking the sheet with him." My cheeks flushed again, just thinking about it.

"And? Did you get a look?"

"A look at what? He fell on top of me."

She laughed. "Oh my gosh. How did that resolve?"

"It didn't. His mom happened to walk in at that exact moment to offer us cookies."

Laughter filled the cab of the truck. "You've got to be kidding me. Did you tell Mom that you already had some cookies?"

"I most certainly did not. Here I thought I might be able to set up shop in Swallow Springs. How can people take me seriously when I botched my first job?"

"You think he'll be eager to spread the news of what happened?"

An image of Dustin's smile popped into my mind. "I don't know. Probably not. He's not what I expected."

"How so? I didn't know you'd spent time musing over what one of your son's idols would act like in person."

"Of course not. I guess I just expected him to be more of an asshole. That's how most of the famous folks I worked for out in LA were. He seemed interested in stuff."

"Like getting naked?"

"Would you cut it out? No, in learning more about me. He asked if I planned on being a waitress for much longer." Granted, he'd asked because I was most likely the worst waitress he'd ever encountered in his life. But I didn't feel the need to share that particular piece of information.

"So the sexy stunt man has a heart. Good to know."

"Would you stop calling him that?" I wasn't sure why it bothered me so much. Probably because it was true. Dustin Jarrett was every bit as good looking in person as the larger-than-life poster hanging on the wall in Liam's room made him out to be. I'd worked around extremely attractive men before. Even spent a whole season as the personal massage therapist for one of the original members of a super famous boy band that I still wasn't allowed to name.

My hands hadn't had much of a chance to explore the contours of Dustin's mass of muscles, but from what I'd been able to tell, he was in prime physical shape. To someone who spent time with her hands all over all kinds of body shapes, types, and levels of physical fitness, it had been a bit of a treat.

"Still there?" Reva's voice pulled me back.

"Yeah."

"So are you going to see him again?"

"I sure hope not. He said he was only staying for a short

time. Hopefully he'll be long gone before he gets another craving for steak and eggs."

"Maybe that won't be all he's craving."

"Cut it out." I reached up to adjust the rearview mirror. It had a tendency to move on its own when I'd been bouncing over gravel roads. "There's no chance of anything happening between me and Dustin."

"Why are you always such a party pooper?"

"Someone has to be. Between you and Liam I guess that's my permanent title."

Reva sighed. "Liam still hasn't come around?"

"No. Although, he's pretty focused on those cute baby raccoons we saved. So he hasn't much time for causing fights."

"I can't believe it. You're barely there a month and you've got a slew of raccoons living in your house."

I couldn't believe it either. Especially when I found out the wildlife rehab place was closed on Sundays. Now we had at least another week of all-night feedings ahead of us before I could try to make the trip to Kansas City next Saturday. I could have tried to fit it in during the week but Liam would never forgive me if I went without him which meant my options were rather limited. "They're technically limited to the garage." That was the rule, but I knew Liam had sneaked the one with the bent leg, the one he called Snap, into his room last night.

"I've got to go. Client in Bel Air this afternoon, and it's going to take me hours to get there on the 405."

"I sure don't miss that."

"What? The fact it takes days to get anywhere out here?"

"That and the mass of people. Rush hour around here might be two cars reaching the stop sign downtown at the same time."

"Sounds fabulous." Reva giggled. "Hang in there, girl-friend. And don't be so quick to knock the sexy stunt man. You might like his cookies."

A low groan rumbled in the back of my throat. "I've spilled on him twice and been caught with him naked by his mom. What could possibly happen next?"

"You really want me to answer that?" she asked.

"No. Please don't."

"Give my love to Liam. I'll try to get my calendar whipped into shape and let you know when I can come for a long weekend."

"Okay. Love ya, girl."

"Love you, too."

She disconnected as I continued to muse over the botched massage with Dustin. If he did have a bruised or cracked rib, I wondered if there was anything in my essential oils reference book or something else that might help him heal faster. Maybe Liam had info on Dustin's latest injury and could help me figure out what was wrong.

Why should I get involved, though? I had enough going on with trying to survive the café and now figuring out how to get my studio space built out. When I added in monitoring my son, that seemed like more than enough to keep me busy. But the way Dustin had leapt off the table when I'd barely touched him—he had to be in major pain.

My mom always said caring too much for people would be my downfall. So far she'd been right about that, at least where my love life was concerned. I'd thought I could help Liam's dad. But I'd told myself I couldn't help someone who wouldn't help himself.

I slowed the truck, getting ready to turn off the blacktop and on to the gravel road that would lead me to Robbie's old home. Although I was grateful to him for providing a place for us to stay, I wasn't one for taking handouts. I needed to come up with a more permanent solution for me and Liam. Maybe once we got settled in our own space he'd feel better about being in Missouri. Or maybe he'd resent me for moving him until he graduated high school and could move back to California on his own.

With thoughts of plans and careers and living arrangements swirling around in my head, I almost didn't notice the sheriff's car parked in the drive until I pulled up beside it.

11

DUSTIN

*H*ow the hell would I ever be able to face Harmony again? Or a better question, how would I ever be able to look my mom in the eye? She might have played innocent with the mud pie patties and tea, but I couldn't help but wonder what she thought she'd walked in on.

After Harmony left, I gathered my clothes and tried to get myself back into the right frame of mind. I'd never been so damn out of my comfort zone around a woman before. Not since eighth grade when I'd tried to kiss with my tongue for the first time.

I cranked up the tunes and set to work on an old engine I'd left behind. Working with my hands, zoning out and letting myself fall into the music, had always been my escape. I'd totally succumbed to the wailing guitar of Eddie Van Halen when a knock bounced off the metal door. Mom wouldn't bother to knock. Maybe Harmony had come back.

I opened the door, surprised to see Dewey Watson, decked out in full uniform, standing on the other side. He'd always been a bit of an ass, trying to make himself more important than he was. Being a sheriff's deputy was the perfect job for him. He'd get to wield all that power he'd tried so desperately to hang onto in high school.

"Hey, Dewey. What can I do for you?"

"Scarlett around?"

"No. She and Mom drove into Nevada today. Had to do some shopping."

He shook his head. "That's too bad."

"What's going on? What do you want with my sister?"

"Your nephew's in trouble. Found him down by the creek bed. He and some buddies were setting off fireworks and caught a truck on fire."

"Rodney?"

"You got another nephew?"

My stomach clenched. "No, not that I'm aware of."

Dewey chuckled. "Wouldn't put it past that sister of yours."

"Hey." My hands instinctively curled into fists. "Leave Scarlett out of this."

"Whatever. Someone's got to come down and get him." His gaze swept over me. "Unless you want to leave him at the station until his mom gets home."

A deep sigh passed through my lips. "Nah. I'll take care of it. Just give me a minute to clean up."

"See ya in a few then." He tipped his hat at me. We'd never seen eye to eye. Looked like he hadn't changed much.

Ten minutes later I'd put on a clean pair of jeans and a fresh shirt and was on my way to town. What the hell could Rodney have been thinking? And where did he even get fireworks? The Fourth of July was still months away. I suppose I couldn't get too pissed off at the kid until I heard the whole story. I'd done more than my fair share of causing trouble and wreaking havoc when I'd been his age.

But that was precisely why I'd better get him straightened out. I'd had a dad with a leather belt to set me on the right path, but I'd still screwed up in every way possible. Hopefully I could save Rodney the trouble, and the juvenile record, by sharing a little more of my experience.

Before I'd managed to settle on a plan of action, I turned into the lot at the sheriff's station and pulled up next to an old pick-up truck. A pick-up truck that looked a whole hell of a lot like the truck Harmony had been driving. The one I'd pulled a family of baby raccoons out of just the other day.

I entered the building. The same gray and white speckled linoleum covered the floor. Still smelled like burned coffee and stale cigarette smoke, even though smoking had been banned indoors for years.

"What can I do for you?" A woman sitting behind a metal desk looked up from her keyboard.

"I'm here for Rodney Jarrett." I shoved my hands in my pockets, still uncomfortable being in this space after all this time.

"Take a seat, I'll let the sheriff know you're here." She pointed to a row of plastic chairs.

Harmony sat in one of them, kneading her hands together. I took the chair next to her. "What are you doing here?"

"Liam got in trouble. Something about fireworks. He's never even been around fireworks. Everything's pretty much illegal in California."

I nodded as I stretched my legs out in front of me.

"The drought. That's why they're illegal. Because there's such a high risk of fires." She rambled, probably trying to settle her nerves.

"I get it. The wildfires have been especially bad this year."

"Right." The conversation lapsed. Then she turned to face me. "What are you doing here?"

"Rodney. He's my nephew. Sounds like they might have gotten in trouble together."

"Wait, your nephew is the kid who's been bullying Liam since we moved here?"

"Rodney?" I frowned. "No. I can't believe that. My mom would tan his hide if he was bullying anyone."

She shifted forward on her chair, her eyes taking on a hint of hardness. "Well, he is. I've been working with Liam on how to handle him, but it's obviously not working."

"Hold on a minute." I put my palms out. "Let's not jump to conclusions here."

Harmony stood, knocking her purse off her lap. Papers spilled onto the floor. Glass tubes rolled under the row of chairs. "Shoot. Now look at what you made me do."

"Hey, that was about as much my fault as your kid getting caught shooting off fireworks."

She glared at me as she crouched down to pick up her stuff. Oh hell. I bent down to help, our fingers closing around the same dark vial. She pulled back like she was afraid of catching something by touching me.

"Here." I handed her the bottle. "What is this stuff?"

"My oils. This one's the lavender oil I put on your burn." She tucked it into her bag. "I'm sorry for over reacting. This whole thing with Liam has me rattled."

"No problem. I get it."

She nudged her chin toward where my hands rested in my lap. "How's that feeling, by the way?"

I flexed my hand. "Great. All healed up. Can't even tell."

"You know, I was thinking."

"Uh oh."

Her brow furrowed. "What makes you think that's a bad thing?"

"Gut instinct?"

"You always listen to your gut?"

"Hey, it hasn't failed me yet. Now go on, tell me what's been rattling around in your brain since you left me on the floor of the garage."

Her cheeks tinged a light shade of pink. Every time she blushed, it hit me right in the gut. Something about seeing her slightly out of her comfort zone made my mouth curl into a grin.

"If you'll recall, it was your fault you ended up on the garage floor. You didn't tell me you were injured."

"Aw, just a couple of bruised ribs."

"Broken?"

"Nah, just a little cracked." This time. That hadn't been the case the last time I took a tumble though. I'd spent a couple of weeks in the hospital after surgery for a broken femur and a repair on a punctured lung from a broken rib.

"Cracked is broken."

"No, cracked is manageable. At least until a good lookin' woman tries to split my ribs in two."

"Well, if you'd told me you had an injury, I would have been gentler with you."

"Is that how you like it? Gentle?"

"Oh my gosh." Her cheeks turned a darker shade of pink. "What's wrong with you?"

I let out a laugh. "I don't know. You tend to bring out the worst in me, I think."

"Great." She settled in the chair, clamping her hands over her middle and focusing straight ahead.

"I'm sorry. Tell me what you've been thinking. I really

want to know." I did, too. She had me curious. The fact she'd been thinking about me at all made me a little tingly inside.

"I was wondering if you'd be open to me trying some oils or a mud pack on your ribs and shoulder." She twisted to face me again. "It could help with the muscle soreness."

"I'm not one for experimental treatments." That was somewhat of a lie. I'd been open to acupuncture when I'd slipped a disc in my lower back a few years ago. It had been the only thing that gave me any kind of relief from the pain.

"It's not experimental. A little alternative, maybe. But people have been using home remedies and nature's resources long before they started using all the synthetic drugs."

"Yeah, I don't know." I flexed my hand again. Although, if her woo-woo oils had done such a quick job of healing my hand, maybe they'd get me patched up in time for that doctor to give me the go ahead. I didn't want to go out on a botched burnout.

"Y'all can go back now." The woman from the desk returned and motioned for us to follow her.

"Think about it?" Harmony asked.

"You got it. Now let's go find out what those boys were doing." I gestured for her to go ahead of me. Not only did it earn me points for being a gentleman, it also gave me a chance to appreciate the sway of her hips as she followed the sheriff's secretary to the back of the building.

My attention shifted as we entered the sheriff's office. Rodney sat next to another kid, both of them covered in dirt and ashes. Harmony immediately crouched in front of the kid I assumed was her son, leaving me to deal with my nephew. Suddenly I had absolutely no idea what I was supposed to do.

12

HARMONY

"*W*hat happened? Honey, are you okay?"

Liam pushed my hands away and sat up straighter in his chair. "Mom, I'm fine. Is that Dustin Jarrett?" His eyes grew wide. "Can I meet him?"

"Now doesn't seem like the time." I ran my fingers over his cheeks, smoothing his hair back, checking him for signs of injury.

"Seriously," Liam muttered under his breath, "you're embarrassing me."

"I'm embarrassing you?" I stood, clamped my hands to my hips and leveled my son with my best mama bear death glare.

He squirmed in his seat.

"I'm embarrassing *you*?" I raised my voice a notch. "I come home to find Sheriff Sampson in my driveway saying my son has been arrested for illegal activity, and suddenly you're the one who's embarrassed?"

"We weren't technically arrested..." Rodney began.

I turned my gaze on him. Evidently mama bear death glare worked on other peoples' kids, too.

"If you could take a seat." The sheriff gestured to two empty chairs.

I took in a calming breath. In and out. In and out.

"Mrs. Rogers, it's nice to see you again." He reached a hand across the desk.

I slid my hand into his, making sure to grip tight. "I wish I could say the same. Maybe under different circumstances."

Sheriff Sampson cleared his throat. "Yes, well, we all know boys can be boys." He glanced to Dustin, like he wanted back up on that.

Dustin held his hand out to the sheriff. "Good to see you again, Turner."

Of course he knew the sheriff. Everyone knew everyone around here. Everyone but me. Feeling at a slight disadvantage, I tried to bring the conversation back to what my son had been doing with fireworks.

"Can you tell me what happened?" I asked.

"I'd like the boys to give their version of events, if that's okay with you." Sheriff Sampson gestured to Rodney. "Why don't you go first?"

Rodney slid his gaze to me and then to his uncle. "The guys and I were down at Miller's Landing, just minding our own business—"

"Bullcrap!" Liam exploded out of his chair. "That's not the way it went down at all."

"Liam Allistair Rogers, sit down right now." I jumped to my feet.

"Allistair?" Rodney snickered.

Before I could turn my fiery glare on him, Dustin had yanked his nephew out of the chair by his shirt front. "You got something to say about that Rodney Walloby Jarrett?"

Walloby? What kind of middle name was that? For a

moment, the two boys glared at each other. Then Liam broke the silence by laughing. Not a snicker, but a full-on, deep-from-the-belly laugh.

Rodney joined him, the two of them howling, doubled over in fits of laughter as Dustin, the sheriff, and I looked on.

"What the hell is this?" Dustin asked.

"Seems in addition to finding the fireworks, the boys also found a sizable stash of weed," Sheriff Sampson said.

"Oh my God, he's stoned?" I bounced my gaze back and forth from Liam to the sheriff to Rodney to Dustin. "My son is high?"

"I'm afraid so." The sheriff stood behind the desk. "I'm not sure we're going to get anywhere today. Why don't you take the boys home and we'll reconvene tomorrow so we can talk this through?"

"You're just going to let them go?" I struggled to make sense of the situation. "What about consequences?"

"I have a feeling you're going to be more than fair with distributing justice, Mrs. Rogers." He rounded the desk, leading with a beer belly that some of the guys down at the café would be mighty jealous of. "Why don't you bring the boys in after school tomorrow? We'll figure out a way they can make up for their actions then?"

"That sounds good." Dustin shook the sheriff's hand.

Sheriff Sampson let go of Dustin's hand then took mine. "Have a good night."

I nodded, temporarily out of words.

We left single file, snaking through the crowded office until we finally made it outside and into the sun. How could the sun be shining so bright? How could the smell of honeysuckle float past me on the breeze? My son had not only set off illegal fireworks...stolen illegal fireworks...but he was also high as a kite.

I wrapped my hand around his arm. "Let's go, Liam."

He giggled. "Mr. Jarrett, it's a pleasure to meet you. I'm a huge fan."

Dustin's lips split into a grin. "Thanks."

"Can I have your autograph?" Liam wrenched his arm out of my grip as he moved toward Dustin.

"Let's do that next time." Dustin turned Liam to face the truck and gave him a gentle nudge.

Liam doubled over laughing. That wouldn't last long. As soon as we got in the truck I planned on making sure he didn't have anything to laugh about for a good, long while.

"Harmony?" Dustin followed me. "Are you okay?"

"Okay? No, I'm not okay. Liam may have gotten into trouble back home, but nothing like this. When I'm done with him, he's going to wish he'd—"

"Hey." Dustin interrupted me. "Let's let them tell their side before we go administering the consequences, okay?"

"You handle your nephew how you see fit. I imagine you'll clap him on the back and congratulate him for corrupting my son."

"Look, I know you're upset. But that's not fair."

Those green eyes asked for forgiveness. Maybe not forgiveness, but they did seem to beg for me to put my emotions aside and handle things in a reasonable adult manner. I wasn't sure I could handle acting like an adult right now, but I'd try for adult-ish.

"Fine. It's not fair. I'm thinking in reptile brain right now."

His eyebrows lifted, like he wasn't sure he wanted to know the answer. "Reptile brain?"

"Yes. Emotion brain. When a person gets overwhelmed it's easy to sink into their reptilian brain, the part they use to react." I waited for some dawning acknowledgment. "Fight or flight? You ever heard of that before?"

"Like that 'go' moment before I kick off into a stunt. Instinct takes over. Is that what you mean?"

Maybe. Not really. "I need to get Liam home. Can we talk about this later?"

"Sure. For what it's worth, I don't know what happened, but I'm sorry—I'll see if I can get Rodney to tell me his side of things when he...when he's back to feeling normal."

At that moment Rodney popped his head out of the passenger side window. "Oh my God. I just realized. Dude, your last name is Rogers."

I looked to Liam who sat in the front seat, stuffing his face with a bag of fiery Cheetos he'd left in the truck the day before. "Yeah, so what?"

Rodney leaned out the window. "That makes you Mr. Rogers." Then he erupted into a fit of snorty, high-pitched giggles, much more appropriate for a six-year-old little girl.

Dustin stepped in front of the window, backing up and forcing his nephew to retreat back inside his truck. He bit back a smile. "Sorry about that."

I blinked, a long, slow, blink—a last-ditch effort to try to make the whole situation fade away. Just erase it like it hadn't happened at all. But then Dustin cleared his throat, distracting me, pulling me back to the unfortunate present.

"Talk to you later, Harmony."

Jaw clenched, I nodded. He gave me one last smile then rounded his truck, climbed in, and backed out of the parking spot.

I stood still, watching them go, wondering how a situation like this would be handled at the Jarrett home front. Would they chalk it up to "boys being boys" like the sheriff suggested? Or would Rodney's mother be just as appalled as I was that her son would be capable of such a thing? Granted, I wasn't totally against the healing powers of a natural substance like marijuana and had recommended CBD oil for several of my clients who struggled with chronic pain. I'd even been known to partake once or twice in the past. For crying out loud, I wore Birks and hailed from California. But laws were laws and I wouldn't have my underage son taking matters into his own hands, no matter what.

Liam dangled the empty Cheetos bag out the window. "Hey, Ma. Can we stop at the store on the way home? My stomach is grumbling."

"That's not the only thing that will be grumbling by the time I get done with you." Defeated, I shook my head and made my way to the door. Maybe we should have stayed in California. Liam had been bullied, but had never sunk to breaking the law.

As I climbed behind the wheel, my son leaned over the center console to put his head on my shoulder. "I'm sorry, Mom."

My heart stretched, shaking off the anger and disappointment. He was a good kid. We all made bad choices from time to time but I had to believe I'd done the best I could to raise him right.

I smoothed his hair with my hand. "I know, kiddo."

Then he grinned up at me, orange powder dusting his lips. "Mr. Rogers. That's funny, huh?" Then he hummed a few bars of the song I knew so well from watching episodes of the original Mr. Rogers as a kid. "Won't you be my neighbor?"

He let out a huge laugh, followed by a snort, followed by a stream of neon orange puke. All over my lap and the front seat of the truck.

Karma needed to get her act together, and soon. Because right now life was being a real bitch.

13

DUSTIN

*T*he next day I sat outside the middle school, waiting for Rodney so we could go talk to Sheriff Sampson again. I hadn't seen or spoken to Harmony since I'd pulled out of the parking lot yesterday. She'd been a whole lot of pissed off then, and I figured it would be best to give her space.

Scarlett and I had sat on the porch swing last night, well after the sun had set and the stars popped out. She couldn't make it today since she had to work, but we'd come up with a plan to pitch to Sheriff Sampson, one that would absolve me from the guilt I felt at not being part of the family for the past several years, and hopefully make things right for Harmony. I wasn't sure why it seemed so important for me to get back on her good side. Maybe because that woo-woo shit she'd tried with me seemed to make a difference. Even though the massage had been short, she'd worked on a few knots under my shoulder blade and it hadn't felt this good since my late night appearance.

The sight of Rodney sauntering out of the front doors of school cut my thoughts short. He had his backpack slung over one shoulder and walked down the steps like he owned them. Poor kid had no idea what a tragic, uncool future he had ahead of him, assuming the sheriff and Harmony agreed to my plan.

Ten minutes later we sat in the same molded plastic chairs as the day before. The air was on the fritz so all the windows were open. Metal mini-blinds banged together in an irregular pattern as the warm, afternoon breeze came through the windows. A bead of sweat rolled down my spine, between my shoulder blades and then lower, all the way to dip inside my jeans.

Hell, if we didn't get to this soon, I might have to reschedule. Rodney sat next to me, punching buttons on his phone, oblivious to the precarious situation he'd soon find himself in. With a crash, the door to the office flew open, banging into the fake wood paneling behind it.

Harmony came in, her kid in tow. He looked rough, like he'd been run over by a combine that turned around and took another swipe at him. She nudged him toward a seat and he slid down into it. She gently closed the door then took the seat opposite me in the small waiting area.

"Running late?" I asked.

"I had to feed the raccoons." She didn't look at me as she answered. Probably still blamed me somehow for what happened the day before.

"I thought you were taking them to the wildlife rehab place?"

"We were. But they're closed on Sundays. So we're stuck with them until I can find a time to run them up there on Saturday or during the weekday hours of nine to five."

Before I had a chance to reply, Sheriff Sampson entered the waiting area.

"You're all here. Should we head back to my office?" He

motioned for us to follow. The four of us crammed into the already sweltering space. A tiny window didn't let in much fresh air. The sheriff turned an oscillating fan on his desk to face us. "Sorry about the air. Hopefully we'll have it fixed soon."

Rodney brushed his hair from his face. I squeezed in next to him while Harmony took the seat beside me. She was close enough the sides of our thighs brushed. Despite the heat, a chill ran down my spine at the contact. Something about her set me off kilter. She must have noticed. Her chair scraped along the linoleum as she scooted it a few inches away.

"Well, boys," the sheriff said. "Now that you've had some time to, well, let's say, cool down, can you tell me what happened yesterday?"

"It was his fault." Rodney jerked his head toward Liam. "He dared me to shoot off one of the fireworks."

"That's not true and you know it." Liam stood, knocking the plastic chair backward.

"Sit down," Harmony growled, already scrambling to set the chair upright.

"Mr. Rogers"—even the sheriff smirked at the name— "how about you give me your version of events?"

Liam focused on a spot between his sneakers. The silence drew out, making me wonder if the kid had fallen asleep.

"Liam." Harmony elbowed him in the side. "Tell the sheriff what you told me last night."

He didn't look up. "I was messing around down by the river and came across Rodney and his friends."

"And?" Harmony pressed.

"And they were teasing some kid, pushing him around in a circle and calling him names."

I bristled at that. Like hell my nephew was going to be one of those kids. Rodney slumped in his seat, arms crossed over his stomach like he'd just finished a twelve-course meal. My elbow collided with his ribcage. He sat up. That was more like it.

"Who was it?" Harmony asked.

"I don't know. Maybe a sixth grader?" Liam briefly glanced up at Rodney who narrowed his eyes, barely shaking his head from side to side.

My elbow not-so-gently nudged his side again. "What?" Rodney asked.

"Let him tell his side."

"Can we get this over with?" Rodney asked, sprawling back across the chair again.

"Son, tell us what happened next," Sheriff Sampson said.

"So I told them to leave the kid alone, but they didn't listen."

"And?" the sheriff asked.

"And I figured if I didn't get them to leave the kid alone, someone was going to get really hurt." Liam looked up, made brief eye contact with his mom, and looked back at his feet. "So I told them I knew where there was something really cool."

"The fireworks?" the sheriff asked.

Liam nodded. "I didn't know there would be pot there. I figured if they got distracted by the fireworks they'd let the kid go. But then they told me if I didn't shoot them off with them, that they'd say I was the one who stole them."

"Liam." Harmony let out her son's name on a whoosh of air. "Why didn't you tell me this yesterday?"

"Um, because he was stoned?" Rodney piped up.

I flicked him on the back of the head for that stupid remark.

Liam continued. "We took some of the fireworks down by the river and while we were setting them out we found a baggie with some joints."

"How in the world did you even know what those were?" Harmony's lips pursed together.

"Mom, I'm thirteen. I know what a joint looks like." He spread his hands open.

"If we could stick to the facts…" the sheriff suggested.

"So they wanted to smoke one, and I said I wanted to leave. And they told me if I didn't do it with them they'd track that kid down the next day and finish what they started with him."

"That's so not true." Rodney lifted his foot and set it down on his knee. "I mean, really, why would my friends and I do something like that?" He looked around, like he was wondering how stupid we'd have to be to believe what Liam said.

"Regardless of how it happened, you both broke the law." Sheriff Sampson shuffled some papers into a stack on his desk.

"But you heard what Liam said." Harmony moved to sit on the edge of her seat. "I know we're new in town, but I promise, he's never done anything like this before—"

"I appreciate you speaking for your son, Mrs. Rogers. But we have rules to uphold around here and with summer coming, I can't afford to have these boys running loose all over town."

"Um, I have an idea about that." I saw my chance to jump in and seized it. "I actually spoke with Rodney's mom about this last night."

"You did?" Rodney scowled at me.

"What if I could guarantee the boys would be busy this summer?"

"How do you propose to do that?" the sheriff asked.

"Yeah, how do you propose to do that?" Harmony echoed.

"I've got a few projects I could use some help with. I want to clear out the practice track I set up a long time ago. Plus"—I made sure I caught Harmony's eye—"I was thinking the boys and I could work on a build out. So you can give your business idea a shot."

Her eyes warmed for a moment, causing my gut to twinge in a weird way I hadn't felt in a long time.

"But, Mom." Liam grabbed her arm, pulling her attention away from me. "I thought I was going to get to go back to California for part of the summer. You said I could go stay with grandma."

Turner cleared his throat. "I was thinking a summer program would work, but if you're willing to take charge of both of them, I'd be okay with that instead."

"Seriously? You expect me to spend my summer hanging out with Kid Rogers? No thanks." Rodney unwrapped a stick of gum and slid it into his mouth.

"Son, I suggest you think long and hard about your options here. If your behavior continues like this, I'd have no problem sending you somewhere else to spend the summer working with some colleagues of mine instead."

Rodney's eyes grew wide and he took a visible swallow.

Turning to Harmony, I put a hand over hers where it rested in her lap. "What do you think?"

She turned away from her son. "I thought you were only going to be here for a few days, maybe a week at the most?"

"The thing is"—I glanced around the office, not sure I

wanted to have this conversation in the present company—"can we talk about this later?"

"Okay." She slipped her hand out from under mine.

"So are you boys in, or should I get some summer detention program set up for you?" Sheriff Sampson slid his gaze from Rodney to Liam and back to Rodney again. "I hear the pig farm out on County Road 87 could use some help unloading the swine trucks this summer."

I almost laughed. Jeff and I had worked that shitty job the summer before he...the threat of laughter fell flat. Suddenly the heat, the closeness, the feeling of history pressing down on me was too much.

"I need to get some fresh air." I stood and stumbled to the front of the building before the past caught up to me.

Free from the stifling heat of the office, I leaned against the building. I'd been so eager to find a solution to the current problem that I'd overlooked one major obstacle to making this work. I hadn't considered what staying in Swallow Springs for a summer might do to me.

The door to the office swung open. Harmony came out first, followed by Liam and Rodney. She handed me an envelope and gave me a tentative smile. "Looks like you've got yourself two free laborers this summer."

I said, "Great," but what I meant was *shit, shit, shit.* So much for leaving the past in the past. I was about to fall headfirst into mine.

14

HARMONY

"*I* couldn't believe he offered." I poured Frank a fresh mug of coffee, without grounds, thank you very much, and slid the carafe back on the burner.

"About Dustin..." Cassie stood on the other side of the half-wall of the kitchen. "You know he and Robbie have some bad blood between them, right?"

I nodded. "Yeah, I can tell. You'd think after all these years they would have figured out a way to get past that."

Cassie worked a rolling pin over the homemade pie crust she was making. "I think Robbie is in a good place now. Though Lord knows, it's taken long enough. He blamed himself for so long for Jeffy's death."

I chewed on my bottom lip. Talk of my cousin Jeff always took me to a sad place. I'd only been in grade school when the accident happened. But my mom and Aunt Karen had been so close. When Jeffy died it seemed like a light went out for our whole family, not just those who lived in Missouri. I'd felt it growing up, too—the loss. The heartache surrounded every kind of family event...the face missing from the Christmas card pictures...the missing signature on birthday cards. No one felt his loss as much as Robbie, but the rest of us missed him, too.

"So are you telling me Liam shouldn't spend the summer working with Dustin?" I asked. "Because it sounds like he can either do that or work at a pig farm."

"A pig farm?" Cassie scowled. "They can't make him do that. What law says juveniles have to shovel slop when they've committed an offense?"

"He needs to do something. If he thinks he can cause that kind of trouble with no kind of consequence…" My voice trailed off. This was exactly the type of thing I'd been trying to avoid by moving to Swallow Springs. Liam had always been a good kid. But the older he got, the harder it was to keep him insulated from the wrong type of kids—the ones who went looking for trouble. The first time he'd been approached by one of the older neighborhood boys—one who I knew for a fact was dealing drugs out of a third-floor apartment in our complex—I knew we had to make a change.

So much for bringing him to a safe, small-town community. Maybe he'd be better off if we'd moved in with my parents. Granted, their active adult community might have some rules around having a thirteen-year-old living there full-time.

"I'm sure Dustin will keep him busy." Cassie continued to work on the circle of dough on the counter. One of these days I'd ask her to show me how to make the kind of flaky, light, buttery crust she was known for.

"I hope so. I've finally got a chance to do something I actually enjoy." I glanced to where she stopped moving. "Oh, I didn't mean anything by that. I'm so grateful for the opportunity to work here."

"Don't worry about it." She blew a breath out,

attempting to blow a chunk of hair out of her face. "I know what you mean."

"You've got to admit, the sooner I can get back to what I'm good at, the better of all of us will be."

"I'll drink to that." Frank raised his coffee mug in my direction then took a sip. "You get a new kind of coffee, Harmony? Tastes different."

I didn't acknowledge his question. "So you're sure it's a good idea to accept the free rent program?"

Cassie shrugged her shoulders. "I think that would be great. You're welcome to work here as long as you need to. Although, you might want to stop offering the customers kale smoothies."

"Why?" I'd only mentioned it to a few of the regulars—the ones who ordered a giant milkshake every time they came in.

"First, it's not on the menu. Second, Mrs. Clements took offense. She said you made her feel guilty for making unhealthy choices."

"What?" I racked my brain, trying to recall who Mrs. Clements was and what I might have said to her that caused such offense.

"It's okay. Let's just stick to the menu from now on, okay?" Cassie set the rolling pin aside and lifted the perfect crust into a pie plate.

"Sure. Sorry about that."

Frank leaned toward me as I walked past. "She could stand to work on her cholesterol, you know."

I knew he was only trying to make me feel better. "Thanks."

"You sure you didn't try a new brand of coffee? This sure doesn't taste the same."

"I'll look into it." I wasn't about to tell him I'd given up on ever learning how to operate the giant coffee machine and had taken to mixing instant coffee in the back, one pot at a time. As I wiped down the counter, the bell on the front door jingled. Dustin. He was early.

He slid onto the stool next to Frank.

"Coffee?" I asked.

Leaning toward Frank, he asked, "Is it safe today?"

Frank shrugged. "It's coffee."

I rolled my eyes. "One time. I serve up a cruddy pot with grounds one time and I'll never hear the end of it."

Both men stared at me, brows lifted.

"Okay, maybe twice." I snagged a mug from the shelf and filled it with the steaming brew. Setting it down in front of Dustin, I leveled my gaze at him. "You're early."

"Just a few minutes. I had to come into town to talk to the sheriff." He took a sip of the coffee. "It's different today. You trying a new brand?"

I executed another eye roll and vowed to practice with the coffee monster later. "What were you meeting with the sheriff about? Does it have to do with the boys?"

"Yeah. Everything's set. As long as they stay out of trouble through the end of summer, he'll forget about putting anything on either one of their records."

"Can he do that? I mean, legally?"

Dustin shrugged. "Don't know. But if I were you, I'd be thankful he's not pursuing it. Something like that, even in middle school, can stick on a kid's record."

True. That's why I'd been so worried about getting Liam out of LA in the first place.

Cassie poked her head through the serving window into the kitchen. "If y'all want to head over now, I can cover things here."

"Are you sure?" I asked. Frank was the only customer in

the place, except for a trio of ladies who chattered away at a booth on the far side of the room. They'd finished their breakfast over an hour ago and hadn't needed anything since then except refills.

"Yep. You two go have fun." She pushed through the swinging door while tying an apron around her waist. "I can't wait to hear what you think about the space."

"Shall we?" Dustin motioned for me to lead the way.

My mouth went dry. Dustin and I hadn't been alone together since he'd rolled off the massage table and all over me.

Naked.

He wasn't the kind of man a woman could easily forget. Especially after seeing him in the buff. Reminding myself this was a professional venture, two adults doing research for a business opportunity, I smoothed my hands over my apron and cleared my throat.

"Let's do it."

He quirked an eyebrow.

My face flamed. Again. Why did I seem to lose whatever basic mastery I had of the English language in his presence?

"I mean, let's go."

His smile sent a fleet of butterflies through my stomach. "After you."

I didn't want to get my hopes up. I'd been hesitant to invest much time in trying to figure out what I wanted to do in Swallow Springs. Clearly I didn't belong in food service. No one would argue with me on that. But was I ready to invest the energy, time, and effort into building my own business?

Cassie and Robbie had been encouraging. There wasn't anything like the kind of place I envisioned within fifty miles of town. My mind raced with the possibilities. Yoga classes, an entire line of essential oils to choose from...and of course, all kinds of massage packages available. Creating a one-stop-shop for health and healing had been my goal since I first thought about becoming a massage therapist all those years ago.

With my dream lodged in the forefront of my mind, I moved past Dustin, through the front door and across the street. He'd stopped by the city office to pick up the keys. If we liked what we saw, all I'd need to do was sign on the dotted line and the space would be mine.

He turned the key in the lock on the front door. The space I was interested in was up a flight of stairs and took over the entire second floor. We traipsed up the stairs single file. Dustin let me walk ahead of him which might not have been the best idea. I'd worn another short skirt today. After the massage incident, I couldn't help but think of him as more than a potential client, especially since I'd seen where those twisty tattoos led and couldn't quite get the feel of his muscles under my palms out of my mind.

The air seemed like it hadn't been disturbed in quite a while, and a layer of dust covered the stairs. As we reached the second floor, I stepped onto the landing. The wood split underneath my foot. My knee went down as I slipped, banging hard against the wooden stair. Dustin's arm went out, catching me around the middle and pulling me against him before I took him down with me.

We bumped down a step or two, coming to a rest with Dustin's front pressing into my back.

"You okay, Harmony?" He pushed up onto one arm, his other trapped underneath me.

I mentally checked over all of my limbs. Other than what would probably develop into an impressive bruise on my knee, I seemed to be okay. "I think so. You?"

"Yeah."

I lifted myself up to get my knee underneath me before I twisted around. Dustin hadn't moved. His face hovered inches from mine. I was close enough to see the individual whiskers that made up the scruff on his cheeks and chin. Broad shoulders closed out the light, making my awareness focus in until it was just us. Just him and me, perched awkwardly, very close, on the narrow set of stairs.

"You sure you're okay?" His breath warmed my cheek. Or was that the heat being generated between us?

His hips rested on top of mine. I became all too aware of every single point where our bodies touched.

I lifted my gaze to meet his. Those green eyes swept over my face, resting on my mouth. I could lose myself in them, drift for days, get swept out to sea in the depths of Dustin Jarrett's eyes. With his free hand, he brushed a piece of hair off of my cheek. It fell away. I instinctively turned my head, nestling my cheek against the palm of his hand.

He wet his lips. My stomach tightened, anticipating the feel of his mouth on mine. If I was reading the signs correctly, Dustin Jarrett was about to kiss me. His head lowered, his mouth moving closer. He held my gaze. I couldn't look away.

And I didn't want to.

I closed my eyes, bracing myself, ready for the moment his lips would meet mine. It didn't come. His finger traced my hairline. My breath stuttered, coming in short bursts. *Breathe, dammit.* I tried to focus on my breath. In and out, in and out.

His finger continued to explore, sweeping along my jawline, igniting a heat deep in my core. *Do it.* I wanted that kiss. Couldn't wait to feel the hard planes of his body pressed against me. His palm slipped behind my head, pulling me toward him.

"I want to kiss you, Harmony," he whispered.

I nodded. I couldn't have denied him, even if I'd wanted to. The pull was too strong.

"Open your eyes."

I seemed to feel his words more than I heard them. His cheek brushed mine, his mouth dipping down to make contact with my collarbone. I let my eyes drift open even as my head rolled back, giving him better access. My arms wrapped around his neck and I clasped my hands, urging his mouth closer.

He pulled back for a moment, his eyes searching. A mixture of heat and something else, something I couldn't quite put my finger on, smoldered under half-raised lids.

Then his mouth was on mine, crowding any thought out of my head. I couldn't think, only feel. His weight pressing me into the step, his hands in my hair, his tongue taking over my mouth, deepening the kiss, demanding more.

I took it all, everything he offered and then some. It had been a long time since I'd felt so wanted, so wanton, so alive. He lowered himself onto his side, freeing up his hand so his fingers could play over my ribs. My hands explored the hard planes of his chest, the sculpted biceps, the ridged muscles lining his stomach. In that moment I believed I could spend the rest of my life doing nothing but kiss Dustin Jarrett and never, ever grow tired of it.

He shifted, helping me up to a sitting position. I wanted to be closer, to feel him everywhere at once. Without breaking our kiss, he pulled me onto his lap. I moved, pushing my skirt up around my hips and straddling his waist. My brain tried to slow things down. What did I know about him? He'd be leaving in a few weeks, what was I thinking?

I let the heat he'd ignited chase any rational thoughts from my head. Desire burned through me, even as Dustin's large hands cupped my ass.

He broke the kiss. My lips sought his, landing on the sweet spot under his ear instead. He groaned. The vibration rumbled through me—all the way to my toes.

"We can't do this here," he finally said. "I want to, but not like this. I don't want our first time together to be on the steps."

That made sense. But I didn't necessarily care about sense in that moment. All I wanted was Dustin's hands on my ass, his mouth on mine, and the eventual release of all the pent-up lust I'd managed to accumulate over the past few years. My lips moved over his neck, pausing to pay homage to his ear lobe. I pulled it into my mouth, giving it a little nibble before releasing it to move farther up his ear.

"Harmony, you're killing me." He shifted under me, breaking contact.

I wanted to moan, whine in protest, pull him back against me and continue my exploration over every gorgeous inch. Instead I opened my eyes.

And screamed.

15

HARMONY

"*I*t's just a skunk." Dustin tried to reassure me.

I'd jumped up at the sight of the skunk, then limped as fast as I could down the steps and out onto the street.

"But why is there a skunk inside? On the second floor? How did it get in? Why did it come in?" Skunks belonged outside. In nature. In the wild. Far from second floor studio space. *My* second floor studio space. I hadn't even seen it yet and already I felt mighty possessive.

"Someone probably left the door open one night and it wandered in." He put his hands on my arms, bending over to look me in the eye. "One way or another, we've got to go back in there if you want to see the space."

"Can't we call the landlord to come take it away first?" My mouth twisted into a grimace. "We can come back later. After the skunk has been...um, relocated."

Dustin dropped his hands, making me realize how much I'd liked the contact. "Well, we've got a problem then."

"Why? Do you have big plans later? I thought you told me you were available all day today?"

"I am." He shifted his weight and tucked his thumb into his belt loop. "The problem is, my mom is the landlord."

"What? How?" That didn't make sense. The city was handling the property. Dustin had never mentioned the fact that his family owned the space. "Why didn't you tell me?"

"It's a long story, but technically the building belongs to my mom. Or at least half of it does. She and my aunt are letting the city use it as part of their revitalization plan." He moved in closer. "And I didn't tell you because I didn't want you to think I was trying to earn your affection with free rent."

Something shifted inside. Something I had no idea I was holding. Something that made me throw my arms around Dustin's neck and yank his mouth toward mine. Our lips touched, sizzled at the contact. His hands went around my waist, jerking me tight against him. Our tongues tangled, taking me right back to that place where I was ready to sprawl out on the steps and let him have his way with me.

He pulled away first, clearly stunned at my improbable reaction. "What the hell was that?"

I smoothed my apron down, realizing I hadn't taken it off when we left the café. "I'm not sure. I guess I was happy to hear that you might like me."

"You weren't sure if I liked you?" His lips split into a wide smile. "After what just happened on the steps?"

"You're not an easy guy to get a read on." My lower lip jutted out in an almost-pout.

He crowded me, moving into my personal bubble of space. "You make a good point." Then he nipped at my lower lip, sending a shock wave of shivers through me. "As much as I'd like to continue showing you just how much I do like you, we've got another issue to take care of first." He nodded toward the door. "Have you ever tried to wrangle a skunk before?"

I let out a laugh. "You're joking, right?"

He didn't respond.

"Dustin?" The expression on his face gave nothing away. "Isn't this something best left to professionals?"

Leaning an arm against the wall next to me, he finally said something. "Professionals as in a crack skunk removal team?"

"Sure. When I lived out in LA there was a mountain lion cruising through one of the neighborhoods where I worked. They cordoned off the area, brought in a team to tranquilize it, and took it to a big cat animal sanctuary." What was the big deal?

"We're not talking about a dangerous animal."

"Dangerous is a matter of perspective, don't you think?"

"I think it can be." His finger made a trail from my ear to my collarbone.

What had happened to shift us suddenly from not-even-friend-zone to what appeared to be much more? I swallowed, resisting the overwhelming desire to continue exploring his mouth with my tongue. "All I'm saying is that I'm not going back in there. Not until you have Mr. Stinky removed."

"Fine. Take off your apron." Dustin held out a hand.

"What? Why?"

"So I have something to wrap the skunk in." His hands went to his hips. "Unless you have a better idea?"

My fingers went to my back, working the ties of the short half-apron Cassie had given me. "What if it sprays? Will skunk smell wash out? Cassie will kill me if I ruin another apron."

"Another?" His fingers closed around the light blue cloth

I handed him. "Do I want to know what happened to the first one?"

"Two."

"Excuse me?"

I held up two fingers. "I've ruined two so far."

Dustin tucked his chin closer to his chest. "Two?"

"One was a coffee machine explosion. The other..." I really didn't want to admit how I'd ruined the other apron. Cassie said if I destroyed any more she'd have to start taking it out of my paycheck.

"Well?" he prodded.

"I'll just say I had no idea that polyester would melt the way it did."

"Stop. Don't tell me." He put his palm up.

I grabbed it, swinging our hands down together. "It was an accident."

"It always is." He let go of my hand to reach for the doorknob. "What do you say we take a look at this space so we can retire your aprons and get you back to doing something you're good at?"

My insides warmed, heated up just like one of Cassie's homemade peach pies. "That would be nice."

"Okay, then. I'm going in." He swung the door open a crack, slipped inside and closed it behind him.

I waited, straining to catch a hint of what might be happening on the other side of the door. Seconds passed, then minutes. I couldn't stand it anymore.

My hand wrapped around the doorknob and I twisted. "Dustin?" I whispered into the crack in the doorway.

"Up here." His voice came from the second story. "Come on in, it's safe."

"You got him?"

"Her."

"How do you know?" Wondering how close he'd have to get to the creature to verify its gender, I poked my head in farther.

"You want me to explain it to you?"

"No, forget it." I ventured in, worried about what I might find. As I walked up the stairs and entered the space, I couldn't help but take note of the high ceilings, exposed brick walls, and huge windows. The place needed work, but I could see beyond the broken panes of glass, layers of dust, and gouged floors. And what I saw made my heart sing.

The space was big enough to split into smaller areas. A yoga studio could take up one side with enough room left-over for a few small massage rooms. I paused for a moment, seeing if I could get a read on the energy. Nothing jumped out at me. Sounds weird, but I could always get a read on a space. I might not know what had happened somewhere, but I could tell if a place harbored any bad mojo. I'd still smudge it with sage, but it felt light, positive, absolutely perfect.

"What do you think?" Dustin moved toward me, a light blue bundle in his arms.

I'd almost forgotten about Mr. Stinky, make that Ms. Stinky. "It's gorgeous."

He lifted his eyebrows, making his forehead crease. "It is?"

"Well, not now. But it will be. I can see it." I looked around the room again, nodding my head. Yes, this would work. This could be what I'd always imagined.

"Good. We should get together later and put some ideas down on paper so we can get a plan drawn up."

"That would be great. But, what are you going to do about that?" I pointed to the squirming apron in his arms. "Aren't you worried about getting sprayed?"

"Nah. She's a sweetheart." He pulled an edge of the apron back. A tiny black nose poked out from under layers of my apron. "I think this is Mrs. Glassard's skunk."

"Who's Mrs. Glassard, and why would she have a skunk in my space?"

"*Your* space?" he asked, his voice dropping a notch.

"Yep. It's going to be stunning. Now, back to the skunk. What gives?" I hadn't moved any closer to him, not while he held that potential stink bomb in his hands.

"She used to live on the edge of town and kept an eclectic assortment of pets."

"What happened to her?"

"My mom used to stop by and bring her meals from time to time. Last I heard she'd moved into the nursing home."

"What makes you think Stinkarella belongs to her?"

He took a step my way. I backed up two. "Relax. She's got a collar." He uncovered the skunk's head enough for me to see a bright pink collar ringing the animal's neck.

"What does it say?"

"Her name is Petunia and she's been de-scented." He took another step toward me. "That means she doesn't have any scent glands. So she can't spray you."

"Well that's a relief. How about rabies though?"

"Not likely." He lowered his arms to show me the black and white ball of fur snuggled into my apron. "Like I said, she's a sweetheart."

"As long as she's not here when I come back later..." I turned, running my fingers along a dusty counter top that must have been left by the last tenant. "When can we get started?"

"How about dinner tonight? Your place?"

"You want me to cook for you?"

"Good point. My place. You and Liam can come over and

we can jot down some ideas. It'll give him and Rodney a chance to make up before they have to spend the whole summer working together."

"Is your mom making mud pie patties?"

He groaned. "I said I was sorry about that."

"I'll never live it down. You naked, your mom offering baked goods..."

"Don't remind me."

"And in the meantime, you'll figure out what to do with Stinkypie?"

"Petunia." He nodded. "I'll check in at the nursing home and see if she's missing her skunk."

"Then you've got yourself a deal." I thrust my hand out to shake on it then thought better of it since he still held onto what could be a rabies-infected oversized rodent.

"See you tonight. Seven o'clock."

"Got it." I left him standing in the middle of the space, holding a skunk. It wasn't until I was halfway across the street on my way back to the diner that I realized he still had my apron. That made number three. Hopefully my apron-wearing days were numbered. An extra skip found its way into my step and I gave one last glance at what I'd previously considered a creepy empty old building across the street.

Now it held magic. Possibilities. Maybe even a future.

Not to mention, a man who kissed like he was made for that purpose alone.

16

DUSTIN

"Are you sure?" I held Petunia close to my chest while I argued with the woman sitting behind the front desk of the nursing home.

"Yes, Mrs. Glassard passed away last week." She clicked her mouse then looked up at me. "Do you want me to pass on a message to her next of kin?"

"Is there anyone in town?"

"I'm not allowed to divulge that information."

"These are unique circumstances, wouldn't you say?" I pulled the apron back to reveal Petunia's small black and white head. "I've got her pet here."

"Sir, you're not allowed to bring animals into the building." The woman rolled her chair back, bumping into the wall behind her.

"She was Mrs. Glassard's pet. See? Her name is on the ID tag." My fingers closed around the silver heart clipped to the skunk's collar.

"I'm going to have to ask you to leave." Her hand hovered on the phone next to her desk. "Before I call security."

"What am I supposed to do with a skunk?"

She shrugged. "I don't know, but you can't leave it here."

At that moment a nurse passed by, her shoes squeaking on the immaculate tile floor. "Is that Petunia?" She doubled back to where I stood at the desk. "We wondered what had happened to her."

"You know her?" Maybe I could leave the skunk with her. Obviously she'd be better off with someone who recognized her on sight.

"Mrs. Glassard loved that animal. She's a sweetheart." She ran a finger over Petunia's nose. "Loves peanut butter cups. I hope you find a good home for her."

"I think you've misunderstood. I'm bringing Petunia back here, to her home. I found her in a building downtown and she can't stay there."

The nurse leaned toward me, muttering under her breath. "She wasn't supposed to be here. A few of us kept her in secret. Poor Mrs. Glassard would have been lost without her. By the way, how's your shoulder doing? I saw you on the Bobby Bordell Show."

So much for flying under the radar. "It's much better. You know I've done that stunt at least a thousand times. There must have been something slippery on the stage that night."

"Sure, sugar." She winked at me, then patted Petunia on the head before walking away.

Damn. I'd already leapt outside my comfort zone by making the impromptu decision to stay in Swallow Springs for a little while longer. I couldn't take on a pet skunk as well.

"Do you need an escort out, sir?" The woman behind the desk eyed me with suspicion.

"I know the way." I cradled Petunia against me, at a loss

as to what the hell I was supposed to do with her now. Maybe Mom would have some ideas. Although, she already had a motley crew of cats at her place.

A HALF HOUR later I pulled into the drive, Petunia on the seat beside me. No one in town had any ideas for me. I'd checked with the local dog foster lead, the sheriff's department, and the feed store. Looked like unless I could find her a new home, I was the temporary owner of a pet skunk. At least the feed store gave me a couple of bowls and a used crate I could keep her in when I wasn't around. I'd learned that since she'd been de-scented it wouldn't be safe to set her free. She wouldn't have any way to defend herself in the wild.

I knew what that felt like. Seemed like my own defenses had been removed, too. At least when it came to Harmony Rogers. What had possessed me to offer up my babysitting services for the summer for Rodney and Liam? A weak moment and years of guilt, that's what. I got out of the truck and rounded to the passenger side to unload Petunia and all of her paraphernalia.

I stopped in at the house before heading to the trailer. "Hey, Mom."

"In the kitchen, sweetheart." The smell of something cinnamon-y wafted to the front room.

My stomach rumbled in response. On the bright side, there'd be no lack of home cooking if I stuck around for the summer. I set Petunia and her crate down on the rug.

"How did the meeting with Harmony go?" Mom asked, her hands encased in oven mitts. She leaned toward me so I could press a kiss to her cheek.

"Good." I ran my finger over the top of a giant cinnamon roll sitting on the counter, swiping a finger full of icing into my mouth.

"Hands off. Those are for the ladies' luncheon tomorrow." Ma leaned down to pull another pan from the oven.

"I bet you made a few extra."

She winked at me as she set the pan down on a trivet. "Of course I did. I can't tell you how much I love having you around."

"Careful, Ma. I might eat you out of house and home."

"That would be a dream come true." She pulled her hands from the oven mitts and dropped them onto the counter.

"You mean that?"

She looked up at me, a questioning smile on her face. "Of course I do. Why do you ask?"

"Well, I've been thinking. Would you be okay with me sticking around for a few more weeks? I kind of volunteered to keep an eye on Rodney and—"

I didn't get to finish my statement before she grabbed me in a hug. "Oh, honey, I've been praying you'd make a decision like this."

Wrapping my arms around her, I inhaled the scent of vanilla, cinnamon, and home, sweet, home. "Just for a few more weeks."

"A few weeks." She nodded against my chest then released me. "We need to celebrate. What do you want for dinner?"

"About dinner. How about I grill burgers? Harmony is going to come over so we can talk about her plans for a studio. I'm assuming the city mentioned they might have found a renter for that building you own downtown?"

"Your uncle's old accounting office?"

"Yeah. We need to start cleaning up the space and getting it built out. I figured Rodney and Harmony's son, Liam, could help me with that."

"What a good idea." Ma turned back to roll out another batch of rolls. "And burgers sound lovely. I'll just whip up a batch of coleslaw, maybe some potato salad, and oh, those peanut butter brownies I know you like."

"Thanks, Ma." I rested my hand on her shoulder for a moment. I'd missed this...being surrounded by people who didn't want anything more from me than the pleasure of my company at dinner. My time in Hollywood was filled with excitement, taking calculated risks, and a constant barrage of new people, new projects, and new stunts to figure out. There was something about taking a step out of the rat race to just enjoy being home.

Hopefully I wouldn't screw it up.

17

HARMONY

I knocked on the door of Dustin's mom's house at exactly seven o'clock. I'd brought one of Cassie's peach pies for dessert, not sure whether I should have brought a bottle of wine instead. That's what I would have done in California. Picked up a bottle of some local Sonoma variety at Trader Joe's on my way to dinner. But around here a run to the liquor store meant an hour in the truck round trip. And the last time I'd checked, they didn't offer much beyond Boone's Farm and the boxed variety.

Liam shuffled his sneakers on the porch next to me. "Why did I have to come tonight?"

"Besides the fact I'm unable to trust you on your own?"

He rolled his eyes. "How long is that going to last?"

"As long as I say it does."

The door opened. I pasted a smile on my face.

"Hey, glad you could make it." Dustin pushed open the screen door to let us through.

"I brought a pie." I thrust it at him.

"Did you make it?" He appeared hesitant to touch it, probably wondering how bad it would taste.

"No. I took one from the café. Cassie's peach pie."

"Oh, thanks." Grabby hands reached for the pie. "Mom, Harmony and Liam are here."

Mrs. Jarrett joined us in the front room. "I'm so glad you could make it."

"This is my son, Liam." I gave him a nudge.

"Liam, it's nice to meet you." She held her hand out to him.

Liam took it, somewhat reluctantly. The screen door squeaked behind us.

"And here's Scarlett and Rodney." Mrs. Jarrett gestured to the kitchen. "We've got dinner set out on the screened porch in back. Dustin, can you show them the way?"

Liam followed Dustin, but I caught the glare he shot Rodney's way. Having the boys work together all summer seemed like a better alternative than a detention program or a pig farm, but it might just blow up in our faces.

Dustin set the pie down on a table laden with food. "How many other people is your mom expecting tonight?" I asked.

"Just y'all." He motioned to the long wooden table in the middle of the room. "Feel free to sit anywhere. Can I get you something to drink?"

"Water would be great." I shrugged my purse off my shoulder and set it on the ground. "This is a beautiful room." Reclaimed barn wood covered the walls. Twinkle lights stretched above us, canvassing the pointed ceiling in glowing light.

"Thanks. Mom added it on a few years ago." He stepped to a side table where a pitcher of water and what looked like a pitcher of tea sat next to each other. "How about you, Liam?"

"Water, please."

At least my son had found his voice. I knew he was excited to have a chance to spend time with Dustin but, knowing my son, he was probably more than a little embarrassed at the circumstances.

Dustin handed us both a glass of water as the rest of his family joined us on the porch. Everyone took a seat: Mrs. Jarrett at the head of the table, Dustin to her right. I'd ended up sandwiched between him and Liam with Scarlett and Rodney on the other side. The chair at the end of the table sat empty.

Dustin held a platter of burgers up to me. "Take your pick. Grilled 'em myself."

I used the tongs to take a cheeseburger off the top of the stack. "Thanks. Liam, do you want cheese?"

"I can get it myself," he mumbled.

I took the platter from Dustin and held it for Liam to take what he wanted.

"Dustin tells me you're going to be taking over the space above the old accounting office," Mrs. Jarrett said.

"That's right. We looked at it today." Heat rose to my cheeks as I recalled straddling Dustin's waist.

"And what kind of business are you going to be running?" She scooped homemade potato salad from a vintage Fiestaware bowl while she talked.

"A wellness studio. I've got a license in massage therapy and have always wanted to combine that with other preventative and healing health offerings. Maybe even some yoga." My heart still sang as I thought about the possibilities. It had been my dream for so long. The thought of it coming true had plastered a constant smile on my lips. Not even Liam's surly attitude could bring me down.

Scarlett lifted a cob of corn from a bowl in the middle of

the table and set it on her plate. "Yoga, huh? I'd be up for trying that. How about you, Rodney?"

Dustin grinned. "Coach always told me flexibility helps with sports."

Rodney shook his head. "No thanks. You won't find me in some leotard doing backwards dog."

"There's no such thing," Liam said, his eyes on his plate.

"What?" Rodney's hands paused, burger mid-way between the plate and his mouth.

Liam looked up. "You can do downward dog or upward dog. There's no backwards dog. If you're going to make fun of something, at least get the name right."

Dustin laughed. Rodney scowled. It suddenly felt like it was going to be a very long evening.

"Y'all finish up with school on Thursday, right?" Dustin asked.

"Yes, sir," Rodney said.

"So we'll get started on renovations Friday morning. Say eight o'clock?"

Both boys looked up. "But that's the first day of summer," Rodney said.

"I've only got a few weeks to get the work done. What better time to start?" Dustin grinned at both of them as he sunk his teeth into his corn on the cob.

Rodney pushed back from the table and stormed into the house.

"That's not okay." Scarlett made a move to go after him.

"Aw, let him go," Mrs. Jarrett said. "He'll come around."

An uneasy quiet descended on the table. Liam continued to take bites of his burger, even asked for a second helping of baked beans.

"I saw Rob in town this morning," Scarlett said. "Have the two of you had a chance to catch up yet?" She focused on Dustin. I was pretty sure this wasn't the first time they'd had this conversation.

"Not yet." Dustin wiped his chin with his napkin. "But now that I'm going to stick around for a while, we'll have plenty of time for that."

"I don't get it." Scarlett sat back from the table. "Why can't you just make things right with the guy? You're both adults now."

"Scarlett." Her mom put her hand over where Scarlett's rested on the table. "Enough."

"I'm going to check on Rodney." She slid her hand out from underneath her mom's and got up from the table. "If you'll excuse me?"

I nodded, not sure if it was my agreement she was waiting on or not.

"Who's ready for dessert?" Mrs. Jarrett asked. "I made some peanut butter brownies."

"And Harmony brought something," Dustin added. "One of Cassie's peach pies."

"Ooh, let's have a little of each, shall we?" she asked, earning a smile from Liam. He may be stubborn as a bull but, when it came to dessert, he could be as agreeable as peas and carrots.

"We can clear the dishes." I pushed back, stacking my plate onto Dustin's as I got up from the table.

"I might even have some homemade vanilla ice cream in the deep freeze. Dustin, do you want to go check for me?" Mrs. Jarrett put her hand to her heart and gripped the edge of the table.

"You okay, Mom?" Dustin stood, putting an arm around his mother's shoulder.

"Just got a little light headed. Do you mind if I go lie down for a few minutes?"

"Of course. You need a hand?"

"No, sugar. I'll be fine. Just make sure everyone gets dessert, okay?" She passed the pan of brownies and the pie to Dustin before she made her way back into the kitchen.

"You sure your mom is all right?" I asked.

"I think so. Scarlett said she's been having some bouts of dizziness. She has a doctor's appointment in the morning. Hopefully they'll let us know if anything major's going on. So what will it be? Brownie? Pie?"

Looked like we might not all agree on everything, but one thing was for sure...there were no hard feelings when it came to dessert.

"I'm going to go apologize to Rodney," Liam said.

"Are you sure that's a good idea?" I asked. It wouldn't do anyone any good if they got into a fight.

"Yeah." He nodded before taking off toward the front of the house.

Alone, Dustin met my gaze. "So do you want to talk about what happened this afternoon?"

My chin tucked against my chest. "Not now."

Dustin nudged a finger under my chin, lifting my head to catch my attention. "We're going to have to talk about it eventually."

"Later," I managed.

"All right, then. I'm going to go cut everyone a slice of pie." Dustin disappeared into the kitchen with the dessert.

My shoulders relaxed and the tightness in my chest seeped away as Dustin left the room. I wasn't ready to face the repercussions of this afternoon yet. As I stacked dishes to carry them into the kitchen, movement out on the lawn caught my attention. It had started raining while we'd been eating dinner. The downpour had stalled, but a light rain still fell from the overcast sky. Something shrieked before disappearing into the stand of trees rimming the grassy area. What the heck was that?

I left the dishes on the table and pushed through the door into the backyard to investigate. Nothing appeared to be out of place. Except for a small mound of dirt in the center of the yard. Either my eyes were playing tricks on me or there was some wild ostrich on the loose in rural southwestern Missouri.

Maybe it was the dust I'd inhaled while previewing the studio space. Whatever it was, I needed to stop hallucinating and start putting ideas down on paper if Dustin and the boys might be starting to work on the space.

I shook the rain out of my hair and ventured back into the porch. Dustin set a plate full of pie, brownie and ice cream down in front of me.

"Oh, I can't eat all of that." I gently pushed it away.

"What? Pie? Brownies? Ice Cream?"

"None of it. Do you know how bad refined sugar is for you?"

"Oh, that's right." He let out a laugh. "Sorry, we don't have any quinoa crumpets or wheat germ suckers for dessert." He sat down across from me and stabbed his fork into a chunk of brownie.

"I just believe in being careful about the kinds of things I put into my body." Preferably, organic, non-GMO, locally-harvested and sustainable food sources. But I didn't want to overwhelm him with all of that. It was bad enough I'd been taking advantage of the free meals at the café.

"Okay." He licked his lips, driving home the point. "But it's good."

"I believe you. But I try to limit my sweets intake." I gathered the stacked plates I'd set down before.

"Sure you don't want just a bite?" He lifted his fork.

The perfect blend of crust and peach filling taunted me from the tines. My mouth watered. "One bite."

He smiled as I leaned across the table and took the entire fork in my mouth. My lips closed around it, relieving it of the pie, before I handed his fork back to him.

Sweetness danced across my tongue. I closed my eyes, savoring the sensation, chewing as slowly as possible to make it last.

Dustin cleared his throat. "Want more?"

Hell yes, I wanted more. But instead I opened my eyes and shook my head. "Nope. Just a taste is enough. Now, where should I put these?"

"Kitchen counter's fine," he said.

"Okay, back in a minute." I wandered into the empty kitchen, plates in hand. As I set them down on the counter, I couldn't help but run my gaze over the pictures lining the wall over the sink. Dustin in diapers. Scarlett holding a doll the same size as her. Years of memories splayed across the wall. Dustin on a small motorbike. Scarlett sitting on top of a pony.

This was the kind of life I wanted to provide for Liam. I closed my eyes and leaned against the counter. The sound of something shuffling along the floor by my feet made me open them again.

I yelled, trying to climb onto the counter.

The skunk scurried off into the front room. Dustin burst through the door. "What happened?"

"The skunk. Why is that skunk in your kitchen?"

Dustin shook his head. "We've got ourselves a little bit of a Petunia problem."

18

DUSTIN

"*I* tried to take her back, but Mrs. Glassard passed away. They wouldn't take her at the nursing home and she's been de-scented so I can't let her go back to the wild." I set my palms on the kitchen counter. I'd planned on waiting until after dessert to bring up Petunia. But, unfortunately, she'd beat me to it. "I was actually hoping that maybe you'd be able to take her—"

"No." Harmony backed up, as if moving away from me would negate my request. "I've already got baby raccoons."

"Right. That's why it would be perfect. You're already equipped to handle a tame wild animal."

"Can you hear yourself? A tame wild animal? What does that even mean?"

"Look, my mom already said she can't stay here. She's hardly ever home and there's no room for Petunia in the trailer with me." I shrugged. "Unless you want me to post online that she's available. Although, you never know what kind of wacko might want a skunk for some nefarious purpose."

"Nefarious?" The space between her eyebrows crinkled.

"It means evil."

"I know what it means. I just didn't realize you knew what it meant." She scraped the dishes clean before loading them into the dishwasher.

"Why not? Because I'm a gearhead who never went to college?" The comment came out a little sharper than I'd intended.

Harmony turned off the tap and put a hand on her hip. "No. Because it's not a word most people use on a regular basis. What do you do, read the dictionary?"

"Actually..."

Her mouth gaped. "You read the dictionary?"

"No. I have an app for the word of the day." Somehow admitting that to her made me feel stupider, not smarter. And as far as I knew, stupider wasn't even a word so that made it twice as bad.

"So what's today's word?" She stepped closer to where I leaned against the counter.

"I haven't looked it up yet."

"Do you have a set time of day you do your word practice?" The corners of her mouth quirked up into a bit of a smile. I recognized the teasing tone in her voice.

"Just whenever I can squeeze it in."

"How about now?"

"No."

"Why not?"

"Because now you've made it into a big deal. And it's not a big deal. It's just something I do, you know? Like one of my daily habits."

"What other kind of habits do you have?"

Hell, I wasn't going to go there, especially not with the woman who'd inspired a new almost-daily habit. "Forget it. How about we pick up where we left off earlier instead?"

"Come on, I want to know the word of the day." She reached for my phone but I spun out of her grasp.

"If I show you, will you leave me alone about it and never ask again?"

"I can't promise. But I'll leave you alone about it tonight."

"Fine." I pulled my phone out my pocket and tapped to open the app. One look at the screen told me there was no way I was sharing that word with her. A trail of fire burned across my cheeks.

"What?" Her eyebrows lifted in question. "You've got to show me now."

"No way." I clicked my phone off but before I could tuck it back into my pocket, she snagged it out of my hand.

Her fingers fumbled with the button. "How does this turn on?"

"Give that back." I wrapped an arm around her, pulling her back into my front.

She held the phone out, away from us. Laughing, she leaned forward, trying to get me to let go. "Come on, you said you'd show me."

I leaned over her, my nose against her hair. The scent of vanilla tickled my nose. Subtle, not so in my face. I liked it. "Okay."

She stopped wiggling and settled against my chest. "Promise?"

"Want me to cross my heart?"

"Is that necessary?" She whirled around in my arms, her back now pressed against the counter. "Can't I trust you?"

That question was loaded. I wanted to be the kind of man she could trust with her hopes, her dreams, her future. But that wasn't me. For a moment I thought about lying. Maybe if I said it out loud it would make it true.

The moment stretched — longer than it should have.

"Forget it." She ducked underneath my arm, freeing herself from my embrace.

"Interpolate." The word left my mouth on barely a whisper. "The word of the day is interpolate."

"That's not so bad. What's the big deal?"

I held the phone out so she could see. "Want me to read the definition?"

"Sure, hit me up."

"Interpolate. Verb. It means—" I cleared my throat, searching for a stall tactic.

"Come on, you can do it." Her smirk smacked of sass.

"Fine. Interpolate. Insert something, typically of a different nature, into something else."

One eyebrow ticked up. "Can you use that in a sentence?"

"Really?"

She nodded.

"Fine." I racked my brain, trying to come up with something that didn't sound dirty. No luck.

"Well? Skunk got your tongue?"

"You're enjoying this."

"A little bit."

I narrowed my eyes, moving in on her, herding her against the counter. "What if I said something like the handsome gentleman wants to interpolate the flirtatious lady's mouth with his tongue."

Her smile spread from cheek to cheek. "I'd say you're being a little forward. Somebody could walk in."

"They're all busy." My palms touched the counter on either side of her, pinning her in place. As I inhaled her earthy scent, my nose nudged into the hair behind her ear.

She wrapped her arms around my neck, letting her

fingers run through my hair. "I don't think that sentence conveys the proper use of the word." She mumbled close to my ear, her lips barely brushing the days' old scruff I hadn't bothered to shave.

I pulled back, meeting her gaze. "Would you like me to interpolate you somewhere else?"

Her mouth parted and I wasn't sure if she was going to scold me or kiss me. Either way, I was all-in.

The screen door slammed shut and footsteps sounded in the front room, heading our way. Harmony ducked out from my arms just as her son entered the kitchen.

"Mom, can I go out to the garage with Rodney? He wants to show me some old motorcycle parts." Liam leaned against the counter, totally oblivious to the fact that I'd been about to ravage his mom's mouth.

"Sure. But no riding. You can look all you want. Just don't even think about going anywhere on one of those things."

He nodded and hesitated like he wanted to say something else.

"Don't go there," Harmony warned.

Liam turned and stomped back through the front room. The screen door creaked then slammed shut behind him.

"Why can't he ride? Has he ever been on a bike before?" I asked.

"Over my dead body."

"What about a mini electric bike? It's probably safer than a riding lawn mower." For sure safer than the dirt bike I'd built myself out of an old mountain bike and a lawn mower engine when I'd been Liam's age.

"No."

"Okay." I backed away, palms raised. At least Liam's entrance had broken up the heat the word of the day had sparked.

"I just—bikes make me uncomfortable, okay?" She glanced up, barely meeting my eyes.

"Just the ones with engines?" I asked. "Or is he not allowed to ride a bicycle either?"

"Look, you might think I'm being overprotective, but being a parent is hard. I've got to keep him safe, no matter what. I'm the only one he's got."

"What happened to his dad?"

She held my gaze for a long beat then looked away. "I don't want to talk about it."

"Okay. Off limits, I get it."

"Should we look at the plans?"

"Sure." That was the whole reason they'd come over. Plans for the studio space. I needed to remind myself of that. It wouldn't do either of us any good for me to give in to the need that seemed to take over whenever Harmony was around. I grabbed the blueprints I'd picked up at the city office and made my way to the table.

Harmony scooted her chair closer as I unrolled the paperwork. "I don't think it needs a whole bunch. Maybe a couple of walls added, some sort of division for studio space so it's separate from the rest of the area. And a big counter for retail sales and for people to check in. Can you do drywall?"

I waited a beat to see if she'd say anything else about the moment we'd shared. She didn't. Ignoring it seemed like the best course of action. "Yeah, I've spent some summers doing construction work. We'll have to have someone do the electrical, but I can move walls or divide up the space."

She pointed to the blueprints. "So if we put up a wall here and enclosed this space over here and made them into massage rooms—"

"I'm getting massages for life out of this, aren't I?"

Leaning over her, I traced the thin purple-blue lines on the paper.

"Sorry, you missed your opportunity to negotiate for that." The tease was back in her voice. "And I've decided I can no longer see you as a client."

"What?" I hadn't even gotten a full massage yet.

"I don't make out with my clients."

"Does that mean you plan on letting me kiss you again?"

Her cheeks flushed. "I'm sure we can arrange something. How's your shoulder feeling?"

"It's fine." Like hell. Usually I could ignore the pain, push through it to the other side. But with this, there was no getting past it. Made me wonder just how likely it was that I'd be able to hang the drywall I'd just promised her. But I'd have two helpers. Rodney and Liam would have to step up.

Harmony switched to therapist mode. She rose from the chair and walked around behind me. "Sit."

I did.

Her hands ran over my shoulders, skimming along my T-shirt. My skin prickled under her touch. I leaned forward, resting my head in my hands as she used her fingers to explore the contours of my upper back.

"You're tight."

The "that's-what-he-said" joke died on my tongue. Her fingers began working on a particularly painful knot so I groaned instead.

"Pressure okay?" she asked.

"Mmm-hmm." I gave a little nod, wanting nothing more than to sink into her capable hands and lose myself to her touch.

"Get all your plans worked out?" Mom came onto the porch, a cup of coffee in her hands. "Am I interrupting something?"

"No, of course not," Harmony said, continuing to work on my back. "Dustin's shoulder has been giving him trouble. I figured I'd spend some time on it. Are you feeling better?"

"Much. Sometimes my head just messes with me for a minute or two. Care for some coffee?" Mom asked, setting the mug on the table.

"No, thanks."

"Harmony doesn't believe in coffee," I joked.

Mom's eyes opened wide. "Really?"

The thought of someone speaking bad about coffee would probably send her to an early grave. "I'm teasing, Mom."

Harmony squeezed the muscles at the base of my neck. "I just prefer tea, especially after dinner. Too much caffeine keeps me up at night."

"Oh, do you want some tea?" Mom got up from the table to head back into the kitchen.

"That's okay. I'm fine, really."

"Too late." I shook my head. "She's already on it."

She came back with a mug of hot water on a saucer, a bag of Lipton perched next to a spoon beside it. "Will this do?"

I didn't want to tell her that Lipton probably wasn't what Harmony had in mind. I'd seen the kind of tea bags she preferred. They looked like they were made out of some sort of sheer material and had all kinds of dried flowers and leaves inside.

"That will do just fine, thank you so much."

Mom took her seat again, sliding the mug of coffee in front of me. "So how's he healing up?"

"I told you, I'm doing fine." Why wouldn't she take my word for things?

"I'm not a doctor," Harmony said. "But it seems like he's

got a lot of tension in his back and shoulders. He can work on it over the next few weeks but it won't go away overnight."

Mom nodded. "I tell him to take better care of himself. One of these days he's going to get really hurt, what with the way he takes the life the good Lord gave him for granted."

"I am careful." And if I wasn't more careful, I'd find myself on the receiving end of unsolicited advice from two strong-willed females as opposed to just one.

Scarlett pushed through the screen door out onto the porch. "What did I miss?"

Make that three. She'd side with them, even though Scarlett, out of everyone, knew how cautious I was when it came to my work.

"Harmony is just working your brother over with her hands."

Scarlett slumped into a chair, laughing. "Mom!"

"What? It's what she's doing."

"Never mind." My sister snagged the mug from in front of me and took a sip. "Get the studio figured out?"

"Just about." Harmony's fingers continued to loosen my muscles. "Is Rodney okay?"

"Yeah. He and Liam are oohing and aahing over ancient motorcycle parts. Dustin told me about what you're doing. Sounds like a really awesome concept."

"I hope so. A colleague and I have talked about doing something like this for years out in California."

"Why didn't you?" Scarlett picked a piece of pie crust off my plate and popped it into her mouth. Ordinarily I might have swatted at her hand. But Harmony had me so relaxed, I didn't want to waste the energy.

"Well, Liam and I ended up moving here instead. Reva told me she had no interest in moving to Missouri, so we parted ways. It's not like we had an agreement drawn up or anything. It was just a dream."

"Would you ever consider having a hair stylist as part of your studio?" Scarlett asked.

"Oh, no you don't." I sat up, not about to let my sister swindle her way into Harmony's plans.

"What? I was just asking." She turned away from me, focusing all of her attention on Harmony.

"I hadn't thought about it, but you never know." Harmony paused, her fingers resting on the ridge of my shoulders.

Keep rubbing. I tried to send her the non-verbal message.

"Do you have a card?" Harmony asked.

"Of course." Scarlett stood, sliding one of her business cards out of her back pocket.

Harmony's hands broke contact with my back as she reached for Scarlett's card. "Great. Let's touch base and see if we can figure something out."

"Thanks." Scarlett took another swig of my coffee before kissing Mom on the cheek. "I'd better get Rodney home. He still has homework to do before tomorrow."

"Goodnight, sugar." Mom clasped Scarlett's hands and pulled them to her lips before she let them go. "You sure you don't mind taking me to the doctor tomorrow?"

"I can take you." It was the least I could do, seeing as how I hadn't been around all those years to pitch in when Mom might have needed me.

"I don't want to bother you." Mom waved me off.

"No, really. I'd love to take you. What time is your appointment?"

"Oh, it's all the way over in Nevada. You'd be gone half the day."

"I want to." But there was one little thing. "Although... Harmony, do you think you could take Petunia?"

"What?" She glanced back and forth from me to my mother.

Mom started to rise. "I don't want to cause anyone any trouble. If Scarlett can't take me then I'll see if I can get a ride with Frank."

"No, Dustin should take you, Mrs. Jarrett. I'd be happy to take Petunia tomorrow." As Mom sat down, Harmony stuck her tongue out at me. I winked back.

I tried to seize that opening. "Do you want to just take her home tonight if that would—"

"Why don't you bring her over in the morning?"

"We'll have to leave for my appointment around eight," Mom said.

"Perfect. That should give Dustin plenty of time to run her over and come back in time to get you wherever you need to go." Harmony gave me a smug grin.

If Mom had to leave by eight, that meant I'd have to head to Harmony's by seven-fifteen at the latest. But if it meant I'd get the skunk off my hands, the extra forty-five minutes in the morning would be worth it.

"Will you at least put a pot of coffee on for me?" I asked.

"No can do. I don't even have a coffee pot, but I can make you a nice cup of herbal tea or a green smoothie."

Harmony probably didn't catch the way Mom's eyes widened at that remark. She was still bent over the blueprint, studying the layout of the space.

"No thanks, I'll fend for myself. I'll see if I can get some new plans drawn up with the changes you want. Ought to take me a few days. How about I give you a call when they're done and we can meet up on site to look them over?" And maybe take another crack at whatever we'd started on the stairs.

"That sounds great. I need to get Liam home, too. We have to feed Snap, Crackle, and Pop again." She turned to Mom. "Thank you so much for dinner. I don't do very well in the kitchen, so it was a treat to have something homemade."

Mom took Harmony's hands in hers. "You're welcome. You and Liam come back whenever you want."

I rolled the plans back up and slid a rubber band around them. "I'll walk you out."

19

HARMONY

I got behind the wheel, grateful to be on my way back home. That little incident in the kitchen with Dustin almost had me throwing myself at the man. I didn't need a lover; I needed someone to help me get my business going. That was all. I didn't have the time or the energy to start something with someone. Not now when the most important man in my life needed to be Liam.

"Thanks again for the dinner invite." I pulled the door to the truck closed behind me.

Dustin leaned on the open window. The rain had stopped for a bit, although the amount of humidity in the air almost made me wish it would start up again. "You're welcome. I'll be by in the morning with Petunia."

"We're going to keep the skunk?" Liam asked as he pulled the seatbelt across his middle to buckle it.

"Just for a little bit," I said. If I wasn't careful I'd end up with a house full of rescue animals. My heart wouldn't let me turn any warm body away—didn't matter if it was the two-legged or four-legged variety.

"Cool." Liam popped his ear buds in, prepared for the twenty-minute drive home.

"See you in the morning, then." I turned the key in the ignition and the engine reluctantly groaned to life.

"I can take a look at that for you later this week," Dustin offered.

I nodded. "That would be great." If I moved forward with the studio it would be awhile before I could afford my own car. Robbie had been nice enough to loan me the truck but had also warned it was on its last leg and couldn't promise how long it might last.

"Be careful on the drive. That last turn can get kind of tricky after it's been raining."

"Thanks." With a final wave, I shifted into gear and eased away from Dustin. The truck bumped over the gravel road as we made our way to the blacktop.

The rain had tapered off but left some major puddles on the drive. I navigated between them, easing off the gas when I had to slow down for a slippery turn. As I headed into the last curve before the drive met up with the paved road, my foot slipped off the brake and pressed on the gas. I tried to adjust but I was too far into the turn to correct. The truck bounced over a rut and lodged into a trench full of mud.

"What was that?" Liam yanked his ear buds away from his ears.

"We just slid off the road a little. Hold on." I put the truck in reverse and pressed on the gas. Nothing happened.

"Back up," Liam suggested.

"I am." The wheels spun, slinging mud everywhere.

Liam hopped out of the truck and landed in a patch of sloppy, dark mud. "It's the back wheels."

"Should I try again?"

"Yeah, give it some gas." He pushed on the back bumper while I nudged my foot on the gas pedal.

The truck didn't budge.

"Try again, Mom." Something thumped against the back bumper. "Ouch!"

"What happened?"

"I slipped in the mud and knocked my head. It's okay, it's not bad."

Damn. I slapped my hands on the dash. How in the world was I going to get myself out of this mess? "Let me take a look."

I climbed out of the truck onto relatively stable ground. The rain had created a sloppy mess, turning the dust into a mass of reddish-brownish-grayish sludge. The passenger side wheels were half-buried.

Liam sloshed through the mud to reach me.

"Where are you hurt?" My hand immediately went to his head, smoothing back the goldish waves already crusted in mud. "You've got a bit of a knot. We need to get some ice on that. I guess we'll have to walk back to the house and see if we can get some help."

Ten minutes later, damp from the lingering drizzle, we caught sight of the house. Dustin must have seen us coming. He rose from his seat on the porch as we came closer.

"Hey, what's going on?"

My gaze roamed over golden brown skin, no doubt bronzed by the southern California sun. I'd seen him shirtless when I gave him a massage. But seeing him in the glow of the porch light, hair messed up from relaxing on the front porch swing, made my heart hammer and my stomach twinge. Abs chiseled from granite, pecs outlined like they'd been drawn on, and scars from what had to be tons of wrecks and wipe outs over the years crisscrossed his chest.

For a moment, I let myself imagine how it would feel to trace those lines with my fingers...with my tongue.

I shook any adult-rated thoughts from my brain. "We got stuck in the mud."

"I warned you about that spot at the end of the drive, didn't I?" He grinned.

"Yep, you sure did. And I managed to hit it anyway. Now, do you happen to have some ice we can put on Liam's head and something we can use to dig ourselves out?"

He came down the steps barefoot, his shirt in his hand. Something about the man looking like he'd just rolled out of bed made my insides twist and turn.

"I bet I've got something in the garage. Mom's gone to bed, but why don't you run in and grab a baggie of ice then I can give y'all a ride back to the truck." He yanked his shirt on over his head.

"That would be great." Liam followed Dustin to the garage while I went into the house to get some ice.

I caught up to them a few minutes later in the garage just as the two of them disappeared behind an ATV. I hadn't bothered to look around much when I'd been out here the other day, so I took the opportunity to see what kind of stuff Dustin felt was important enough to hang onto after all the years he'd been away.

Motorcycles in various stages of completion lined the perimeter. A huge workbench took up the entire back wall. The smell of grease, oil, and exhaust lingered. I wondered how long he'd had this set up and if he'd always been into bikes.

"Let's go." Dustin returned, his feet encased in tall rubber boots, carrying a few long pieces of wood and a shovel. He handed them off to Liam before grabbing a coil of rope from the edge of a table.

We followed him out to his truck where he tossed the rope in the back and gestured to Liam to do the same with the stuff he carried.

"Want to squeeze in tight or do one of you want to climb in the back?" he asked.

"I can climb in back," Liam offered.

"We'll squeeze in the cab." I gave my son a look that told him not to argue with me before opening the passenger door. Bucket seats. Wonderful. I scooted as close to the center console as I could. "Come on, Liam. Get in here."

Liam grumbled but climbed in behind me. I pressed the bag of ice to his forehead. "Why can't I sit in the back? We're just going down the driveway."

Dustin closed the door behind us before walking around to the driver's side. "We'll make this as quick and painless as possible, okay?"

As soon as we reached the truck, Liam sprang from the passenger seat.

Dustin walked halfway around the lodged vehicle, deep in thought. "I think our best bet is to wedge the board underneath the tires and see if I can pull you out. Liam, you want to help me with that?"

"Sure." He grabbed a board from the back of Dustin's truck and followed him around to the other side.

While they debated the best angle to put the board, I leaned against Dustin's truck to wait. A huge glob of mud sat on the ground in front of me. I reached out and picked up a handful. It was smooth, the consistency of the mud packs I paid big bucks for online. I spread some over my arm, wondering if it might possess any type of healing benefits.

Some sort of disturbance in the strand of trees on the other side of the drive caught my eye. Leaves rustled, a chirp carried across the road. I waited, wondering what could possibly be causing such a ruckus.

"Hey, you guys hear that?" I asked.

Dustin and Liam continued to volley ideas back and forth, ignoring me. With nothing but time on my hands, I decided to investigate. I crept across the gravel road, making sure to avoid the bigger puddles. Reaching the line of trees and bushes on the other side, I paused. About ten feet ahead, the leaves parted. A beak appeared. A large beak, about four feet off the ground.

"Um, Dustin?" I called.

No response.

I parted the limbs and peered into the tangle of bushes and trees. A ball of feathers burst through a break in the trees ahead. Was it really an ostrich? It had been a long time since I'd seen one in person. Probably not since I was a kid and my parents had taken me to the San Diego Zoo. I held my breath, waiting to see what it would do. Once clear of the trees, it paused, cocking its head toward the noise coming from the truck.

Then it turned and ran back into the brush. I followed, just in time to see it run headfirst into the trunk of a huge oak. The giant bird fell backward and landed on the wet grass with a thud.

I waited for it to get up, but it didn't. Looked like it had knocked itself out.

"Um, guys?" I yelled a little louder. This didn't appear to be something I could handle on my own.

When neither one of them responded, I inched closer to the animal. I got about three feet away when it lifted its head and scrambled to its feet. With a squawk and a furious flapping of wings, it ran through a break in the bushes.

I stood there for a long moment, long enough for my

heartbeat to stop thundering through my chest. This is why I avoided sugar. It could mess with me in the weirdest ways.

Fairly sure I'd hallucinated the entire event, I picked my way through the overgrown brush back to the driveway. I was about to ask if they'd seen an ostrich run by, but my words died on my tongue.

Liam sat behind the wheel of Robbie's truck while Dustin tried to pull it out of the mud. The wheels spun round and round as Liam pressed on the gas. Slowly, the truck edged out of the rut. As far as I knew Liam had never been behind the wheel of a vehicle before. I rushed over, hoping Dustin had shown him how to work both the gas and the brakes.

"What are you doing?" My hands grasped the window frame as Liam eased the truck to a stop.

"You weren't here, so Dustin let me drive out of the ditch."

"I see that." And I wasn't happy about it. My shoulders tensed. "Why don't you get out of the truck now?"

Liam's forehead creased. "But, Mom, I did it. Did you see me driving? Dustin says maybe he can take me out sometime—"

"Get out of the truck, Liam. Now." I jerked on the door handle.

Liam climbed down just as Dustin walked over.

"Good job." He held out a hand to Liam who shot me a glance full of disappointment. "What did I miss?" Dustin asked, clapping Liam on the shoulder instead. "You did a great job there. You should be proud of him." He nudged his chin toward the truck. "You were really stuck."

"Liam, get in the truck, please."

"But, Mom."

"Now." I didn't use my serious mom tone all that often, but when I did Liam knew better than to argue.

He disappeared around the truck and climbed in.

"What's going on?" Dustin asked.

"He's thirteen years old. You had no business putting him behind the wheel. He could have hit your truck."

"But he didn't. He's a smart kid, Harmony. I showed him the gas and the brake. You don't have to be a rocket scientist to get a truck out of a ditch."

"No, but you don't have to encourage him to get behind the wheel either." My stomach hitched itself into a hundred knots. "He's just a kid."

"No, he's a young man who wants a little freedom from his overprotective mom, if you ask me." Dustin placed a palm on the hood of the truck and leaned closer. "What do you think is going to happen? You either give him a little bit of freedom, encourage him to grow in positive ways, or he's going to—"

"You don't know anything about raising a kid. He's all I've got. It's my job to keep him safe, to protect him, to—"

"To smother him so he turns away?" He moved closer, invading my personal bubble of space. "I don't know anything about raising a son, but I do know about being a kid who's lost, who went searching for something to help me feel alive again. And I found it, too. Trust me, you want him to find something positive, not the kind of crap I turned to when the pain got too much to bear."

He turned away, but not before I saw the agony in his eyes. I wanted to pull him to me and hug away all the hurt he must have felt after Jeffy died. Instead, I stood there, absorbing the pain he'd left between us, letting the anger and frustration he must have felt as a teen wash over me.

Dustin walked to the front of the truck and bent to

unhook the tow rope. I wanted to say something. Something that would ease away the years of hurt. But in that moment, I couldn't find the words. So I climbed into Robbie's truck and turned the key in the ignition.

As we pulled away, Dustin lifted his head. I gave a little wave of thanks then put both hands on the wheel to navigate around the curve that landed us in the mud in the first place.

He'd be by tomorrow with the damn skunk. Hopefully, by then I'd come up with something to say.

20

DUSTIN

*a*t seven-fifteen the next morning I pulled into Harmony's drive. It had been years since I'd been to the Jordans' house. When I said I'd run Petunia over to her I didn't think about the fact I'd have to come face to face with a two-thousand square foot reminder of my past.

"Better get it over with." I wrapped my hand around the handle of the cage. Poor Petunia could barely turn around inside, but it was better than letting her have free reign of the cab of my truck. "We'll get you settled and find a place where you'll have some room to move around."

Harmony met me at the door. "About last night—"

"No big deal." I set the cage on the ground. "You want to keep this in case you need to take her somewhere? Or do you have something else you can use?"

She opened the door wide so I could step inside. I paused, glancing past her, my gaze running over the living room I'd spent so much time in as a kid. Memories flooded my mind. Jeffy and me fighting over the remote, Mrs. Jordan pulling a pan full of fresh-baked cookies out of the oven. My heart thundered in my chest, the sound so loud I was sure Harmony could hear it.

"Do you want to come in?" she asked.

"No." The urge to leave, to run as far and as fast as I could, took over. That's what I would have done if I were still a kid. But I wasn't so I tried to gain control of my feelings. I took a deep inhale, recognizing the familiar scent of the Jordans' living room—a mixture of lemon Pledge and Windex. "I've got to get my mom to the doctor. Thanks for taking care of Petunia."

She smiled, a crooked grin that lifted one side of her mouth. "Want to see the raccoons before you go?"

"You let them in the house?"

"No way. They're in the garage. Want to peek real quick?"

"Sure."

She led the way to the side door of the garage. I'd probably spent just as much time in the Jordans' two-car attached garage as I had in my own. As we entered, I couldn't help but think of all the good times we'd had. Regret filled my heart, and something that sounded like a strangled sigh wrenched its way out.

"Are you okay?" Harmony turned to me, her concern evident in the creases lining her forehead.

"Yeah." I took in a deep breath, filling my lungs. "It's just...I haven't been back since..."

"Oh my gosh. I'm so sorry. How insensitive of me." She grabbed my arm, whirling me around and leading me away from the garage. "I had no idea."

My hand went to my eyes. I wasn't going to cry, but it felt like the weight of the world had just slammed into my chest and left a hole the size of a monster truck. "It's okay."

"No, it's not. I didn't even think." She pulled me in for a

hug, her arms wrapping around my middle, clutching me to her.

I let her. It felt good to have someone care. I lingered for a beat before breaking loose. "I'm fine, really." I summoned my best "don't give a shit" expression, the one I used to psych out my competitors when I used to ride the racing circuit.

"Oh, okay." She backed away. I wanted to pull her close again, lose myself in her hair and let her erase the deep-seated ache that wouldn't go away no matter how hard I tried to ignore it.

"I'd better get back before Mom thinks I abandoned her." I attempted a smile.

"Will I see you around later?" she asked.

"Maybe. I might bring Mom to the diner for lunch if we get back in time."

"Sounds good." She followed me to the truck. "Hey, Dustin?"

"Yeah?"

"Thanks for getting us out of the mud last night. What you said about Liam, I'm thinking about it, okay?"

"I didn't mean to overstep." That was kind of a lie. I didn't mean to tell her how to raise her kid, but I also saw so much of myself in him, I felt an obligation to try to speak up. I knew what it was like to not be able to put my feelings into words at that age. Hell, I wasn't any better at it all these years later, either.

"I know." Her hand touched my arm. "He's everything to me." She looked up at me, her eyes welling with unshed tears. "It's hard trying to be mom and dad to him."

"I wish you'd tell me what happened to his dad," I muttered before I could stop myself.

She ran a finger under her eye, wiping away any sign of

tears. "He didn't want to be part of our lives." Her gaze met mine. "He wasn't a good guy. It's for the best."

I tried but couldn't get a read on exactly what she meant by that last comment. "Did he hurt you?" I asked, suddenly feeling more protective of Harmony and Liam than I had about anyone else in a long time.

"It was forever ago." She managed a weak smile, one that didn't make it to her eyes. "I sometimes forget, though, that Liam isn't a little boy anymore."

"Looks like he'll always be a bit of a mama's boy."

She gave me a skeptical look. "Like you?"

I chuckled. "Hey, you grow up without a dad and you can't help but be a little more protective of your mom."

Harmony nodded. "Speaking of your mom, shouldn't you get going?"

"Yeah. She'll be pissed if I make her late for her appointment." I climbed into the cab of the truck and leaned out the window. "He's a good kid."

She smiled. "Thanks. He is."

I wanted to say more, to tell her that she was a good mom and that things between her and Liam would be just fine. Was that how it had worked out for me? I'd left my mom when she needed me most. I didn't have anything left to give. Now that I was back, I had to figure out a way to make it up to her. Fit fifteen years of good deeds into a couple of short weeks. Before I left her again.

THE DOC PUSHED a piece of paper across the desk toward us. "You're healthy as a horse, Mrs. Jarrett."

"Then why does she keep getting dizzy?" I asked.

"We'll keep an eye on things," the doc said. "Start with

taking it easy. Maybe take some time off work and let the kids help you more at home."

"She will," I promised.

The doc shook my hand before ushering us out of the office. Mom didn't waste any time, just hustled out to the parking lot.

"Mom?" I caught up to her easily. "How long has this been going on?"

She kept her gaze ahead. "A few months. Don't worry, I've got it all under control."

"I don't think it's something you can control." I beat her to the truck and held the door for her. "The doc said you need to make sure you're not overdoing it."

"Honey, you know me. I couldn't sit still if I tried. When I start to feel lightheaded, I take a break. Otherwise I'd prefer not to dwell on it."

Not to dwell? Damn, my mother could be stubborn as a mule sometimes. But even a mule would rest when it got tired. "I'm not trying to dwell on it. But you've got to take better care of yourself."

"I do." Mom pulled the door shut, essentially ending the conversation.

How much did Scarlett know about this? She'd been taking Mom to her appointments. Why hadn't they told me? I rounded the front of the truck and climbed in.

"You need to stop anywhere on the way home?" I asked.

"No. It's Tuesday. I need to get the wash done this afternoon. Frank comes for dinner on Tuesdays, and I promised pork chops with caramel apples tonight."

"Frank can figure out how to feed himself. And I'll do the wash."

"Don't be ridiculous, Dustin."

"Who do you think does my laundry when I'm not at

home?" My housekeeper did, but Mom didn't need to know that. I'd been on my own since I was seventeen. There was a time when I had to do everything for myself, and I hadn't forgotten how.

Mom folded her hands over her stomach. "Frank was just widowed last year. I'm pretty sure the meal he eats with me is the only well-balanced meal he gets all week."

"Then I'll make dinner. Pork chops and what else?" I asked.

"Apples in caramel sauce. It's his favorite."

The way Mom held herself while we discussed Mr. Blevins made me wonder if there was more behind her fixing him dinner than her concern over him getting a well-balanced meal. I'd have to ask Scarlett about it later.

"Want to stop in at the diner for lunch on the way home?"

"You sure do seem eager to get me to the diner today." Mom narrowed her eyes as she glanced over at me. "What exactly is going on with you and Harmony?"

"Nothing. Assuming the city lets her have the space, I'm going to help her build out the studio, and she's going to make sure I get back in shape before..." I almost said before I lost the part on the movie my agent had pretty much guaranteed was mine.

"And?" Mom asked.

"And what? That's all." Brow furrowed, I turned to face her as I came to a stop at a red light.

"Hmm." Mom looked out the window.

Hmm? That was it? Didn't matter what Mom thought she knew about Harmony and me. Bottom line was we were exchanging services, bartering one specialty for another. That was all. It didn't make a bit of difference that the sight of her kick started my heart. Or that being around her made me ache for something deep inside.

"So is that a yes to lunch at the diner, or do you want to go home?" I hadn't gotten a response.

"If it's okay with you, I'd rather just go home. This trip into town pretty much wore me out. I think I need to take a rest before I get started on the wash."

I groaned. "Mom, I'm doing the wash this afternoon. And making pork chops."

"If you say so, honey." She reached across the console and patted my arm, a complacent smile stretched across her mouth.

I'd show her. I was going to rock that laundry room and cook the crap out of those pork chops. Just as soon as she told me how.

21

HARMONY

"We'll have a couple of massage rooms in the back and a studio space where I can teach yoga or do classes." I finished sketching a rough layout of the design Dustin and I had worked on the night before.

Cassie leaned over the counter to check out the drawing. "That sounds amazing. And you're sure Dustin can do all of that himself before he leaves again?"

"He said he could. Why? Do you not think he's capable?" A coldness flowed through my heart, leeching outward to fill my limbs with lead. Was there something Cassie knew but wasn't telling me?

"I have no idea." She shrugged. "Robbie hasn't talked to him in years. But if you need help, Robbie can probably fit you in." She pushed away from the counter. "Somewhere between finishing up the farmhouse remodel he's working on and revamping the courthouse."

"So sometime in the next five years?" I asked.

"Eighteen months." She spun around to finish setting up the coffee monster. "It's nice his business is going well. There was a time when he thought he'd lose it all."

"I know. I'm glad the two of you are doing so well. And grateful for you taking Liam and me in."

"We didn't take you in, we just happened to be able to help out a bit. Robbie's dad's old place isn't exactly a dream house."

I let out a laugh. "True. But still"—I paused until she met my gaze—"I want you to know how much I appreciate it."

Cassie lifted one shoulder then let it fall. "You're family."

It was good to have family. Out in LA we'd been on our own. My parents had moved to an active adult community in Hemet, but even though they were only about ninety miles away, it could still take three to four hours to get there due to traffic. So we didn't see them nearly as often as I would have liked. Being here, in Swallow Springs, definitely had its perks. Life was slower, less complicated, more predictable. I just hoped the good people of Swallow Springs would be open-minded when it came to accepting a wellness center like the one I envisioned.

"Want me to take the deliveries today?" I asked. Cassie offered box lunch service and usually had a standing order from several places around town.

"Sure. I have one going to City Hall. Maybe you can check in on the zoning office while you're there and find out what kind of permits you'd need to get started on construction."

"Good idea." I'd planned on dropping by on my way home this afternoon anyway. That would save me some time. I untied my apron and hung it on a hook. "Where else do you have me going?"

Cassie handed me a clipboard. "City Hall, then a couple of orders at the Cut 'N Curl. Oh, and the chiropractor on the outskirts of town."

"There's a chiropractor in town?"

"Yeah, we've actually got two. Dr. Hank is a quack. He's been around for years. But there's a new guy who opened up shop about a year ago. He's the one who ordered the veggie club." She leaned close and raised her eyebrows. "With a side of fresh fruit."

Tingles raced down to my toes. "Veggies and fruit? You're kidding." Most of the diner crowd preferred their chicken-fried steak with country gravy or a meatloaf sandwich with garlic mashed potatoes on the side. Cassie's recipes were mouth-wateringly delicious, but even though she sourced local produce and kept everything organic, they still contained a gazillion calories. We offered healthier options but usually the only ones who went for the lighter side of the menu were under strict doctor's orders. How refreshing to hear of someone who preferred a meal containing all four food groups.

"Oh, and he's single, too." Cassie added that nugget of info like an afterthought, but I knew better.

"Is that why you want me to do the deliveries today?" I asked. "This isn't a veggie sandwich hook-up attempt, is it?"

Cassie rolled a lemon around on the counter, working on a batch of fresh-squeezed lemonade. "Of course not. But he's kind of cute. And if a sandwich delivery happens to turn into something more..." She smiled as her words drifted away.

I shook my head. "And I thought I'd escaped the fix-ups by moving out here."

"It's not a fix-up, I swear. Just take the man his sandwich, will you?" She winked at me as she cut the lemon in two and reached for another.

"Fine." I wasn't about to tell her I'd had an almost-hook-up with Dustin. From what I'd gathered, she wasn't a huge fan of his.

"Y'all can talk about your studio. Maybe he'll have some ideas." Cassie didn't look up as I grabbed the handles of the big brown bag.

"We'll see." No promises. With the studio space becoming a real possibility, I felt like I was finally following the path I'd always wanted. I wouldn't let anything knock me off course, not now.

I navigated the truck around the streets of Swallow Springs, stopping at the Cut 'N Curl first. Scarlett sat at the front desk, her phone tucked under her ear. She gestured for me to set the food down on the counter in front of her and held up a finger, signaling me to wait.

As she finished up her call, I glanced around. I hadn't been in the Cut 'N Curl yet, I usually just trimmed my own split ends and didn't see the need to spend a small fortune for someone to cut my hair. The inside of the shop made me think it could have been lifted straight out of the 1950s. Light pink floral wallpaper covered the walls. Customers sat in teal vinyl chairs, a few of them under iconic dryers I'd only seen in the movies. While I looked around, Scarlett's conversation caught my attention.

"We've been doing fine so far. Now all of a sudden you think you can come back in town and tell me what I've been doing wrong all this time? That's not fair, Dustin."

I didn't want to eavesdrop, but anything having to do with Dustin Jarrett kind of related to me. At least that's how I justified not walking away when Scarlett continued.

"I've got to go." Her gaze cut to me. "We can talk about this later."

She jabbed at a button on her phone then tossed it into something under the counter.

"Sorry. My brother is being an asshole." She lifted her gaze to mine. "Again."

Not sure how best to respond to that, I nudged the bag forward. "Three meatloaf sandwiches and two bowls of the soup of the day. Utensils are in the bag."

"Thanks." Scarlett stood and reached into the bag, then turned to announce to the other women in the shop. "Lunch is here."

"I'll see you later."

"Hey, Harmony?"

"Yes?"

"He's a good guy."

When I didn't respond right away, she leaned forward. "Dustin. He's just being all over protective right now. Thinks he can stay away for years and then come back and tell all of us what we've been doing wrong all this time."

I took a step closer to the counter. "I don't know what's happening, but maybe he feels bad for not being here. Maybe he's trying to fix that by showing he cares."

"Maybe. It's just not fair. Mom and I have been doing just fine. Now he's bitching because she's been having these dizzy spells. They started right after he got back. Thinks she needs to be evaluated by some hoity toity doc out in California."

"I'm sorry. But I'd better get going." I didn't want to get caught up in some family battle. "I have a couple more deliveries to make before heading back to the café."

She nodded. "Thanks for the delivery. See you later."

Next up, City Hall. Two loaded clubs going to the city inspector's office. I snagged the bag of sandwiches and made my way into the building.

"Lunch. Thank goodness." A middle-aged woman stood

as I approached. "I love Tuesdays. It's the one day a week I let myself order from Cassie's place."

I couldn't help but grin as she enthusiastically took the sandwiches out of the bag.

"Boss, lunch is here," she shouted in the direction of the office behind her.

"Is this where I ask about building permits?" I asked.

"I can help you with that." A man not much older than me came out of the office. "We can also license your dog, help you apply for a garage sale permit, and sell you a cemetery plot."

"Wow, you're a real one-stop shop."

"Hi, I'm Jake Duncan." He reached over the counter to shake my hand.

"Nice to meet you. Harmony Rogers."

"I know. I coach baseball with your cousin, Rob. I'm surprised we haven't run into each other yet." He grabbed his sandwich from the desk. "Sounds like you're going to be making some changes to the building that housed the old accounting office downtown?"

"I hope so. Word travels fast around here, doesn't it?"

He nodded. "The good and the bad. And you'll be working with Dustin Jarrett on the remodel?"

"Um, yeah." He wasn't kidding. Dustin and I had barely made that decision ourselves.

"So depending on what changes you're planning on making, we'll just need some time to go over the plans. Usually we ask for two weeks before construction starts, but I'm pretty free right now so I ought to be able to fit you right in."

"Well that's good news. I'll send Dustin your way once he's got the plans drawn up." I left the office, my step a little lighter. At least something was starting to go my way. This had to work out, otherwise I'd end up serving diners at the café until I couldn't stand straight any more or accidentally burned it down by never figuring out how to work the coffee pot.

My mind wasn't on the road ahead; I was working out how we'd advertise the wellness center grand opening, what kind of mini tarts we could serve, and mulling over options for a name. So when something large and feathered ran across the road, it caught me by surprise. I veered right, onto the bumpy shoulder and slammed on the brakes. Whatever it was, I'd nicked it. Turning back, I covered the distance to where a large mass of feathers lay in a clump in the middle of the two-lane road.

I approached with caution, not sure if I'd hit a giant raptor, a heron, or some sort of prehistoric beast. It was too big to be a hawk. The coloring and shape wasn't right for an eagle. As I got closer, it raised its head. Two cloudy eyes gazed out at me, attached to a long, U-shaped neck. Good Lord, I'd been right—it was an ostrich.

"Hey there." I put my hands out, trying to assure the bird that it was okay.

It made a noise deep in its throat like a mix between a growl and a hiss before swiveling its head around.

"It's okay. I'm not going to hurt you." I walked around the animal in a wide circle, looking for any signs of injury.

Its beak opened slightly and a clicking noise came out. It made me think of the sound a rattlesnake made right before it struck.

"We need to get you out of the middle of the road."

The bird might have understood or maybe it was just scared shitless, because it tried to hobble to its feet. Over and over it pushed up on one leg, only to fall down again. The injured leg wouldn't hold weight. I must have hit it right before it made it across the road. My heart ached to see an animal suffer. *What to do, what to do.* Considering I only had contact information for a few people in town, my options were limited. The most logical choice would be to call Robbie. But he was working a job all the way over in Springfield and I knew if I reached out, he wouldn't hesitate to drive all the way back.

That left Cassie, who probably wouldn't be much help in a situation like this, and Dustin. Reluctantly, I pulled up his number on my phone. It rang twice and I tried to think of what kind of message I might be able to leave.

"Hello?"

The sound of his voice made my core light up, sending heat radiating outward. "Hi, are you busy?"

"No. Just got back from running Mom to her doctor's appointment. What's going on?"

"I'm not sure you'll believe me."

Warmth filtered through the phone. I could picture him with that smirk on his mouth, a hint of humor in his gorgeous green eyes. "Try me."

"I hit an ostrich while making a sandwich delivery, and it's lying in the middle of the road."

"Is it dead? An ostrich? Are you sure it's an ostrich?"

I glanced toward the lump of feathers. "It's a big bird—"

"Is it yellow?"

"Yellow? No. It's gray and brownish. Why would you ask if it's yellow?"

"Yellow, like Big Bird. Get it?"

"Dustin, I'm standing in the middle of the highway with a giant injured bird. Are you going to sit around cracking Sesame Street jokes or can you come help me out?"

"Where exactly are you?"

I gave him my approximate location. It was the best I

could do seeing as there weren't exactly any reference points and I hadn't been paying attention when I passed the last mile marker. While I waited, I squatted down to take a closer look at the bird.

Its head continued to swivel around without stopping to focus on anything. At one point it stared right at me, a vacant look, like it could see right through me. When would Dustin get here?

Fifteen minutes later his truck eased to a stop behind mine.

22

DUSTIN

"What the hell is that?" I hopped out of the cab and strolled toward where Harmony crouched down in the middle of the road.

"It's an ostrich. I think it's hurt. Do you think we can get it into the back of the truck?"

"That's not an ostrich." The woman grew up in California but surely they had books. Couldn't she tell the difference between an ostrich and an emu?

"Then what is it?" Her eyes squinted and she shielded her face from the sun as she turned toward me.

I moved closer, leery of the giant bird. "Looks like an emu to me. Similar to an ostrich but smaller."

"Are you sure?" Her head swiveled back and forth between me and the bird.

"Pretty sure. There used to be an emu farm west of town. Maybe it's from there." How else would we be able to explain the presence of an emu in the middle of Missouri?

"Do you think it escaped? Or maybe it was someone's pet. It seems pretty docile." She reached a hand toward the bird. It didn't flinch.

"I don't think it's still around. There for a while people were going crazy over emus and ostriches. We had a ton of farms pop up around town."

"Then what?"

"Then they all went out of business to make way for the next craze. Bison became the next red meat." I shrugged. Seemed to be the norm around here. Some know-it-all from the city would get a wild hair and decide they wanted to live the simple life. They'd sell their giant McMansion and move out to the country. After a while they'd get bored and flee back to the city.

"So they just left the birds?" She moved even closer. The emu rotated its head around. That beak sure looked sharp.

"They probably sold them. Maybe this one got out. Whatever happened, we need to get it out of the road." And her. Sitting in the middle of the blacktop made me nervous. At any moment a truck could come over the crest of the small hill and take all of us out. "Let me see if I have a blanket in the back."

As luck would have it, I didn't have a blanket, but I did have a towel. It would have to do.

"Is that it?" Harmony asked when I returned. "You really think that's going to protect us?"

"You know, if you want to call someone else to help you, I'd be all for it." I knelt down next to her, the hot asphalt burning through the knees of my jeans. "I've had more encounters with wild animals in the few days since I met you than I have in the past fifteen years."

"I'm sorry. I just can't seem to catch a break here. What's with all of the crazy animals this week?"

"I don't know. Some people just seem to be a magnet for weird shit."

Harmony let out a laugh. Sounded like sunshine to my

ears. Why didn't she laugh more often? "Is that me? A magnet for weird shit?"

"Maybe. I've never seen someone get stuck with baby raccoons, a skunk, and an emu all in one week."

"Have you ever heard of anyone getting stuck with all three *ever*?"

"Got a point there. Can't say that I have."

We grinned at each other, caught up in the ridiculousness of the moment. I wanted to kiss her. I hadn't been able to get those few precious minutes we'd spent on the stairs out of my head. Before I had a chance to lean over and capture her mouth with mine, the pavement trembled under my legs. Something was coming. Something big.

"Here, toss the edge of that towel over its head." I flung the corner of the ragged towel toward her.

She pulled it over the bird, pinning down its head. The towel whipped back and forth before flying across the road.

"I'll go grab it."

"Harmony, no!" I reached out, grabbing her by the arm as a semi pulling a full trailer rumbled over the hill, heading right toward us.

She struggled to lift the bird. I got my hands underneath and levered it up. The three of us scrambled for the side of the road just as the truck roared by.

"That was a close one." I shifted the weight of the giant bird in my arms. It didn't appear to be frazzled at all. Harmony on the other hand, didn't look so good. She leaned over, her head resting on the hood. "Are you okay?"

"Yeah. Just a little lightheaded."

"Come here." I set the bird down on the grass and pulled her into my arms, letting her lean against my chest.

She pressed her cheek to my pec, making me wish we

weren't standing on the side of the road with an awkward bird.

"I'm okay. That just scared the crap out of me."

"You and me both." I brushed my hand over her cheek.

The bird squawked. "What should we do with it?"

"You're the one on a first name basis with the wildlife rehab center. Want to give them a call?"

"I think they might have blocked my number. I still haven't had a chance to get the raccoons up there, but I've been calling them all the time with questions." She squatted down next to the emu. "He looks injured."

Dropping down next to her, I took a look at the bird. One leg had a nasty cut. "A vet ought to take a look at that. The sooner the better."

"You're right." She pulled her phone out of her back pocket. "Lucky for me I added Dr. Hobert's number to my contacts earlier this week."

While Harmony talked to the receptionist at the vet's office, I studied the bird. No matter where I moved, its eyes didn't follow, which was strange for an animal, seeing as how it had to feel threatened. I leaned in, trying to get a better look. A layer of cloudiness covered the poor bird's eyes. I'd bet my competition bike that the damn bird couldn't see a thing.

Harmony rejoined me. "They said to bring it in. Do you have time to handle that? I've still got a delivery to make to the chiropractor's office."

"But I've got laundry going and have to get home in time to make pork chops and apples in caramel sauce."

She stepped back, appraising me with raised eyebrows. "What happened to you? Laundry and pork chops?"

I shook my head, dropping my gaze to my toes. "It's my mom. I took her to the doctor this morning. All of a sudden she's been getting these dizzy spells and they can't figure out why."

Harmony placed a hand on my arm. "I heard Scarlett talking to you on the phone. How bad is it?"

My shoulders slumped, the guilt of not being around threatening to bowl me over. "I don't know. Mom wouldn't admit to feeling bad even if she were on her deathbed."

"Well that's not happening." Harmony's hand brushed over my arm. "I may have some oils or something else that can help."

"You really think those little oils are going to make a difference?"

She ran her thumb over the spot where the coffee had burned my hand. "They've worked in the past."

"I suppose it's worth giving it a shot."

"So how about I run lunch over to the chiropractor while you handle the bird?" I gave her my best grin, hoping we could swap errands.

"Fine. I wouldn't want you to be late on getting the laundry done or not have time to make your pork chops."

"You and Liam want to come over for dinner?"

"Two nights in a row? People might talk."

"Let 'em." I leaned in, wrapped my arm around her waist and drew her close. Her breath tickled my skin.

"Do you think this is a good idea?"

"No." My nose nudged into her hair, breathing in that earthy combo that hovered around her.

"Then why start something?" She spoke into my chest.

I put my finger under her chin, tipping her face up so she'd meet my gaze. "I can't not start something. I'm drawn to you, Harmony, craziness and all. Did I see this coming? Hell no. Do I want to get caught up in something that's going to have to come to an end? Hell no on that, too."

"Then why?" Her eyes told me everything I needed to know about how she must be feeling inside. A mix of hope, hurt, and helplessness pulled at my heart.

I didn't want to hurt her. And leaving in a couple of weeks would do that. But how could I deny the feelings she stirred up inside? I wasn't that strong. At that moment, another possibility entered my mind.

"I was planning on going back to LA in a couple of weeks."

"Even more of a reason not to get involved."

"But with my mom not feeling well...what if I stuck around for a while longer?" As I said the words out loud my mind was made up. I could spend the summer in Swallow Springs, give my shoulder ample time to heal before I went back to the doc. "If you don't want this, just say so. Tell me to leave you alone and we'll keep things professional." I brushed my finger along her jaw. She shivered.

"What if I can't?" Her gaze met mine again. She felt it too.

"Then we go into it with eyes wide open. Have a bit of fun while it lasts."

"No regrets?" she asked.

"No regrets," I confirmed. "If we're both on the same page, how could it go wrong?"

She nodded. "Okay. Let's do this. A summer fling with no commitment and no regrets."

"So can I count on you for pork chops tonight?" I asked.

"Caramel apples, too?"

"All the caramel apples you can eat."

"I think I'd better avoid the sugar."

"Sugar, no sugar, it's up to you."

She nodded, her head barely moving against my shirt. I snugged her against me and lowered my head to meet her lips. The heat, the humidity, the awkward bird at our feet...it all faded into oblivion. I could have stood there for fifteen seconds or fifteen hours. Time lost all meaning as Harmony wrapped her arms around me and met my mouth with hers, time after time.

We only broke apart when a truck rolled by. A horn sounded, invading the private dimension we'd carved out between us.

"Oh my gosh, I've got to go." She wiped her fingers over her lips. "Can you put the bird in the back of the truck? I need to get to the vet and head back to the diner before Liam's out of school."

"Sure." The bird didn't move as I attempted to scoop it up in my arms. My shoulder twinged and I grunted.

"You need some help?" Harmony asked.

"I got it." Staggering to my feet, I readjusted my grip before loading the feathered beast into the bed of the truck. "Where am I going for that delivery?"

She reached into the truck and pulled out a brown bag. "The chiropractor just down the road. Watch out though, Cassie said he's cute."

I kissed the top of her head. "Even more of a reason for me to make the delivery instead of you."

"Don't go getting all possessive on me now. Nobody can know about this. I don't want Liam to get any ideas."

That's not exactly how I would have done things, but if we kept it a secret then I wouldn't have to handle questions from my family either. And it would make it easier to leave when the time came if no one knew we'd been involved except us.

"Fine. So tonight? Pork chops at seven?"

"I have a better idea," Harmony said. "Why don't you

sneak out after dinner and swing by my place? Liam's out like a light by ten."

"You've got yourself a deal. Now go take care of Big Bird."

She fired up the engine and blew me a kiss. As I watched her drive away, I couldn't help but wonder what would go wrong. Because if history had taught me anything, it was that Swallow Springs and me didn't add up to a happy ending, no matter what. For a moment I thought about texting her and calling the whole thing off. She obviously didn't need a guy like me in her life, even in secret. But the anticipation of having her in my arms in a few hours, of getting to explore every inch of her with my eyes, my mouth, my tongue, shot that idea down faster than I could have scarfed down one of Mom's mud pie patties.

I'd be careful. Not let Harmony get attached. No strings meant no guilt. And I needed to leave Swallow Springs without a ton of regrets hanging over my shoulder when the time came. This time.

23

HARMONY

I smeared a thick layer of mud over the emu's leg. Poor bird stood still, letting me run my hands over the wound. It was healing up nicely, thanks to Dustin's magic mud. For a moment I wondered how my life had come to this. I'd gone from a busy life in LA to feeding a trio of raccoons, catering to a needy skunk, and harboring a giant, blind bird.

Either the fresh country air was making me crazier than normal or I was starting to actually enjoy my newfound life. I reached a hand out and smoothed down the soft feathers on the emu's back. He twitched then swiveled his head around, seeking out the dried apricot I held in my hand.

"Goodnight, Magoo." I let myself out of the makeshift pen we'd rigged on the side of the garage and made my way back to the house.

Exhausted, I peeked in on Liam to make sure he was asleep. Out like a light. That was the one thing I could count on with my son. He slept like the dead. And thank goodness for that. Dustin would be knocking on my door—I checked my watch—any minute.

That didn't give me much time to get ready. I ran a tooth-brush over my teeth then took my ponytail down and tried to fluff my hair. What he saw would pretty much be what he got with me. I'd never been one to fluff and primp, and I wasn't about to change my ways.

It had been a long time since I'd entertained a man. The last guy I'd even kind of dated had been a few years back. I wasn't into swiping left or right and preferred to meet poten-tial dates the old-fashioned way—in person. That put a severe limitation on the possibilities. Reva had introduced me to one of her clients—a relatively normal guy with a tennis injury. We'd hit it off but he bailed when he found out I had a kid. At least Dustin knew what he was getting into, even if we were going to keep it under wraps.

I walked back to my bedroom. Maybe I should change my shirt. I had to keep reminding myself that it wasn't like we were going to be dating. I didn't need to try to impress him or even look good. What I wanted from Dustin was purely physical, and evidently he felt the same. I ditched the idea of changing into something less unisex. My LA Kings T-shirt would do just fine.

With nothing left to do but wait and second guess myself, I sat down on the edge of the couch. Maybe this was a bad idea. I'd never done a pure hook-up before. Some-thing was bound to go wrong. Liam would find out or Mrs. Jarrett would suspect something. I snagged my phone from the coffee table, ready to call the whole thing off.

Someone tapped on the front door.

I'd have to have this chat in person. I pulled open the door to find Dustin on the porch, a bouquet of flowers in his hand. The last man who'd given me flowers had probably been my dad when I graduated from college.

"Hey." He stood in the doorway, looking entirely lickable

in hip-hugging jeans, a form-fitting T-shirt, and holding a colorful bouquet of wildflowers.

"What are you doing?" I grabbed the flowers out of his hand. "You aren't supposed to bring me flowers."

"Sorry. I thought you might like them."

"I do. But it doesn't matter. We're not doing flowers."

Dustin grinned, tucked one thumb in his belt loop and reached for my hand. "What exactly are we doing?"

I let him pull me out onto the porch. "I don't know. It seemed like a good idea earlier today, but now—"

"Now you've changed your mind?" He stepped close, too close, crowding into my space.

I turned, resting my back against the door frame. He didn't touch me, just stood there, his body lined up with mine. The ache I'd felt for him earlier in the day returned with a vengeance, throbbing between my legs. My arms itched to wrap around his neck. My lips tingled in anticipation of another kiss.

He moved in closer. I didn't even think it was possible. I might have been able to slide a piece of paper between us, but that would be about all that would fit. His fingers traced the outline of my cheek in the air. I could almost feel them. Almost, that was the problem.

"Did you change your mind, Harmony?"

The way he said my name, all gravely and wispy, was the final straw.

"No." I managed to say the one word before his mouth captured mine.

His hands went behind my head, cushioning me against the door jamb while the rest of him pressed into me, all hard planes and rigid lines. I let the flowers fall to the porch before I moved my arms up, circling his neck. His lips moved from my mouth to my cheek, trailing down to my collarbone.

"Not here." How I could even think rationally at that moment was beyond me. But I knew we couldn't do the kinds of things I wanted Dustin to do to me out in the open of the front porch. "The bedroom."

He pulled away long enough to eye the doorway to the house. "I can't. I haven't been in there since...since that day. I'm sorry. Is there somewhere else?"

Somewhere else? "Like where?"

"The truck?" he asked.

"No." I'd been there, done that.

"Give me a second." Dustin let go, taking his warmth with him, giving me a moment to consider where this was headed. It was crazy. This wasn't the kind of thing I'd done in the past. Which was precisely why I wanted to.

Dustin returned, a blanket draped over his arm. "Trust me?"

We seemed to keep coming back to that question. I did trust him. I trusted him to get my truck out of the mud. I trusted him to take apart my engine and put it back together again. But did I trust him with my feelings? Did I trust him not to break my heart?

"Yes." I twined my fingers with his before I let myself over think things.

He led me around the house to the backyard and down a well-worn path. The pond sat behind the house, halfway between Robbie's dad's place and where Robbie and Cassie lived now at her grandparents' remodeled farmhouse.

"Have you been out here before?" I asked.

"Just to skip rocks and swim on a hot summer's day." He held my hand, leading me away from the house.

I turned back as it disappeared beyond the ridge of a

small hill leading down to the water. There would be no way Liam could see us from here. The tension drained from my shoulders.

Finally, he stopped at the end of a small dock. He spread the blanket out and moved to stand in front of me. Taking my hands, he bent to kiss my neck. I couldn't help but respond.

Within moments he'd pulled me down to the blanket. The hard boards of the dock pressed against my back but it didn't matter. His hands worked up and down my side, his fingers finding their way under the edge of my shirt. Goosebumps pebbled my skin, and a spark of desire ignited in my gut before slowly spreading through my limbs. When was the last time I wanted a man like this? The thought entered my mind but was immediately pushed away by the sensations flooding my nervous system. What Dustin was doing with his tongue along the rim of my ear crowded out any rational thoughts.

I let my hands roam over the sculpted muscles of his shoulders, being careful not to touch his injured ribs. His groan reverberated through me, making me even more eager, more desperate to feel him everywhere.

His mouth moved down my neck, over my collarbone, stopping at my chest. "You all in on this with me?" he asked.

I nodded, incapable of speech.

His fingers undid my button. I lifted my butt so he could slide my shorts down my legs. He kissed my navel, moving lower, avoiding the place I most wanted to feel his touch. With a grin of someone who enjoyed teasing way too much, he lowered his face and kissed his way down my inner thigh all the way to my ankle.

I sat up and reached for him. He kissed his way back up my other leg then paused to wriggle out of his own pants.

Did the man not own a pair of underwear? His shirt followed, landing on top of the accumulating pile of clothing. The light of the moon bathed him, turning him into a mixture of shadows and smooth planes. He took pride in keeping his body in shape and it showed in the curve of his muscle, the definition of his pecs.

For just a moment I gazed in appreciation. Then he reached for my shirt, lifting the edge up and over my head. I crossed my arms over my breasts, suddenly slightly chilled with the full force of his gaze bearing down on me.

He settled on the blanket, pulling me closer. With a final nod to my reservations, I dismissed them. Told them to take a hike. Before I had a chance to change my mind I took the foil packet he held between his fingers and ripped it open. While he unrolled the condom in place, I slid my underwear down my legs and tossed them toward the rest of our clothes. Then I straddled him, wrapped my legs around his waist and lowered myself onto him.

He leaned back, his palms flat on the dock, watching me move against him. I didn't care. The need to feel him deep inside shredded my inhibitions. It had been so long, too long, since I'd taken pleasure from something that didn't require batteries. He waited, letting me find the perfect angle.

With my knees on either side of his thighs, I was in complete control. He moved slightly, his arms wrapping around my back, pulling me into him. His mouth found my breast, and he scraped his teeth over my nipple, teasing me. Two could play at that game. I lifted up and lowered myself fully onto his lap. His breath came out in a heavy exhale, blowing over my naked chest, stirring something deep inside. My fingers dug into his shoulders and I lifted myself again, over and over, taking him deeper and deeper each time.

He held back, his restraint clear in the clench of his jaw, the tightness of his shoulders. Then finally, my release washed over me. I drew it out as long as I could, riding that wave of pleasure until I'd wrenched every last possible sensation from it.

Breathless, I leaned against him, feeling his hands run up and down my back, the sweet heat of his kisses falling on my cheeks. Gently, he urged me back. I stretched my limbs, satiated and satisfied, like a cat who'd just enjoyed an afternoon nap in the sun.

Dustin hovered over me, then nudged my legs apart with his knee. I lifted my hips, welcoming him. He pushed into me, driving into me with a force I hadn't expected. I wrapped my legs around his back, pulling him in with each thrust. My back rubbed against the blanket and we scooted across the dock. With a final thrust and a shudder, he collapsed on top of me and let out a sigh.

"Are you okay?" he asked, his breath blowing across my neck, cooling the sweat I hadn't even noticed I'd worked up.

"Yeah, you?" My fingertip traced a lazy, scrolling path over his twisty tattoo.

"I don't want to hurt you." He rolled off and nestled into my side. With a hand propped under his cheek, his other cupped my hip, pulling me against him.

"You're not. Although we seem to have lost the blanket." It had bunched up underneath me and we'd scooted off the edge.

He chuckled into my hair. "Sorry about that."

"It was worth it." I stared up at the inky blackness of the sky. A billion stars dotted the darkness, like tiny pinpricks of light.

We stayed like that for a long time, our breath returning to normal, my heartbeat slowing to a steady, comfortable thump. Finally, the sweat cooled and my backside grew tired of the uncomfortable dock.

"I should go in."

"You sure?" He lifted my head to snuggle an arm underneath it. "I swear, I could stay out here with you for hours, maybe even days."

I landed a playful swat on his abs of steel. "You don't think Liam would wonder where I was? Cassie might miss me if I didn't show up for my shift."

"Being a grown up sucks sometimes."

I stretched to plant a kiss on his scruffy chin. "That's the truth."

We laid there for a few more minutes. I tried to soak it all in, the feel of his breath on my cheek, the warmth of his palm on my hip.

"I need to get back." I pushed up off the dock, reluctantly getting to my feet.

He held out a hand and I pulled him up with me. Then the awkward aftermath descended. He handed me my shorts, I tossed him his shirt.

Finally, both of us dressed, he held out a hand. "Can I walk you home?"

"Sure." I finished folding the blanket.

"What's wrong?"

I squirmed, trying to figure out what was going on with my backside. "I don't know. Something's not right. I think I picked up a splinter or two."

"Want me to take a look?"

"No. I'll check when I get inside."

"All right then." He slung an arm over my shoulder and we made the short trek back to the house. When we reached the front porch he turned to face me. Grabbing both of my hands in his, he nestled his mouth against my ear.

My stomach dipped as his breath floated over my neck.

"See you tomorrow?"

Cold clammy hands seemed to squeeze my throat. Tomorrow. I'd have to see him tomorrow and pretend like none of this had happened. "Oh, um—"

"We'll just pretend like nothing happened. Piece of cake, right?"

Piece of cake? Maybe for him. He hadn't been relieved of the main role in his elementary school play for bad acting. And I'd only had one line to say then. How would I possibly be able to convince everyone that there was nothing more going on between me and Dustin than him helping with the build out of the studio space?

"I think maybe it would be better if we didn't see each other tomorrow."

"Really?" His fingers left mine to wrap around my backside and nudge me into him. "I'm going to have to see you, Harmony. One way or another."

"What are we doing, Dustin?"

"Right now? I'm copping a feel and hoping to convince you to let me interpolate you again in the near future." The cocky grin I'd grown to expect graced his lips.

"You're awful."

"Awful hot and bothered. Tomorrow?"

I nodded, not trusting myself to speak.

His lips made contact with my cheek before he let go. I picked up the flowers I'd abandoned during the heat of the moment. Then I stood there while he disappeared down the drive to where he'd parked his truck, wondering how in the world I was going to be able to pull this off.

24

DUSTIN

*T*he next few days passed by in a whirlwind of drawing up plans, getting permits, and helping out around Mom's place. And the nights flew by in a tangle of limbs on the dock out at Harmony's place. By the time I got back to LA, the doc would probably marvel at my state of physical fitness. Harmony and I spent hours on the dock, talking, snuggling, and burying ourselves in each other. I'd enjoyed myself—too much I sometimes worried—but that was all about to come to a screeching halt. Today was the last day of school. For the next several weeks I'd be under constant supervision from both my nephew and Harmony's son.

"Did you get my list?" Mom called out from the kitchen.

"Yeah." I skimmed the handwriting covering the small piece of spiral notepad paper in my hand. "Need anything else while I'm in town?"

"That should do it." She sat at the kitchen table, still in her housecoat and slippers.

"You sure you don't want me to stay back and go later once Scarlett stops by?"

Mom waved her hand. "Don't be ridiculous. I'll be fine. It's just a little dizzy spell."

Her little dizzy spells had been happening more and more frequently. Had me on the verge of calling in a favor from one of the high-powered docs I'd seen out west. But Scarlett and Mom both said I was overreacting. If it got much worse, they wouldn't have a choice—I'd get her to the doctor if I had to take her myself.

"All right. Call if you need me." I leaned over and kissed her forehead. Being around the past couple of weeks had given me a glimpse of what I'd been missing. When I thought about my apartment out in LA it seemed so empty —the opposite of everything I'd left behind in Swallow Springs.

A half hour later I stood in front of the Lovebird Café. Harmony and I had plans to do a final walk-through of the space across the street after the lunch crowd died down. But I'd been in such a hurry to be on my way I'd arrived a half-hour early. With nothing to do but sit outside and twiddle my thumbs in the ninety-eight degree heat or take a stool at the counter inside, I opted for the latter.

As I walked in, the conversation took a nose dive, settling at a low murmur. I thought talk of my botched burnout had died down. What had happened now to make me the laugh-ingstock of Swallow Springs? I took the only empty seat at the counter, next to Mr. Blevins. As I settled onto my stool, conversation picked up around me.

"Hi, Mr. Blevins, what's going on today?" I set my keys on the counter as Harmony placed a coffee mug in front of me.

"Coffee?" she asked, already pouring.

"I guess so. Sorry, I'm early." I caught her eye for a half-second and smiled.

"It's okay. I'll be a little while, we've got a bigger than

usual lunch crowd." She tilted her head, motioning to something behind me.

I twisted in my seat to see Robbie Jordan. He sat at the head of a table of what appeared to be contractors and builders. No wonder my presence had shut down the chit chat. I'd been in town a couple weeks already and had yet to come face-to-face with Robbie. I gave him a nod of acknowledgment and he reciprocated. It was only a matter of time before we sat down for a chat. The kind of conversation we needed to have was long overdue.

But not today.

Today was my last free day to wrap myself in Harmony's arms without the fear of being walked in on by her son or my nephew. Nothing would get me down today.

I took a sip of my coffee and put the mug back down. It hadn't tasted the same since that first day I'd arrived.

"Coffee's different," Mr. Blevins said. "I think she's poisoning us with wheat germ or alfalfa sprouts."

Harmony laughed as she swept by, her hands full of the daily special. "Oh, Frank. If I wanted to poison you, I'd use something much more deadly than wheat germ."

"Told you so." He turned his attention back to his newspaper.

"Now what can I get you for lunch?" Harmony stopped in front of me, pencil poised over her notepad. "We've got a seven superfoods salad or turkey on sprouted toast with a side of fresh fruit."

"How about the meatloaf sandwich?" I licked my lips, almost able to taste the heavenly concoction of ground beef and spices.

"We're out of meatloaf." She leveled me with that blue-gray gaze. "What'll it be, salad or a sandwich?"

At that moment Cassie bustled by. I craned my neck to

see her tray full of meatloaf sandwich platters. "Thought you said you were out of meatloaf?"

"We are. That was the last batch. Now what'll it be? Salad or sprouts?"

"Tuna melt?" I asked.

She shook her head, her lower lip captured between her teeth.

"Turkey sandwich then." I leaned back on my stool while I took another sip of coffee. "And what's with this coffee?"

"You don't like it?" she asked.

"It's just...different."

Mr. Blevins raised his mug next to me. "Different."

"Different can be good." Harmony tucked her pen back into her apron and whirled around to hang my order ticket on the spin rack.

I watched her move around the diner. She still hadn't mastered the fine art of waiting tables. A plate clattered to the ground, smashing into pieces, followed by Harmony making a mad dash to the back for a broom and dustpan. For her sake, I sure hoped she'd be better at running the wellness studio than she was at waiting tables.

"She's not getting any better, is she?" Mr. Blevins didn't look up, just kept his eyes trained on the sports section.

"No, sir. She's not." I couldn't help but smile. "We'd better get her place across the street built out before she wears out her welcome here at the Lovebird."

"You ever had one of those massages she talks about?" he asked, barely glancing up.

"Um, yeah, I've had therapeutic massage before. Helps keep your muscles loose."

Mr. Blevins grunted. "If you ask me, it's probably a front for something."

"Really? Like what?"

"I don't know. But we've made it decades without a sleazy place where you pay for a rubdown. I can't say I've been missing that."

Harmony slid my plate in front of me. "One turkey sandwich platter. Extra honey dew on the side."

"Thanks." I took a napkin from the dispenser and spread it over my lap. "Looks fine."

"Fine?" she paused.

"Yeah, it's not a meatloaf sandwich."

She let out a frustrated sigh before heading to the back.

"You're not winning any brownie points, if you ask me," Mr. Blevins volunteered.

I bit into the sandwich and chewed. Not bad for a plain turkey sandwich. But meatloaf would have been a hell of a lot tastier.

"A woman like that wants to be romanced a little bit."

I forced the dry toast down my throat. Wouldn't have killed her to put a little mayo on it, would it? "I'm sorry, are you talking to me?"

"Who else?" He leaned away from me and poked me in the arm with his finger. "You may as well embrace it."

"Embrace what?"

"The legend."

"What legend?" I took another bite of sandwich, wishing I'd thought to wash down the last one with a sip of bad coffee.

"The legend of the Lovebird Café. Ever since Patsy and Duke took over the place, people who meet here tend to fall in love and get married."

I squinted at Mr. Blevins as I reached for the mug of coffee. "How is it I've never heard of this legend?"

By that time Harmony had stopped in front of me on the other side of the counter. "How's your sandwich?"

"Dry."

"You know about the legend, right, Harmony?" asked Mr. Blevins.

She rolled her eyes. "I've heard about it. But hearing about it and believing in it are two entirely different things."

Before I could ask her about it, she'd moved on to greet a table full of customers who'd just sat down.

"Since when is there a legend?" I set the oversized sandwich on the plate and turned to the stranger on my right. "Did you know there's a Lovebird Café legend?"

"Sure. Young lovers who meet at the Lovebird Café fall in love." The woman next to me on the stool shrugged. "Sorry, sugar, I didn't catch your name."

"It won't work for you, Eloise," said Mr. Blevins. "Not unless you plan on knocking off your husband."

The two laughed like they were in on some joke. A joke that somehow involved me. "Well I think that's bullshit," I said.

"Worked for Cassie and Rob." Mr. Blevins tilted his chin toward the back where Rob dipped Cassie into a kiss.

"Whatever. Why don't you get back to your sports stats and I'll get back to my sandwich?" I suggested.

Mr. Blevins refocused on his newspaper while I choked down the rest of my lunch. By the time I'd finished, Rob and crew had left. I waited for Harmony to bus her tables and get the dining area back in order. What had that whole deal with the legend been about? Had Harmony put him up to it? I followed her path through the café. She stopped to pick up a tab then clear dirty dishes off the table. No way. Harmony and I were on the same page with regard to our arrangement. Weren't we?

Why mess with a good thing? And we had a good thing going. Not just good, great. Maybe it was the fact that both of us had been around the dating block enough times, but we'd cut through all the bullshit and made it straight to the "comfortable in our own skin" part. I wasn't just enjoying spending time with her naked, I also enjoyed chatting with her. She had a great sense of humor and had somehow made my word of the day app into one of the most anticipated moments of my day.

Speaking of...Harmony untied her apron and hung it up behind the counter. "Ready to take one more look before you start on the build out?"

"Yeah."

"You need more coffee first?"

"No. I think you're turning me off coffee."

"Good. It's bad for you. You should try tea instead."

"That'll be the day." I held the door for her as she passed through in front of me.

"The day that what?"

"Huh?"

"You said that'll be the day. What do you mean? What's got to happen to get you to try swapping your coffee for tea?"

I kicked at a rock, sending it rolling to the other side of the street. "I don't know. It's just an expression."

"Well, think about it." She stepped onto the opposite curb and turned to face me. "What would it take?"

"Something big." We were almost behind the safety of the doors, away from the threat of prying eyes. My arms ached to wrap around her and pull her up against me. But not yet.

"What if I rubbed your shoulders for you?"

"Naked?" I slid the key in the lock and turned it.

"Is that all you can think about?"

"No." My lower lip stuck out in a pout. "I think about you rubbing my feet, too."

"Rubbing your feet?"

"Yeah, naked."

"You're incorrigible." She moved into the space. I pulled the door shut behind us and flipped the lock.

"I'll show you incorrigible." I gathered her up in my arms, my hands cupping her ass. She wrapped her legs around my waist and I carried her up the fourteen stairs to the second level, avoiding the top step that still hadn't been repaired.

The light coming in through the large windows slanted across her face. She smiled at me and I was lost. In five seconds I had her shirt up and over her head. In less than ten her back was flush against the exposed brick and her fingernails raked long streaks across my back. We had to stop doing this. Deep down I knew that. But I didn't want to. Didn't even know if I could.

My addiction to Harmony kept me up at night, had me imagining scenarios I never even would have considered a month before. Scenarios that looked a lot like what playing house used to look like when I was a kid. I wasn't ready for that. It had never been something I wanted. Never been something I needed. Had that changed?

A groan ripped through her as I gave a final thrust, losing myself inside her. She clung to me, clenched around me until we both came down from our climax. As our breathing returned to normal, a lazy smile spread across her face. Knowing I was the cause of that smile made me want to start all over again.

"We've got to stop meeting like this." I pulled out, setting her feet back down on the ground.

"You're absolutely right. My ass can't take it." She peered over her shoulder, trying to catch sight of her perfectly rounded butt.

"Did I do that to you?" An angry red scrape covered half a butt cheek.

She eased her underwear up over her thighs. "I definitely didn't do that on my own."

"I'm sorry. I'll take the wall next time."

"First splinters, now this. I'm beginning to think you're too dangerous for me."

She had no idea. Up until now we'd been having fun. But with the boys about to be out of school, it was time to put a stop to our daily trysts. I *was* too dangerous for her. She needed stability, safety, security. The last thing she needed was a guy who couldn't even give her a piece of his heart.

"Listen, about us."

"Us? There's an 'us' now?" She smirked as she pulled her shirt on over her head. "I thought we were anti-us."

"Yeah, we are. You're right. Technically there is no us."

"But..." She came up behind me, wrapping her arms around to the front of my chest and snuggling her head against my shoulder. Her breasts pushed into my back.

I fought the need to spin around and claim her again. My overwhelming desire to possess her battled with the logic of keeping this purely physical, simple.

"But it feels like the anti-us isn't quite working."

Her breath brushed against my back. "That's because you can't keep your pants on around me."

I laughed. She wasn't lying. The more time we spent together, the fewer clothes I seemed to need. "While that is true, I need to figure out how we're going to handle ourselves with Rodney and Liam in the picture."

"What they don't know won't hurt them. We don't owe anyone anything, right?"

"Riiiiiiiiiiight." It couldn't be that easy. But as she pressed against me, making my heart thump in time to hers, I wondered if it might be. Maybe I was making it too complicated. "So you don't want to change anything?"

"I do want to change the height of that wall over there." She pointed to the taped off area we'd marked on the floor. "Not everyone is as tall as you. I think we need to lower it by a few inches."

And just like that she was back to business. We went over the plans, checking and double checking that I had things just how she wanted them. Despite my thoughts in the café, I had no doubt she'd succeed—she had that perfect combination of creative vision and realistic business sense. But I did have my doubts that I'd be able to keep my heart as shielded as I'd originally thought. And that might prove to be a problem.

25

HARMONY

I snagged a big box of cookies out of the back of Cassie's van then shifted it on my hip to get a better grip on Petunia's leash. For some reason I'd let Liam convince me that bringing the skunk to the annual last day of school carnival wasn't a horrible idea. Cassie had made enough cookies to feed a crowd twice the size of the one they were expecting. I was just glad Liam actually wanted to go. That must have meant he was making friends. I tried to find him in the sea of kids and baseball caps as I made my way to the covered shelter at the park.

Though I'd known about the carnival for a couple of weeks, he'd only asked me to come the day before. So here I was, cookies and skunk in hand. Petunia was eager to explore, pulling taut on her leash and sniffing at anything and everything she came across in the grass. She paused at an oversized clump of clover and I took that opportunity to pull out my phone and dial my son.

He answered on the second ring. "Hey, Mom."

"Where are you? I'm at the park and there are kids everywhere."

"Oh, I'll be back in a few minutes. I went with Dustin to get the drinks."

"What? Went with Dustin where?" I twirled around, half expecting to see my son materialize out of thin air.

"Just to the store. He asked if I'd help haul back some water bottles."

"You'd better not be on the back of one of those bikes." I'd told both Liam and Dustin that under no circumstances was Liam allowed on a motorcycle.

"Chill, Mom. We're in the truck. You can't take cases of water on a bike."

I stumbled back a step, relieved. He was in the truck. That meant he was safe. "Fine. Get back here as soon as you can, though."

"We will."

Petunia lunged toward a morsel of something that fell to the ground in front of her. I went with her, catching myself before falling flat on my face. As I stood, Cassie waved to me over the crowd.

"Hey, why don't you set those down here?" She smoothed out the plastic tablecloth she'd taped down to the picnic table.

"Thanks." I set down the box of cookies, glad to be relieved of the burden of sniffing all of that sugar and frosting.

"Who's that?" Cassie straightened, her eyes on Petunia.

"Meet Petunia, the skunk. The one Dustin and I found in the studio across the street from the diner." Even saying his name out loud had me feeling all sorts of warm and tingly nonsense inside.

Cassie knelt down to run her hand over Petunia's back. "That's right. Mrs. Glassard's skunk. She's a sweetie. Used to bring her into the café before she had to move into the nursing home."

"You let a skunk come into the restaurant?" My jaw dropped. I couldn't imagine Cassie risking a health code violation for letting a skunk in the Lovebird.

"I didn't *let* her do anything. You should have met Mrs. Glassard. She never asked permission, just did as she pleased."

"No wonder she ended up being able to keep Petunia at the nursing home."

"I guess she had a pet hedgehog too."

My head jerked up. "What?"

"Yeah." Cassie continued to run her palm over Petunia's stripe. "I'm not sure where he ended up. How are the raccoons, by the way?"

"Getting big. I had to move them to the dog kennel outside. Pretty soon they should be able to go back into the wild."

"I bet you never thought you'd turn into a wildlife rehabilitator when you moved here."

"I never thought a lot of things that have happened would have when I moved here," I mumbled, more to myself than to Cassie.

"What?"

"Oh, nothing. Just the studio space and the mud..." I shook my head. "It's been a whirlwind, that's for sure." Not to mention the self-contained whirlwind that was Dustin Jarrett. I'd never anticipated how he'd crash into my life. I thought I'd be able to handle it. But the more time we spent together, the more I doubted my ability to keep my heart safe and secure.

"Well, I sure am glad you're here. Oh, and look, here

come Misty and Jake." Cassie walked around the table to wrap her arms around a woman holding a baby in a carrier and a pulling two kids in a wagon. "You made it."

"Barely. I never thought I'd get out of the Cut 'N Curl today. One of the regulars saw Dustin Jarrett tripping around town without a shirt on, and I thought the whole damn building was going to combust."

"Misty and Jake, meet Harmony." Cassie put an arm around my shoulder and gave me a not-so-gentle nudge toward Misty.

"What the hell is that?" She jumped back as Petunia walked around the wagon.

"Petunia. Mrs. Glassard's skunk," Cassie said.

"Well bless her heart, we wondered what became of her. Mrs. G used to bring her into the Cut 'N Curl for her weekly appointments."

"The skunk had weekly appointments?" I asked.

Misty looked at me, opened her mouth to speak, then turned back to Cassie. "Who's she again?"

Cassie groaned as Jake stepped forward. "This is Harmony, Robbie's cousin. We met the other day at City Hall. Did Dustin tell you he stopped by to pick up your permits today?"

"No, not yet." I let out a sigh. "Thank goodness."

"Good. That means y'all can get started." Cassie leaned toward me, dropping her voice a notch. "And Petunia didn't have weekly appointments, Mrs. Glassard did."

"Oh." That made so much more sense. Hanging around all of the wild animals was getting to me. "Well it's nice to meet you, Misty."

She eyed me with a healthy share of skepticism. "Nice to meet you, too."

Before I embarrassed myself further, Dustin and Liam pulled in. They unloaded cases of bottled water into the coolers Scarlett had dropped off earlier. Liam gave me a quick half-hug, bent to pet Petunia then ran off with his friends. So much for us hanging out together at the carnival. I tried not to let my disappointment show.

"You need any more help setting up?" I asked Cassie.

"Nope. Misty and I are going to hang out here with the boys until the cookies are gone. Why don't you walk around? Have a good time?"

Dustin smiled at me. "What do you say, Harmony? Want me to win you a stuffed animal over at the midway?"

"Midway? Just how big is this carnival?" I asked.

"It's just a couple of games," Cassie said. "Probably take you all of ten minutes to walk the whole loop."

"May as well, as long as I'm here." I switched Petunia's leash to my other wrist and let Dustin lead me away from the park in the middle of the square.

"So what's your pleasure? We can do the cake walk or try our hand at the milk jug toss." Dustin acted like he was about to take my hand, then must have thought better of it.

"I'm not much for cakes. But I'd love to see you try your hand at throwing a ball. Think your shoulder can handle it?"

He stretched his arm then rotated his shoulder forward. "It's been feeling much better lately, thanks to my personal massage therapist."

"Hey, I'm just rubbing your back because I like you. Don't you dare go around telling people I'm your therapist. I told you, I don't date clients."

He stopped, taking my hand in his. Petunia continued to walk forward, sniffing at the grass. "What are we doing here, Harmony?"

"What? Taking a skunk on a walk? That's not part of your typical day?"

He managed a grin before his forehead furrowed. I wanted to smooth out the line between his brows with my finger. Or better yet, a kiss. "Seriously. I don't know what I'm doing."

"I think you know exactly what you're doing. And you do it well. Why do we have to define it?" Every part of me ached to do just that. He'd carved out a spot in my heart—a heart I thought I'd shut off from being able to have feelings for a man again. And even though technically it was supposed to be a punishment, I could see the admiration Liam had for Dustin. And it was only going to get worse the more time they spent together. But what was the alternative? Tell him not to bother building out the space? Call things off between us?

The thought of ending things with Dustin, whatever it was we had going, seemed like a horrible alternative.

"Harmony." My name on his lips did things to my insides. Things that were best experienced in private, not in the middle of a makeshift midway with dozens of my son's classmates looking on.

"Let's enjoy the carnival. We can talk later. Now's not the time or the place." I glanced around. Tonight was a night for celebrating. The joy and exhilaration of the last day of school was almost tangible. Laughter bounced around us, everyone we passed had a smile from ear to ear.

"All right. But we have to talk about this later."

"Later," I agreed. "For now, why don't you show me how well your shoulder's healing?"

We'd stopped in front of the strength tester game. Liam's science teacher, Mr. Ridley, held out a giant mallet. "Want to give this a shot?"

Dustin glanced to me. "Come on,"—I nudged him with my elbow on his non-injured side—"Let's see if you can ring the bell."

His expression changed, his eyes darkening to a deeper shade of green. He leaned close, whispering against my cheek. "I bet I can ring your bell."

I laughed, thankful no one else had heard him. "You ring this one and maybe I'll let you take a shot at mine later."

He peeled a few dollars from his wallet and handed them over, then stepped back to size up the game. When he was ready, he took the mallet and gave it a couple of practice swings.

"You get three tries." Mr. Ridley moved to the side. "Make them count."

Dustin held the mallet up, hoisting it over his shoulder. His biceps flexed, and I felt like I might pass out right on the spot from the overabundance of male showmanship and testosterone on display. As he swung the mallet down, it struck the platform. His gaze went to the top of the tower where the metal bell clanged. I kept my eyes on him, my gaze running over the taut muscles of his neck and chest, imagining him putting in that same amount of effort in that promised attempt to ring *my* bell.

"Congratulations." Mr. Ridley reached for the mallet. "You're welcome to take two more swings if you'd like."

Dustin rubbed a hand over his shoulder. "That's okay. I'd hate to miss the next one."

"Well, since you got it on the first attempt, you get the big prize."

I looked around. This wasn't a fancy set up like the state fair so there weren't any prizes on display. "What's the big prize?"

Mr. Ridley stepped behind the tower and came back holding a cage. A birdcage.

Dustin reached for it. "Here you go, Harmony."

"No, absolutely not. You've already been responsible for three raccoons, a skunk, and an emu."

"How do you figure? The raccoons climbed into *your* engine."

I crossed my arms over my chest. "And how did Petunia end up in my care? Should I jog your memory? You dropped her off for me to skunk-sit for a morning and never came back."

"Skunk-sit?" The edges of his mouth tipped up, threatening a grin.

My eyebrows lifted. "You abandoned her. There's no way I'm taking on a bird, too."

"Lovebirds," Mr. Ridley said. "Not just one bird, it's a pair of lovebirds. We thought it was appropriate seeing as how we've got the Lovebird Café in town and all."

Who was on that committee? What happened to tiny stuffed animals filled with Styrofoam beads?

Dustin held onto the cage and peered inside. "Don't you want to take a look? They're super cute. Besides, you've already got an emu. What's another bird or two?"

"Fine." I unwound Petunia's leash from my legs and bent down to peek inside the cage. Two greenish-orangish birds looked back at me.

"Lovebirds are special. They form a very strong bond with their mate." Mr. Ridley handed Dustin a bag. "There are supplies in there. Make sure they have something to keep them busy. Oh, and you'll probably want to get them a bigger cage as soon as you can."

"I'll make sure she has everything they need." Dustin

grabbed the bag in one hand, the cage in the other. "Wow, where to next?"

"You're joking." The birds were cute enough, but there was no way they were coming home with me. No. Freaking. Way.

"Lovebirds, Harmony. What should we name them?" His grin told me he was enjoying this way too much.

"I think your mom would love some company. You should give them to her."

"Mom's allergic to birds." He bit his lip like he was barely even trying to suppress a smile. "Yeah, as I recall, she breaks out in hives."

"What's your end goal here? To saddle me with one of each species before you leave town?" I'd been kind of kidding but the mention of him leaving town wiped the smile off his face.

"If you don't want the birds, I'll give them to someone else." He glanced around, like he was willing to pass them off to the next person who walked by.

"Hey, Mom." Liam approached from out of nowhere. "Can I have ten bucks to buy a snack?"

Not exactly thankful for the interruption, I turned to face my son. "I gave you twenty this morning."

"I know. I spent it already."

"On what?"

"Here." Dustin held the bird cage out to Liam. "Hold onto this for a sec, and I'll give you an advance on your wages."

"Cool. Where did these come from?" Liam put his face close to the cage.

"I won them for your mom, but I don't think she wants them." Dustin handed Liam a twenty-dollar bill as I looked on, my jaw clenched.

"They're cool. We should keep them." He passed the cage back to Dustin.

"What are you doing paying him? That wasn't part of the agreement." Now I wasn't sure who to be more irritated with, my son or Dustin.

"Can't expect him to work for free." Dustin took the cage back and clapped a hand on Liam's shoulder. "Have fun."

"Thanks, Dustin." Liam broke out in a grin before he took off again.

It was nice seeing him excited to be at the carnival instead of moping around, but still... Dustin had no right to give him money. No right to decide he'd pay the boys for helping out.

"So who's supposed to be paying for labor? I can't believe you didn't talk to me about this. I've barely got enough to cover the supplies for the build out. I can't afford to pay Liam and Rodney to work, too."

"Hey, calm down. I'm covering it." He set the cage down on the ground and put a hand out.

I avoided his grip. "What about consequences? They're supposed to be working as punishment. Don't you get it?"

He gave me a blank look, proving we obviously weren't on the same wavelength. "I'm trying to help here, Harmony. What do you want me to do?"

What did I want him to do? Stop meddling in my relationship with my son. Stop trying to fix everything. Stop being so nice? The more involved he got in Liam's and my life, the more it would hurt when he would inevitably leave. Yes, it pissed me off that he'd inserted himself into the conversation and made a decision about paying the boys without consulting me. But what scared me the most, what had me the most rattled, was that I was letting him. I let him get involved. I let him make decisions. Despite my reservations, I'd let him in.

And sooner or later, even though I'd gone into this with my eyes wide open and my heart closed tight, I was going to be the one left reeling.

26

DUSTIN

I left Harmony at the fair, along with the birds. She'd gotten a wild hair up her ass about me saying I'd pay the boys. Maybe I was minimizing the fact that they were supposed to be doing penance for past transgressions. But I was trying to help. If someone had come along and offered me a decent job when I'd been their age, maybe I wouldn't have been so damn self-destructive before I finally found a way out of town.

The muscles in my shoulder pinched as I got behind the wheel. Damn if I hadn't come to rely on Harmony's healing touch to keep the pain bearable. And relying on someone was exactly what I'd been avoiding in the first place. But she was right, I'd overstepped when it came to her son. I didn't want to interfere or make things worse between them. I knew Liam had a thing for bikes. It was a shame she wouldn't let me teach him how to ride. But she was in charge where Liam was concerned. All I could do was respect that if I wanted to stay a part of their lives.

That right there was the billion dollar question. Did I want to stay a part of their lives? I'd been running so hard and so fast from anything that looked like a commitment to anyone beyond myself. Was I ready to change that?

As I walked into the house, I heard scuffling in the kitchen. Mom stood at the kitchen sink. When she saw me she put a hand to her forehead.

"You okay?" I moved closer, not sure if she was about to pass out.

"Just a little dizzy, honey."

I took her hand and helped her to the table. "What happened?"

"I don't know. I was going to take my vitamins and as I stood at the sink, I just got a little lightheaded. I'm sure it's blood sugar or something. Nothing you need to worry about."

Mom might want to pass it off as something simple, but I knew better. Even if the doc hadn't been able to find anything, something was going on.

"What can I do to help?"

"Oh honey, I don't want you to worry about me. You've got your own things going on. All those jobs coming up. Although..." She paused and slid her hand over mine.

"What, Mom?"

"It's just been so nice having you around. Not having to worry about things for a while. It sure has eased my mind."

"I'm here for you. Even if I'm out in California, I can still find a way to pitch in. I'll hire someone to do the lawn and come in to help take care of the house."

Mom's nose wrinkled. "I just don't like strangers around."

"Well, I'm not a stranger and I'm here now. Everything going on out in California comes second. I'll stay as long as you need me."

Her eyes sparkled, and I got a little kick out of bringing a moment of happiness into her life. "I don't want to come in the way of your job."

"You're not. Being back here has made me realize something."

"What?" She leaned toward me.

"Just that I missed y'all. Yeah, California is great. The weather sure is better. But it's nice to be around people who like me for who I am."

Mom's hand rubbed mine. "Your nephew's glad you're back."

I stifled a grin. "I'm not so sure about that. Or at least he might not be once we get started on that job tomorrow."

"What you're doing for him, and for Liam, it's going to make a big difference for both of them."

"What do you mean?"

"You're being a role model. Neither one of those boys has a father-figure in their lives. Your dad was a bit of a crackerjack, but at least he was around."

I considered that statement. Crackerjack didn't begin to describe my dad. Most folks thought he was nuts. He'd been obsessed with the caves on our land, always telling people that some of Jesse James's long lost treasure was hidden somewhere underground. Didn't matter that people called him a loony tune. He believed in that legend with all of his heart. And Scarlett had seemed to catch that bug, too.

"Yeah, I don't know that I'm ready to be a role model."

"Of course you are. Rodney and Liam will be lucky to have you. Everything that happened all that time ago"— Mom shook her head—"I didn't realize how much it affected you."

"It's okay, Mom. I'm over it."

"Are you?" Her gaze drilled into me, the softness around her eyes pulling at the bound up bundle of memories I'd managed to suppress all this time. "Talking to Rob might help."

"Yeah." I stood, needing to step away for a moment. My efforts at soothing my mom had suddenly turned into a deep dive into my own personal hell. "I need to get that over with."

"You'll find the right time." Mom stood from the table and scooted her chair in. "I forgot to ask. Did you have a good time at the carnival?"

I cleared my throat. "Yeah. It was fun."

"Was Harmony there?"

Her question appeared innocent on the front end, but she'd loaded it with meaning. I knew enough about my mom to know that she had a way of getting the answers she wanted even without coming right out and asking.

"Yeah, I saw her and Liam."

"Mmm hmm." Mom moved back to the sink to fill a glass with water. "She seems like good people."

Good people. That was her way of giving her approval. Not that I needed it. Not that I wanted it. "Yeah, I'll be glad when she has a space of her own."

"What you're doing for her, honey, that makes you good people, too."

Good people. The last thing I felt like was good people. I might be working on a build out for her for a few weeks, but I was getting plenty in return. Free physical therapy for my shoulder. Plus free physical therapy for the hard-on I always seemed to have when Harmony came around.

Heat pricked my cheeks. I dismissed the thought and turned my attention toward my mom. "You feeling better?"

"I sure am. I'm headed to bed. Early day tomorrow. I need to run into the office and wrap things up."

"I'll drive you."

"Don't be silly. I'm perfectly capable of driving myself."

"I know. That's why I'm offering."

She wrapped her arms around me to pull me into a hug. "Did I tell you how much I love having you around?"

"Only about every five minutes." I smiled and kissed her forehead.

After Mom went to bed, I couldn't decide whether to head to the trailer and crash or take another crack at the engine I'd been piecing back together in the garage. Neither option held much interest. The only thing I wanted to do in that moment was bury myself in Harmony's arms. I'd grown too used to our nightly get-togethers. So instead of drowning my sorrows in a beer or aimlessly flipping through the cable channels, I went out to the truck.

We hadn't made plans, so I wasn't sure what I'd find when I got to Harmony's place. When I pulled into the drive, all the lights blazed in the front room. With any luck Liam would be in bed so we'd have a chance to talk...or maybe even more.

Before I could reach the door, it opened. Harmony stood in the doorway, the light from the living room glowing behind her.

"What are you doing here?" She had on a nightshirt with some sort of blobs of color on it.

I focused on the green blob centered between her breasts. "Couldn't sleep. I didn't want to leave things weird between us."

"Weird, huh? Is that how they are?" She shifted her stance and the light behind her filtered through her nightgown.

"Feels weird." I moved closer, my feet crunching on the gravel as I approached. "Doesn't it feel weird to you?"

"I don't know. With all those new vocabulary words

you're picking up, I'd think you could come up with something more interesting than weird."

I grinned. Teasing was a good sign. "You're absolutely right. Weird is too simple a way to describe the complex situation going on between us. Things have felt a bit anomalistic."

"Oooh. Have you used that in a sentence before?" She leaned against the door frame. Her hair was down, all messed up and sexy. Begging for my fingers to comb through it.

But not yet. It was time for sucking up, not time for sucking...*damn*... "First time."

"Well, keep practicing. You know what they say..." Her words drifted off as I moved even closer.

"What's that?" My whisper landed in her hair.

"About practice?"

"Yeah." I leaned down to nibble her ear lobe. She smelled like sunshine and blue summer skies.

"That practice makes perfect?" Her arms snaked up around my neck.

"Right." I ran a hand over the back of her nightshirt, feeling her ribs through the flimsy cotton material. "Where's Liam?"

She aligned her body with mine. "Stayed in town tonight. He's spending the night with a friend."

"Really?" My cock practically wept at this news. "All night?"

"All night," she confirmed. "Are things still weird, or have we made up yet?"

I put my hands on her hips and backed her against the door. "I vote yes. Now can we have make-up sex?"

She palmed the front of my jeans, running her hand over the line of my hard-on. "Are you going to come inside?"

"Hell, I'm ready to come anywhere you want. Inside, outside, upside down." I might joke about it, but the meaning of her question definitely wasn't lost on me. Hesitating, I dipped down to meet her mouth with mine. She tasted like strawberries, sweet and addictive. Was I ready to take that next step? To start facing the demons of my past?

Harmony didn't push, just stood there kissing me, doing her best to work me over through a thick layer of denim. The kissing, the stroking, the feel of her breasts pushing up against my chest...I wanted her. I always seemed to want her.

I picked her up, and carried her into the living room. "Where's your bed?"

She laughed and pointed to the back of the house. Made sense she would have taken over the master. At least that was one room in the house I'd never spent any time in. I ignored the rising panic in my gut, the way my shoulders tensed at the sight of Jeff's picture on the wall. Instead, I focused on Harmony. The way her lips skimmed my cheek, the way she felt like nothing in my arms, the way her nightshirt slid up her backside, allowing me to cup her gorgeous ass with my hand.

Down the hall and into the master bedroom. I let her fall to the bed, then I followed. The only light coming in from the window was from the huge motion-sensing lantern that hung over the outbuilding. We melded together, a tangle of limbs and lips. Her mouth trailed over my neck, leaving heat and a deep need to have her in its wake. I wriggled out of my jeans, once again grateful I didn't have boxers or briefs to contend with. She straddled me. I could feel her wet heat through her panties. She bent over me, running her hands down my chest. The feel of her fingers made me throb, aching for more. With her on top, there wasn't much I could do.

I wanted to touch her, slide my fingers through her slick heat. She leaned down, kissing her way over my stomach, not stopping until she got to my cock. I hissed as she rimmed the head with her tongue then took me into her mouth. We hadn't crossed this bridge yet, though the thought had crossed my mind. Multiple times.

I tried to relax as she took me deeper. Heat surrounded me. Her lips slid up and down, priming me, pushing and pulling me to my release. I held back, wanting to extend it as long as I could. Her hair tickled my thighs, her finger traced around my balls, but nothing could distract me from the momentum building inside. I tapped on her shoulder, straining to maintain control.

"I'm close. You want me to..." Fuck. Any ability to speak was obliterated when she took me deep into her throat. Her tongue, her lips, I couldn't make out one sensation from the next. She literally fucked me with her mouth, taking me deeper and deeper each time. My hips thrust, so close, so fucking close.

Then I was gone. My hips bucked one last time before settling back on the bed. Harmony held on, sucking me off until the last tremors left me.

"What the fuck was that?" I managed.

She looked up at me, a sexy smile on her lips. "You liked it?"

"Like isn't a strong enough word, baby." I wasn't willing to say the "L" word. I'd never said that to a woman, not even about giving head, and I wasn't about to start now.

"Use your big words. You know how much they turn me on." She snuggled up next to me, her damn nightshirt still in place.

"Get naked and I'll give you something big."

She snort-laughed at me.

"What?"

"You're not supposed to call yourself big."

"Why not? It's not exactly small."

"You're right. It's huge, gargantuan. Epic in proportion."

I snugged her closer to me, trailing a finger from her belly button to her breast bone. "Are you mocking me?"

"Maybe just a little?"

Groaning, I nudged my head down her stomach, sliding her panties off her legs. Hovering on my elbows, I took her in, splayed in front of me like a damn dessert buffet. But where to start? I licked my way up her leg. She started to giggle. In the many nights we'd spent together, I'd learned her inner thighs were a playground where I could make her squirm since she was so ticklish.

She tried to swat my hands away as she laughed. But I persisted, trailing my tongue up her leg, nudging her thighs apart until she spread open before me. Then I wet my lips and dove in.

27

HARMONY

*H*oly shit. Holiest of shits. The man's tongue could win an Olympic medal. I'd been ready to go since taking him in my mouth. Seeing how turned on he got, how crazed I could make him, was the best kind of foreplay I'd ever known. And now, he had me hovering on the edge of something so big, so huge, so gargantuan, all I could do was brace myself for the impending impact.

It started slow, a flare, sparking a burn that coiled through my core. As he nipped and licked and used his fingers in the most creative way, it spread. Then he sucked. Hard. And I exploded. Tremors rocked through me. Stars sparked across my eyelids. I clenched my eyes shut, concentrating on following that feeling wherever it would take me.

"Oh, Dustin. Right there. Just like that."

He didn't let up, didn't give me any relief until the waves crashing over me subsided.

"You okay?" he asked, climbing up my body from between my thighs.

"Yes. I think so. But you may have broken my vagina."

His mouth dropped open. "What?"

"I don't think it's going to work the same after this. It's done. Nothing can top that. Wrap it up, stick a fork in it." I put my arm under my head so I could see him better. "I mean, not a literal fork."

"Yeah, I figured that. But we can't have you shut down for good. What am I supposed to do?"

My shoulders lifted in a semi-shrug. "You'll have to take matters into your own hands. You've ruined it. You've totally shut down my vagina."

He blew a raspberry into my belly button. "I'll send a repair crew in. We'll get you back up and running in no time."

"There's a forty-eight hour waiting period. It needs to rest." I ran my free hand through his hair as he nestled his cheek onto my stomach. His whiskers scratched against my skin, making my afterglow that much glowier.

"That's all right. I'll be busy with the boys tomorrow anyway. I'll probably be too worn out tomorrow night to want to play in your gorgeous vagina."

"Forty-eight hours." I sighed, relishing the feel of his weight, of not being alone in my bed. I hadn't had a man in my bed for a long time.

"Do you want me to leave?" His fingers traced circles around my navel. The rough pad of his finger reminded me this man worked with his hands. He wasn't mine to have and to hold.

"No. Can you stay tonight?" I was almost afraid to ask. We'd shared plenty of sexy times on the dock and in the tall grass and even once or twice in the bed of his truck. But this, him being in the house, had to be hard for him. It was easy to overlook that in a moment of passion, but now that we'd both floated back down to reality, would he want to stay?

"Yeah." He bit his lip, suddenly looking like a much

younger version of himself. The way his brow furrowed, worry lines creasing his forehead, told me more than he could with words.

"Then get up here." I put my arms under his armpits and tried to tug him closer.

He obliged, kissing his way up my body until he reached my mouth.

I tugged my nightshirt down, covering myself up.

"What the hell is on your shirt by the way?"

"Oh, it's my chakra nightshirt. The different circles represent the seven different chakras of the body." I touched the purple circle at the top. "This one's the crown chakra, the purple one."

He put his hand next to mine. The heat from his touch seared my skin through the flimsy cotton. "What's the green one? I like the green one best." His fingers slid to the green circle, centered between my breasts.

My breath hitched as he traced the edges of the circle, moving back and forth from one breast to the other. "That's the heart chakra. It represents love. It's my favorite too, since green is my favorite color."

He lowered his head, kissing the center of my heart chakra. "Nice shirt, now take it off."

I laughed. "What are you talking about?"

"I mean, if we're going to do this, we're sleeping naked." He worked my nightshirt up, sliding it over my head, then tossing it aside. Then he pulled me into his side, spooning my back with his front. "So is your shirt more of that woo-woo shit?"

"It's a little woo-woo. Do you not like it when I talk about woo-woo stuff?"

His fingers moved my hair off my shoulder and he snuggled his neck in that spot instead. "I like your woo-woo."

My heart glowed. Some people found the woo-woo side of me hard to take. But it was a part of me, and I wasn't willing to change myself for anyone—at least not any more. What he saw would be what he got.

"Good." I wrapped my hands around the arm he'd flung over me. "What else do you like about me?"

His lips played along the shell of my ear. "I like that you're a horrible waitress."

"Horrible is a strong term."

"Strong, but surprisingly accurate."

"Fine. Anything else?"

"Hmm." His whiskers tickled my neck, reminding me how they'd tickled my inner thigh as he performed that amazing homage to my lady parts. "I really like your vagina."

"Even if it's broken?"

"I'm going to nurse it back to health. A little massage, maybe a nice, warm bath or two. It'll be back in top-notch condition in no time."

"I look forward to it."

"Not as much as me." He pulled me just a tiny bit closer, securing me against him. "Goodnight, Harmony."

"Goodnight, Dustin."

His breathing evened out. I lay there, more comfortable than I'd been in a very long time. Safe, secure, warm and cozy, in Dustin's arms.

I COULDN'T HAVE SLEPT for more than an hour or two, when some sort of vibration woke me. Used to the faint rumblings of a California earthquake, I opened my eyes, ready to run for the doorway to brace myself. Instead, I saw Dustin crouched on the ground, feeling around for something on the floor.

"What's going on?"

"My phone. It's in my pocket. Somewhere over here." He must have found it because the noise stopped.

I rolled to a seated position as he walked to the kitchen.

"What's wrong, Mom?"

My heart pitched in my chest at the thought of something happening to his mother. Those dizzy spells had been coming more and more often. Without wanting to intrude, I tiptoed to the doorway.

"No, don't call the police. I'll be home in a few minutes. Just stay inside." He stopped at the edge of the table and ran a hand through his hair. Even in the urgency of the situation, I couldn't help but warm inside as my gaze ran over his chiseled, naked body.

He clicked his phone off and walked across the kitchen to the bedroom.

"Everything okay?" I reached for him, putting a soothing hand on his arm as he passed me on his way into the bedroom.

"I don't know." He tossed the phone on the bed and shoved a leg into his jeans. "Some assholes are messing around at the end of the driveway. Woke up my mom and she panicked when she couldn't find me."

"Do you want me to come with you?"

The T-shirt went over his head and he thrust his arms through the holes. Any softness he'd let show during the night had disappeared. He was all hard angles and tension. "No. You stay here. I'll call you once I figure out what's going on."

He was down the hall and in the front room before I had a chance to follow. "Hey."

"Sorry. I've got to go." Keys in hand, he opened the door.

"I get it. I hope everything is okay with your mom." I walked to him and pressed a quick kiss against his mouth. "Be safe."

He wrapped me in a fast hug, already distracted by what might lie ahead. "Go back to bed."

Then he was gone. The darkness behind him swallowed him up, making me wonder if he'd ever really even been there at all.

DUSTIN

*H*aving to leave Harmony pissed me off. The one night we'd finally managed to spend together and some asshole had to go and blow it for me. By the time I pulled off the main road and onto the dirt road that would take me home, I'd worked myself into such a foul mood I might have had steam coming out of my ears.

Mom was right. Sure enough, some jerk in a half-ton truck had pulled off the driveway onto the side. As my head-lights swept over them, a couple of people scrambled behind the truck. I stopped, wishing for the crowbar I usually kept under the front seat. Never knew when you'd need that out in LA. Around here I'd let down my guard.

I stepped onto the running board and looked out over the scene ahead. Buckets and shovels scattered over a stretch of mud. What the hell was going on?

"This is private property," I shouted into the darkness. "You've got five seconds to tell me what you're doing before I get Sherriff Sampson over here."

Nothing but silence.

I started to count. "Five. Four."

"Hey, no need for that, neighbor." Lou, one of the regulars at the café, stepped out from behind the truck.

"What are you doing here? You've got my mom scared half to death." Seeing a familiar face sent my pulse down a notch, but I was still worked up over getting interrupted in the middle of the night.

He shrugged his shoulders. "Sorry, Dustin. It's the mud. My wife heard that new waitress down at the café spouting off about this healing mud she'd found."

"What are you talking about?"

"Yeah, she said it fixed up her son's head. Even worked on an animal." He leaned on the handle of his shovel. "You know we've got that cow who's about to split in two. I tried some on that heifer and it works better than bag balm. The missus sent me over for more."

"Wait." I put my hand to my forehead. Maybe I'd hit my head or mom's dizzy spells were wearing off on me. "You're stealing mud?"

"It's supposed to help with wrinkles, too." Another man stepped out from behind the other side of the truck. "When Lou said he used it on his cow, I figured I'd pick some up for my wife. She's been bitchin' about wanting some of that pricey wrinkle cream. Why spring for that when we've got miracle mud, right here in Swallow Springs?"

"Where did y'all hear about this again?"

"That new gal, Harmony." Lou leaned on his shovel. "She said something about it at the café. You want us to pay you for it?"

"No." I waved a hand at the two men. "Take what you want, just be quiet about it, okay?"

"Sorry, we didn't mean to cause a fuss."

"Why didn't you just ask? Why sneak over here in the

middle of the night?" Mom would have gladly let them take what they wanted. Why'd they have to ruin my night?

"I don't know. I guess I figured if it's a miracle mud like that gal said, you might be charging a pretty penny for it." Lou lifted his shovel. "We'll be done here in a bit."

I shook my head. Wait until Mom heard about this. I left the men to their mud harvesting and drove the rest of the way to the house. Mom met me on the porch. I felt a little bit like a kid who'd gotten caught sneaking out.

"What's going on?" She clutched her hands to her heart. "All I could hear was clanging and laughing. Like someone was having a heyday down the drive. I figured it was some drunk teenagers celebrating the last day of school."

I followed her into the kitchen where she already had a pot of coffee going. "Worse than that."

"What?"

"It's Lou and one of his buddies."

"Good heavens, what are they doing out at this hour? And causing such a ruckus?"

"They're stealing your mud." I grabbed onto the back of a chair. It still hadn't quite sunk in. How did I go from holding Harmony in my arms to talking about miracle mud at three o'clock in the morning with my mom?

"Whatever for?" She snagged two mugs from the cupboard and poured us both a cup of coffee.

I hadn't planned on getting such an early start to my day, but it looked like I wasn't going to have much of a choice. Wrapping my hands around the mug she offered, I leaned against the counter. "Evidently Harmony mentioned we have some sort of miracle mud on our property. Said it cured Liam's cut and even helped with that crazy emu."

"Mud?"

"Yep, just plain mud." I didn't get it. "You going to go back to bed?"

"Oh, I don't think I can. All of this excitement, I don't think I'll be able to fall back asleep now. How about you? You can go catch a few winks before you drive me into town."

"That's okay. I need to get the truck packed up anyway. Today we start work on the studio space." That's what I should have been doing last night. But the need to see Harmony had pushed every other priority out of the way. Since when had I become so hung up on a woman that I couldn't get her out of my mind?

"All right. I'm going to work on my cross-stitch for a bit before I get ready for work."

I kissed my mom on the cheek then transferred my coffee to a giant travel mug. With more than packing the truck on my mind, I headed for the garage.

An hour later I'd put together some sort of demo kit. Today we'd tear out the existing cabinets and bust through a non-load-bearing wall. There were also a few larger pieces of furniture we'd need to get out of the space. On my way out of the garage I snagged the small handsaw off the shelf. No telling if we'd need to take stuff out in pieces or not.

With another hour before I could even think about leaving to get Mom to work, I decided to hit the shower. Part of me didn't want to wash away the scent Harmony had left on my skin, but I needed something to wake me up. Seemed like I'd been walking around in a stupor since I'd found Lou and his friend digging in our front yard.

As I grabbed some work clothes out of the trailer to head in for a shower, I checked my phone. Damn. Two missed calls and three texts from Harmony, wondering if I was okay. I'd completely forgotten to let her know how things turned out. The last one had come through twenty minutes ago. I picked up the phone and called her back.

"Is everyone okay?" Her voice came out a little breathless.

"Yeah, it's fine. Turns out it was just Lou and some other guy trying to steal some of your miracle mud from the end of the driveway."

"What?"

I pictured her, woo-woo nightshirt back in place, worry causing her brow to wrinkle and making lines across that gorgeous face. "Yeah. I guess they heard you talking about it at the café."

"Wow. I must have mentioned it. I swear, that mud must have been what healed Liam's head so fast. And I slathered some on Magoo, too."

"Who's Magoo?" The idea of Harmony slathering anything on anyone besides me wasn't so appealing, especially after the night we'd shared.

"The bird. We're calling him Magoo since he can't see anything."

I let out a half-laugh. "That's a good one."

"You could have called. I've been worried about you. The way you left...I didn't know what was going on." An edge of hurt sliced through her words.

"I'm sorry. I got back and had to fill in my mom. Then she made coffee—"

"Your mom thinks coffee can heal just about anything, doesn't she?"

"Usually, in her world, I guess it does. Have a fight? Make up over a pot of coffee. Get bad news? Discuss it over a cup of coffee." If only life were that easy all the time. Fuck up on national television? Drink a gallon of coffee.

Harmony sighed. "Maybe I need to start actually drinking coffee."

"Maybe you should figure out how to make it first."

"What? I must still be dreaming because I know you didn't just insult my coffee-making abilities."

I smirked as I pictured her all worked up, that shirt bunched up around her hips. "Will I see you later on this morning?"

"Yes. Liam is supposed to be meeting you at the studio at eight. I'll be at work before that, but maybe if you're nice to me, I'll bring over some lunch."

"I was pretty nice to you last night." Just thinking about tasting her again had me on the verge of a hard-on.

"Yes, you were. See? Even you can be sweet from time to time."

"I'll see you later then."

"Sounds good. Oh, hey, will you do me a favor?"

"Sure." At that moment, I probably would have done just about anything for Harmony Rogers.

"Bring me some of that miracle mud?"

Except that.

29

HARMONY

I stood in the café, watching Liam, Rodney, and Dustin unload the back of the truck. I hoped my son was up for the full day of work he had ahead of him. I'd already been on the job for a couple of hours and that was after making the rounds and feeding all of the animals. We were going to have to figure out what to do with a few of the critters Dustin had saddled me with. Running a full-time animal rehabilitation clinic wasn't in the cards for me.

Although, as I faced down the giant commercial coffee pot, maybe I'd be better at that than I was at waiting tables. Cassie came by, a full tray of breakfast platters in her hand. "Watch your back."

I stepped out of the way. Too tired to mess with the monstrosity, I pretended like I didn't notice it was out and made my way to the back to prep a fresh pot of instant. As I stepped to the sink with the carafe of hot water, Ryder caught my eye.

"You can't keep doing that, Harmony. Someone's going to find out sooner or later. They're already talking about how the coffee tastes different when you're around."

"You keep your mouth shut if you want me to mix up those scented bath bombs for your girlfriend's birthday." I measured out several tablespoons of instant coffee and stirred them into the carafe. "Hopefully my coffee pouring days are limited now. I've given up on trying to master that monster of a machine."

He laughed as he flipped a trio of flapjacks on the griddle. "I'm sure Cassie would go over it with you again."

"Shh." I tucked the instant coffee crystals back in my cubby. "No one will be the wiser, and I'll make it through my shift without scalding myself. Win-win."

"If you say so." He went back to cracking eggs into a bowl to mix up another one of his omelets. My secret would be safe with Ryder. He was head over heels for his latest girlfriend and wouldn't do anything to jeopardize the bath bombs I'd promised.

"More coffee?" I made my way down the counter, filling mugs as I went. As I reached the end closest to the window, I peered out at Dustin. He had on a regular T-shirt and faded blue jeans. Nothing special. A Swallow Springs baseball cap sat backward on his head. Even from this distance I could tell he hadn't bothered to shave yet. My thighs rubbed together as I recalled the feel of those whiskers between my legs.

"Why don't you go see how they're doing?" Cassie gave me a gentle hip bump as she stepped beside me. "I can cover you for a few minutes."

"I don't want to get in the way." I turned, making my way to the coffee machine where I nonchalantly slid the carafe into place, like that's where it belonged. The truth was, I didn't want to get in the way, but I also didn't want to distract myself by spending more time with Dustin. Even knowing he'd be across the street all day was enough to put me on edge. I needed the perspective of some distance, even if it was only about fifty yards.

"Okay, then. Suit yourself." Cassie pushed past me to enter the kitchen.

The rest of the morning passed so slowly that I could have sworn time was standing still. Frank stopped in. Based on a few comments he made, it sounded like he might have a little thing going for Dustin's mom. I promised I wouldn't say anything, although senior love was just about as cute as young love in my opinion. He blushed when I asked about Mrs. Jarrett, and mentioned that he'd been invited over for dinner the following Tuesday. For a moment I wondered if Dustin would be cooking again and if so, what he might make. Then I brushed that thought away and refocused on putting something together that Dustin and the boys could have for lunch.

By the time I took the box lunches across the street, I could barely suppress the tingly feeling that had plagued me all morning. I walked up the stairs, ready to be surprised by the amount of progress, only to find nothing much had happened. Liam and Rodney sat on two crates, tossing an orange back and forth between them.

"Hey, Mom." Liam glanced up as I entered the space.

"Where's Dustin?" I asked.

Rodney's chin jutted to the back. "He's talking to somebody back there."

I set the lunches down on the counter and followed the sound of Dustin's voice. Laced with frustration, he was arguing with someone about construction.

"So how long until we can get that taken care of?" he asked.

"I'll have to check. Could be a couple of weeks. Or if we

have to wait on a crew to come in from out of town, might take a couple of months."

"That's ridiculous."

I caught a glimpse of Dustin's backside as I rounded the corner. His arms crossed over his chest and his shoulders set tense and rigid.

"Hey, what's going on?" At the sound of my voice, both men looked over.

"Oh, Harmony, you're here." Dustin gestured to a man holding a clipboard. He had on a helmet and protective goggles. A mask hung around his neck. "This is Sam from the City Inspector's Office. Looks like we've hit a snag."

"Already? You just started this morning."

"Asbestos." Sam checked something off on his clipboard. "Until we get it taken care of, we're going to have to close up the building."

"But—" I struggled to understand what that would mean for my potential business.

"But nothing." Dustin moved my direction, spreading his arms wide as he came closer. "First wall we hit we came across some old asbestos insulation. They'll have to bring in someone to remove it before we can do anything else."

My vision went fuzzy at the edges, and I reached out for something to grab onto to steady myself. All I could feel was Dustin latching onto my arm.

"You okay?"

"Yes, I'm fine." I waved him off. "You're saying we're pretty much stuck now? Nobody can do anything until this asbestos is taken out, right?"

"Yes, that's exactly what I'm saying." Sam gave me an apologetic grin then glanced at Dustin. "Why is it the concept is so easily grasped by Ms. Rogers here and you're having such a difficult time understanding?"

Dustin shook his head, gesturing widely with his hands. "I'm not having a hard time understanding, I'm having a hard time accepting the fact that you can't tell me when we'll be able to move forward. I'm only going to be around for a few more weeks. We need to get this project going so we can wrap it up."

"I understand your concern. We'll do what we can to try to move things along as quickly as possible." He scribbled something else across the clipboard then looked back and forth from me to Dustin. "I'll be in touch. Until then, I suggest you remove what you need from the space. I'll have a crew come by to seal it up later on this afternoon."

My hopes, my dreams, my escape from the Lovebird Café...it all came to a grinding halt in that moment. Dustin waited until we could hear Sam clambering down the steps before he met my gaze.

"Harmony..."

"It's done, isn't it?" With my heart free falling into my shoes, I moved back to the front room. "So much for keeping you boys away from the pig pen."

"What?" Liam caught the orange Rodney tossed at him then stood. "What's going on?"

"Asbestos." Dustin came up behind me. I could feel him there, even though he kept his distance. "Inspector is sealing this place off until they can get a crew in here for asbestos removal."

"Aw, shit." Rodney whacked his hat on his knee.

"Hey," Dustin said. "We'll figure something out. I promise I'll keep y'all away from the pigs."

Despite the humidity and heat in the air, my body felt chilled, like the temperature had dropped twenty degrees. I'd bet my savings, my sanity, and my future on this place.

Being stuck in limbo, not knowing when we'd be able to move forward, had thrown me for a major loop. A double major loop, like the kind on that roller coaster at Six Flags I rode one time that made me want to toss my cookies all over the place. "Well, why don't you at least come over here and grab a sandwich? I made lunch."

"Thanks." Dustin gave me a smile.

Instinctively, I reached for him, stopping myself before I wrapped my arm around him. So much for being careful. Thankfully Liam and Rodney were too interested in the box of cookies I'd tucked into the bag to pay much attention to us. Dustin noticed though. I could tell by the way his mouth twitched up at the corners.

"You okay?" he asked, letting his hand linger on mine as he took the sandwich I handed him.

"I will be." Taking in a deep breath, I nodded.

"I may have to stick around a little while longer, based on how this asbestos cleanup goes." He tilted his head to the side, studying my reaction.

My skin tingled as his gaze drifted over me, making me feel deliciously exposed. "Are you sure you're up for that?" I teased.

His voice dropped a couple of notches and he leaned in close. "Oh yeah, I'll be up all right. I might even be kind of glad for the delay."

"Would you cut it out?" I might chastise him for being so forward with the boys around, but my thighs quivered, already anticipating what extra time with Dustin might entail.

While Liam and Rodney grabbed their lunches and started packing up the equipment they'd barely unloaded, I let my gaze drift around the room. I'd already become so attached. But I'd experienced setbacks before. This would be a minor problem. A week or two to do clean up and we'd be back to work. And if that meant spending a couple of extra weeks with Dustin, I could handle that, too. I might even enjoy it.

30

DUSTIN

*I*t had been three weeks since they shut down the studio. Three weeks since they'd promised to get someone in there as soon as possible to clean up the space. If something didn't happen soon, one of two things would occur: I'd go crazy trying to keep two thirteen-year-old boys out of trouble for eight hours a day or I'd bail and find myself halfway back to LA before Harmony even knew I was gone.

Option one was the more likely of the two. The more time I spent with Harmony, the less likely I was able to picture myself without her in my life. And that was a problem.

"What's on the agenda for today?" Mom asked. Her dizzy spells seemed to have evened out a bit since I'd been helping more around the house.

"I guess we'll start clearing the back part of the track." Without something to work on at the studio, I'd taken to having Liam and Rodney help me clear brush and debris from the practice track my dad had helped me build all those years ago. It's where I first learned to ride and Scarlett had given me permission to start Rodney on a bike. A baby bike. Liam had been working on Harmony, but I didn't see her ever giving him the green light to ride.

In the meantime, he seemed content to help out. I'd also given them both an overview of the bikes I had in the garage. By the end of the summer, they'd probably be ready to do some modifications of their own, assuming we weren't back to swinging a sledgehammer soon.

"You're doing a good thing by keeping those boys out of trouble." Mom poured her coffee then offered me a cup.

"Thanks. I didn't realize how much energy it would take to keep up with the two of them." The first week I'd been more of a referee. Liam's attitude wasn't too terrible, but my nephew was kind of an ass. We'd been working on it though, and with any luck, the two of them would stop bickering so much and start getting along.

"How's Harmony handling the setback?" Mom sat down at the table, her crossword in front of her.

"She's doing okay. Obviously she's not happy about it, but what else can she do?" We'd had a few heart-to-hearts and Harmony was hell-bent on getting out of waiting tables as soon as possible. In fact, she'd asked if we could get together this morning so she could tell me about an idea she had—something to keep her busy while we waited for the asbestos crew to do their job. "She's going to stop by in a little bit."

"Good. I'd love to see her. Make sure you invite her in for a cup of coffee." Mom held her pencil poised over her crossword, ready to get started. I didn't bother to remind her Harmony didn't do coffee.

"I will." I grabbed my mug and headed for the front. Rodney must be here.

"Hey, Uncle Dustin." Rodney climbed down from his

mom's truck. She'd started dropping him off with me in the mornings before she headed to work.

"Hey, kid. Ready to work on the hill today?" I waved at my sister as she turned the truck around.

"Once we get it cleared off, can I try a jump?" His eyes shone with enthusiasm. Reminded me how I felt when I was first learning how to ride. I hadn't had a teacher though. Hopefully I'd save him a few rough tumbles by showing him the right way to do things.

"I think you'd better master puttering around the yard first, don't you?" I reached out to ruffle his hair.

The smile disappeared, replaced with his standard scowl. "I suppose."

Just then tires sounded on the gravel. Harmony must be coming up the drive. Her truck appeared around the last curve before the house. I couldn't help the warm glow that started in the center of my gut at the sight of her. I'd been getting used to seeing her just about every day. And I'd be lying if I said I didn't like it.

She eased to a stop and then both she and Liam hopped out.

"Hey, Rodney, why don't you and Liam run in and see if your grandma has anything you can snack on for breakfast."

"Come on." Rodney held the screen door for Liam and the boys disappeared into the house.

"Good morning." Harmony moved to where I stood at the edge of the porch.

"Good morning to you."

Her eyes sparkled. Something had her all worked up. "So I dug around a little bit in the city's files."

"Oh yeah?" I reached out to straighten the collar of her shirt. "Find what you were looking for?"

"I did." She pulled a folded piece of paper from her back

pocket. "I knew there had to be a reason that mud works so well. Looks like the original Swallow Springs flowed through a part of your land. Did you know people came from all over to take a dip in the springs?"

"Sure did. We learned that back in grade school when they talked about the history of the town. But then they dried up. There's still a tiny trickle that runs through a pipe in the town square." I pointed to the area on the map where the center of town rested.

"I've seen it. Not very impressive."

I nodded in agreement. "I'm assuming this has something to do with what you wanted to ask me about?"

"You're a quick one, Mr. Jarrett." She gave me a playful poke in the stomach. "I want something only you can give me."

My mind exploded with possibilities, the majority of them triple X-rated. "Say the word, darlin'. I'm your guy." I leaned in to try to kiss her.

"You perv. I want your mud. I figure the spring must still be running underground somewhere, and that's what's making the mud at the end of your driveway so fantastic."

"So you want to get dirty with me?" There had to be some way I could spin this to my naughty advantage.

She rolled her eyes as she shook her head. "Whatever. Can I have your mud? I can pay you for it. I just thought it would give me something to get started on while I wait for things to get going again on the studio. Orders for those mudpacks I'm making are coming in faster than I can keep up. I need more dirt."

"If it's dirt you want, it's all yours." I leaned toward her to kiss her. She dodged me instead. My lips landed on her hair, right behind her ear. "What was that for? The boys are inside."

"I know. It's just"—she looked toward the sky, maybe waiting for some sort of divine inspiration on what to say next—"it's just, I keep getting more and more comfortable around you. I'm afraid I'm going to slip one of these days and they'll see us."

I moved in, giving her a proper kiss. One that involved tongues and even a little moan—hers, not mine. "What's so bad about that?"

"About someone seeing us together?" She pulled back, sliding the map into her back pocket while she considered my question.

"Yeah. I mean, we started off not wanting people to know we were seeing each other. But I've been thinking about it."

"What about it?"

"About us." I shrugged. "What's the big deal if people see us together? We're both adults. It's not like we're going to get in trouble."

"No, it's not that. Keeping it between us has been nice. No questions. No assumptions. Nobody gets hurt."

I slid my hand along her cheek. "If we walked away from each other now, do you think neither one of us would be hurt?"

She tilted her head, nuzzling her cheek into my hand. "It's not that easy. Liam would get hurt. He's so attached to you already. If he thinks there's a chance that you and me..."

"That we what?"

"That we'd stay together, okay? If he thinks there's a chance that you would stick around, it would get his hopes up. I don't want to do that to him."

"What if I did?" I didn't consider my words before they fell out of my mouth.

She stared up at me, her brow furrowed. "You don't mean that."

"I don't?"

"No." Twisting away, she walked along the edge of the front flowerbed. Mom had planted a variety of annuals that provided a show of color all season long.

"What if I do?"

Her head jerked back to face me. "What are you saying, Dustin?"

My heart sputtered, like the gas had just been cut and it was about to stall out. "I'm saying I might want to stick around. I've had fun with you."

"Yeah, fun with me on the dock, fun with me on my knees." Her lips stretched into a thin line. "We've been having a lot of fun. But being in a relationship is a lot more than figuring out who's in charge of buying the condoms."

"Don't you think I know that?"

"Look, I think it's better if we just keep things as they are. Unless you're serious about sticking around. But you'd have to be one-hundred percent sure before I'd tell Liam. Not even ninety-nine point nine percent sure, but a full hundred percent. Otherwise, it puts him at risk of a heartbreak."

I reached for her hand, twining my fingers with hers. "I'd never hurt him."

"Not on purpose."

My other hand went to her cheek and I smoothed her hair away. "I'd never hurt you either."

Our eyes met. Hers held hope, along with a tiny bit of unease. I'd give anything to chase that lingering doubt away. But would I be willing to give up my job? My life in California? I leaned in, pressing my lips to hers. She responded by wrapping her arms around my shoulders. Her fingers played with the hair at the base of my neck. I deepened the kiss, trying to give her everything she wanted, everything she needed.

The screen door squeaked then slammed.

"What the hell?" Liam shouted.

Harmony pulled away. A glint of guilt shone in her eyes before she turned to face her son. "Liam. I thought you were getting something to eat?"

"I did." He held out a banana. "What's going on?"

Rodney snickered. "Looks like my uncle was about to bone your mom, dude."

Liam glanced from Harmony to Rodney. His hands clenched into fists. I saw it coming before my nephew, but neither one of us had a chance to stop him. Liam put everything he had into that punch. It cracked across my nephew's smirk, sounding like a shotgun blast.

Rodney staggered backward, his hand covering his nose. Blood spurted between his fingers. We all stood there for a split second, probably in some sort of shock, before Harmony and I sprang into action.

"Liam!" Harmony rushed to Rodney's side. He pushed her away, struggling to stand.

"You okay?" I put my hands underneath Rodney's shoulders, hoisting him to his feet. "Tilt your head back. Liam, go get some paper towels from inside."

Liam shook out his fist, hung his head, and retreated inside the house.

"Is it broken?" Rodney yelled. "Did he break my nose?"

"Let me see." I peeled his fingers away from his face, trying to take a look. Please don't let it be broken. I'd never hear the end of it from my sister if it was. Although, it wasn't my fault Liam decided to man-up and finally defend himself against the verbal onslaught Rodney had been subjecting him to for the past few weeks.

Liam returned, a wad of paper towels in hand, with Mom behind him.

"What happened?" she asked.

"He broke my nose," Rodney shouted, pointing at Liam.

"Let me see." Mom brushed us all away, took a quick look at Rodney, and declared it just a bloody nose. "Come on in to the house and let's get some ice on that." She led Rodney by the arm, up the steps and into the house.

"Liam, what got into you?" Harmony asked.

Liam kept his eyes on his feet. "He didn't have to say that about you, Mom."

"I'll be inside." I didn't want to get in the way of whatever needed to be said between Harmony and her son, so I followed Mom and Rodney into the house. My nephew sat at the kitchen table, a bag of peas pressed to his face.

"Are you going to do something about that, Uncle Dustin?" Rodney asked. Splotches of color dotted his cheeks, and I almost felt sorry for the kid.

"Yeah, I am."

"Good. He can't go around punching people like that. If I hadn't been so off-guard I woulda popped him in the face with—"

"Cut it out. You had no business saying what you said to Liam."

Rodney glared at me. "You saw what he did to me."

"And I heard what you said about his mother. That's unacceptable."

Mom looked on, probably waiting to see how I'd handle this, ready to run interference if necessary.

"Liam and Harmony are part of our lives now. You've got to accept that."

"Or what?" Rodney let the peas fall to his lap. "And just whose life are they a part of? It's not like you're sticking around. And once you go, I'm not gonna put up with that asshole anymore."

"Rodney." Mom didn't have to yell to get someone's attention. All she had to do was lower her voice and let that sharp edge come through.

"I'm sorry, Grandma, but it's true." Rodney glanced to my mom as his eyes filled with tears. "Uncle Dustin won't stay. He'll go back to California and leave us here again." Then he jumped up from the chair and ran to the back porch.

"You ready to tell me what happened?" Mom asked.

I shook my head and rubbed at my temple. The beginnings of a headache pulsed at the edges. "Liam and Rodney saw me kissing Harmony. Rodney spouted off something I won't repeat, and Liam decked him." I internally braced myself for the tongue lashing Mom might unveil.

"Good." She folded the hand towel she'd had wrapped around the peas and set it on the counter. "It's about time the boys figured out you and Harmony are interested in each other."

"What?"

"Oh, I may be getting on in years, but I've known you've been sneaking out at night to go somewhere. Now it makes so much sense." She took her seat at the table again.

"So now what?" I let my arms fall to my side. "What am I supposed to do to fix things?"

Mom smoothed a hand over the paper. "How's Harmony with all of this?" Her gaze drifted to the front room.

"I don't know. She didn't want to tell Liam we were seeing each other unless I was a hundred-percent sure I was going to stick around."

"That sounds smart. It's a mama's job to protect her kids from getting hurt."

I thought about what Mom went through when my dad

walked out. All the sacrifices she made so Scarlett and I could stay in the home we'd grown up in. "I suppose."

"So now what?"

I tried to wrap my head around that question. "That's what I want you to tell me. What am I supposed to do now?"

"What do you want to do, son?"

I let out a long, slow breath while I thought about the possibilities. Harmony and I holding hands as we walked through the carnival. Teaching Liam how to take an engine apart. Spending every night in Harmony's bed. "I don't know. I've never tried sticking around before."

Mom reached for my hand. "Then don't you think it's about time you did?"

I chewed on the inside of my cheek while I thought about that. Could I stay in Swallow Springs? Could I give up the adrenaline rush, the emotional high, the flat-out charge I got from competing? Could I give up the spotlight, the awards, the recognition of a job well done when it came to my job?

"I don't know, Mom."

Mom patted my hand. "You'll figure it out, sugar."

Her faith in me seemed misguided. Could I really stay in Swallow Springs? The hometown where I'd failed so miserably as a teen? The one place I'd never wanted to set foot in again?

31

HARMONY

I got up from the table to answer the door. Dustin. Of course. After Liam decked Rodney I couldn't leave him there. So I called in to work to let Cassie know what happened, and she told me to take the day off and spend it with my son. As soon as we got home, Liam hightailed it back to his bedroom. I'd tried to talk to him but he refused to engage. All I got was a headache from the pounding bass he had blaring on his radio. I knew my son. He needed space before he was ready to process everything.

"Hey." I held the door open for Dustin to come in.

He hesitated, letting his gaze drift around the room before taking a deep breath and brushing past me. The birds squawked as he stepped into the living room.

"I see you've still got the lovebirds," he said.

"Lucy and Desi."

He tapped a finger on the side of their cage. One of the birds cocked its head, studying Dustin. "Those are cute names."

"Well, she drives him crazy so I figured it would work." I

crossed my arms over my chest while I waited for him to get to the point.

"I wanted to stop by and apologize for the way I handled things this morning."

"Apologize for what? Liam's the one who owes everyone an apology. All this time I was thinking it was LA that was the problem. That if I could just get him away from the city and away from the bad influences, he'd be fine."

Dustin turned away from the birds and crossed the room to me. He laced my fingers with his then held my hand to his lips. "It's not him. It's me. I think you're right. I think he probably has gotten attached this summer. Maybe if we'd been up front with him from the start—"

"And told him what? That you're my regular late-night hook-up?"

"No." Dustin squeezed my fingers. "That we've been seeing each other. He's not a little kid, Harmony."

"Don't you think I know that? Of course he's not a little kid. That's why I brought him here. To keep him safe and out of trouble."

Dustin pressed a kiss to the back of my hand, sending a shiver up my arm. "I'm just saying, I think he can handle it."

My throat squeezed shut. I forced a breath. "How do you know what he can and can't handle? You can walk away any time. You've never had to put the pieces back together when..." I bit my lip, forcing myself to stop.

"When what?" Dustin put his finger under my chin, nudging my face up.

I stared at his mouth, not wanting to meet his gaze. My chest tightened. I couldn't cry...I wouldn't. "Nothing."

"When are you going to tell me what happened with Liam's dad?" He tucked a strand of hair behind my ear. I wanted to turn into his touch, nestle my cheek against his hand and let him tell me everything would be okay. But the last time I put my trust in a man like that, I'd learned my lesson.

"It doesn't matter. It's in the past." I pulled away to settle on the couch. My finger traced the intricate floral pattern on the overstuffed cushion.

Dustin sat down next to me. "It does matter. Liam said his dad left when he was three or four."

My head snapped up. "When did he tell you that?"

"While we were working out at my place." He put a hand on my knee. "He said he doesn't remember him anymore."

"Good."

"What happened between the two of you?"

"You really want to know?" I searched his face.

"If you're willing to tell me."

"Fine. I was young, just out of high school. He was the bad boy. Rode a motorcycle"—Dustin cringed—"stayed out too late, skipped all of his classes. He had a horrible family life. Didn't even know his dad and had been in and out of foster homes since he was a kid." I hugged a throw pillow to my stomach. "I got caught up. Thought I could help him heal the hurt in his past. He said he loved me. For the first time in my life I felt needed. Next thing I knew, I was pregnant and he was gone."

"I'm so sorry."

I put up a hand to silence him so I could continue. I'd started, I may as well get the whole sorry story out of the way. "I dropped out of college and moved back in with my parents. Mom watched Liam so I could get my massage license. He came around occasionally and kept telling me he was going to find a way for us to get our own place, to be a family. For a while I even believed him."

"Where is he now?" Dustin rested his hand on my knee. The pad of his thumb brushed my skin.

I didn't want to make eye contact, didn't want him to know how gullible I'd been. But the physical proof of my naivety and stupidity was in the next room, all thirteen years and five-foot-seven of him.

"I don't know where he is and I don't care. Liam and I have been fine on our own."

"Why didn't you tell me, Harmony?"

"Tell you what?" I glanced up at his face. His jaw clenched. This wasn't his battle to fight. "Tell you that I got sucked in by some sweet-talking, no-good charmer who didn't give a crap about anyone but himself?"

"No." His brow softened, and he met my gaze. Those green eyes held a world of words. "It makes more sense now, how protective you are of Liam."

"He's the only good thing that came out of that time in my life."

"I understand." Dustin bent his head toward mine until our foreheads touched. "I'm not that guy, you know."

"I know." The emotion I'd been squelching down bubbled up. I tucked my head, not wanting Dustin to see the threat of tears. I'd cried enough in the past. I didn't want to waste any more tears on Liam's dad.

We sat like that for several minutes, until my breath evened out and I felt like I could look at Dustin without bursting into tears. Yes, I'd been hauling some bitter baggage around with me for the past several years. And Dustin was right—he wasn't that guy. After seeing the way he was with his mom, with Liam—he'd never treat anyone like my ex had. I relaxed against him, breathing in his scent, taking comfort in his presence even though it was temporary.

"So here's what I propose we do." Dustin slid his arm around me, pulling me closer. "I say we come clean with Liam and let him know what's going on."

"But how can I be honest with Liam when I don't even know what we're doing?"

Dustin brushed the hair from my shoulders. His breath blew across the back of my neck. "I've been thinking."

"Uh oh." I stifled a half-laugh. "Last time you did that didn't I end up with some four-legged creature?"

"Two. The last critter I saddled you with had two legs."

"Two birds. Four legs." I shrugged.

"Hear me out on this, okay?" He took my hand. "What if I split my time? I could go back to LA and try to stack my appearances so I'd have bigger chunks of time off."

I shook my head, already knowing where he was going to go with this. I didn't want a part-time boyfriend. What we'd been doing all summer might have woken up a part of me I'd been ignoring for the past decade, but when I was ready to commit to someone, it would be a real commitment, not a half-assed booty call. "We're enjoying each other's company with the time we've got left. Let's not mess it up by trying to make it into something else."

"But—"

"It'll be better this way."

"I'm not sure I agree with you on that. Spending time back here, with my family, it's made me realize what I've been missing."

"Look, I don't want to foster Liam's hope just because you're feeling a little nostalgic."

"You're right. I'll be more careful with Liam. I don't want to hurt his feelings." Dustin pressed a kiss to my forehead. "As for the rest, can we just see how it goes?"

"If you're serious about spending more time in Swallow

Springs, isn't there something you need to do?" I hadn't wanted to push him, but it was obvious that Dustin had a huge weight on his heart.

"I need to talk to Robbie." He let his head drop. "I've been putting it off, but it's time."

"For the record, I'm not telling you to do anything." I didn't want him to blame me if things didn't go well with him and my cousin. But I knew he'd never be at peace until the two of them made amends. They'd been friends once, almost like family. If he meant what he said about sticking around, there was no way he could do that without prying that massive monkey off his back.

"Will you go with me?"

"To talk to Robbie?" I asked.

"I could use a little moral support." He met my gaze, his eyes revealing the uncertainty he must be feeling.

"Okay." He might make things right with Robbie, but I wouldn't get my hopes up that he'd be sticking around. I'd been left in the past, and I was done giving a man the power to hurt me again.

"So does that mean we can still...you know..." Dustin nuzzled my neck with his mouth.

Heat simmered through my veins. "Yes. But we need to be more careful."

"You got it." He lowered his chin, and nibbled on my ear lobe.

I let myself relax into him for a moment, knowing it wouldn't last. Dustin would get bored. The novelty of being around family, of being around me, would wear off. How could it not?

32

DUSTIN

*H*armony reached the door to the truck before I had a chance to run around and open it for her. She must have been watching for me from the front window. The sight of her loosened the dread that had been gripping my heart all day.

"Hey, give a guy a shot, why don't you?" I closed it behind her then leaned through the open window to give her a peck on the cheek. "You look gorgeous tonight."

She had on a flowery sun dress that tied in back. Her hair sat on top of her head, leaving her neck exposed. I wanted to nip at the spot right behind her ear—a spot I knew she favored. But if I did that we'd be late for dinner and she'd never forgive me for ruining our double date with Robbie and Cassie.

"Thanks." Her cheeks flushed. When would she get used to accepting a compliment? "You sure you're ready for this?"

"Ready as I'll ever be." As I walked around the front of the truck, my fist landed a thump on the hood. I'd been trying to convince myself all day that I could do this, yet I'd almost called to cancel twice. The other night when she'd been snuggled in my arms, it seemed like a good idea. But now, now I wasn't just getting cold feet, it seemed like they were frozen in solid blocks of ice.

I climbed in and got settled behind the wheel.

Harmony rested her hand on my thigh. "It's going to be okay. He won't bite, you know."

"I know." I picked up her hand and flipped it over before pressing a kiss against her wrist. The scent of her skin filled me with resolve. I kissed my way up the inside of her arm and into the crease of her elbow before she giggled and jerked away.

"Stop that. You're not getting out of going tonight, no matter what you try."

"Damn. May as well get it over with then." I turned the key in the ignition and the truck rumbled to life.

Harmony kept the conversation going on the way into town. Or at least, she kept talking and every once in a while I'd respond with a nod or some other sort of short reply. My mind was on the task ahead. Robbie knew I wanted to chat. It was high time we talked about what had happened that day with Jeff. Past the time I should have asked for forgiveness.

Too soon I pulled into the parking lot of Sal's Steakhouse. As the truck came to a rest, Harmony put her hand over mine.

"It's just dinner and some conversation."

I glanced over. Her smile offered reassurance. I didn't deserve her faith. Everyone knew it. Everyone but Harmony, it seemed.

"Come on, let's go." She squeezed my hand and was out the door before I had a chance to even open mine.

My mouth went dry like I'd just stuffed a wad of cotton inside. I tried to swallow. Dinner. A little bit of small talk.

Surely we wouldn't start off with the big stuff. We'd work our way up to that.

I shook my hands out, trying to get rid of the jitters as I caught up to Harmony. She'd painted her nails a bright turquoise color. For some reason that made me smile. As I relaxed, I was able to force a few deep breaths into my lungs.

"Looks like they're already here." Harmony nodded toward Cassie's SUV parked on the other side of the lot. No mistaking it for someone else's—not when she had a license plate that read LUVBIRD.

Forcing myself to put one foot in front of the other, I made it to the door and held it open for Harmony. She passed by, brushing against me, leaving a flowery scent trailing behind her. This woman was such a mystery to me. She touted kale smoothies and hemp hearts yet painted unicorns on her toenails and tried to pass off instant coffee crystals as the real stuff. The more time I spent with her, the more I wanted to know her—and that was a first for me.

"Y'all made it." Robbie stood from the table as we approached the booth. He gave Harmony a hug then stuck his hand out for me to shake.

"Thanks for agreeing to meet." I gripped his hand in mine for a moment before letting go.

"We're thrilled to have someone to double with." Cassie pulled me in for a hug. "Jake and Misty never have time to get together any more. Not with three little ones running around."

I wrapped my arms around her loosely. Cassie had always been good at making people feel comfortable. A long, long time ago I'd even crushed on her a bit. That was the whole reason Rob and I had got in a fight that day. The day of the accident. Because I liked Cassie enough to give him shit about her.

"Go ahead, sit down." Robbie gestured to the opposite bench.

Harmony slid in first and I followed. An awkward silence descended for a brief moment before Rob and Cassie spoke at the same time.

"We ordered—"

"Hope you don't mind—"

"Go ahead." Rob stretched his arm along the back of the booth, letting it rest on Cassie's shoulder.

She smiled at him, then turned her grin on us. "We went ahead and ordered a couple of appetizers."

"Oh, thanks. I hope you got the fried onion straws. That always used to be our favorite. Remember when you and Jeff—" I stopped myself before launching into a detailed account of how he and Jeff had split one of those giant fried onions right down the middle at one of our baseball banquets. They both stuffed half of it into their mouths. Jeff chewed his up and swallowed. Robbie had dipped his in the horseradish sauce first so he ended up spitting onion through his mouth and his nose before getting cuffed upside the head by his dad.

Robbie looked up at me, a glint of pain slicing through his eyes. It disappeared as soon as I saw it. "Yeah, those were some good times."

I figured I'd better try again. "Hey, Rob, I—"

"Getcha y'all somethin' to drink?" Saved by the waitress. Harmony and I placed our order and by the time the server left the table, the moment had passed.

Through fried onions, stuffed peppers, and a full meal of steaks and all the sides, I smiled and nodded, contributing as little to the conversation as possible. Between Harmony and Cassie, there wasn't much chance to get a word in anyway. The two of them acted like they hadn't seen each other in weeks—not like they didn't spent six to ten hours a day together.

Finally, the bill arrived. I scooped it up before Rob had a chance to snag it. "My treat."

"You don't have to do that." Rob held out his hand for the bill.

"I want to." I dug my wallet out of my back pocket and slid a platinum card into the folio.

"Well, thank you for dinner." Cassie pulled Rob's arm back. "Do you mind if I scoot out to the ladies' room?"

Rob stood so she could slide out of the booth.

"I think I'll do the same." Harmony put a hand on my arm.

"Okay." I held the folio close to my chest while I stood to let her by.

The waitress appeared and took the check. That left me and Rob and a deafening silence. I fidgeted with the straw wrapper, twisting it around my finger over and over until the paper ripped. Now was my chance. Unless I wanted an audience of Harmony and Cassie to witness my apology, I needed to force it out.

"Rob, I...I just wanted to say..." Damn, it was hard. Not the apology itself, but what it represented. "I need to tell you that I'm sorry." There. It was out there. My eyes stayed trained on the table, examining the barely perceptible scratches in the thick polyurethane they must have slathered on the commercial grade tables.

When he didn't respond, I chanced a look up. Rob's gaze locked on his hands which were fiddling with the edge of a napkin. He must be just as uncomfortable as me.

"I'm sorry, too." His voice came out barely above a whisper.

"For what?" Why the hell did he need to apologize? "You did nothing wrong."

"No." He glanced up. Blue eyes locked on mine. Any hint of softness that had come through in his voice had disappeared. "What happened to...what happened was just as much my fault as it was yours. More even."

"No." I shook my head. "I was the reason you got in the fight. If I hadn't been giving you shit, we wouldn't have gotten detention. You don't get to take the blame for this."

He leaned back against the booth. "Bullshit. Truth is, it's both of our faults. We knew better than to fight on school grounds. And if my dad would have answered his phone, Jeff never would have tried to come and get me." His head shook slowly from side to side. "It sucks. But you're no more to blame than anyone."

I sighed, forcing out my frustration. "How can you even say that? It was my fault you got in trouble. My fault you had to stay after. My fault Jeff tried to come get you. I've been living with this for so long. If I hadn't been such a dick that day, he might still be with us."

Rob put his hand over mine. "You can't keep blaming yourself. It'll eat you alive from the inside out. I know that for a fact because I almost let it."

I slid my hand away. "Every day. Every fucking day I think about it. What I could have done different..."

"I know," Rob said. "I still think about him all the time. Remember the time he talked us into pooling our money and buying that lobster at the Piggly Wiggly?"

A snort escaped my lips. "Damn. He told everybody it was his new pet and walked it around the playground during recess for a week."

Robbie doubled over in laughter. "And then that girl

found it in his desk and he had to do community service for a month."

It felt good to laugh about Jeff. So good I didn't want to stop. "How about that time he decided to move the manure pile in back of your dad's place with that new ATV?"

"Dad pulled out the belt for that one. Jeff had to wash and wax every patrol car at the station."

Waves of laughter subsided. My stomach ached. I hadn't laughed like that in years. "He was one of a kind."

"Yeah, yeah he was." Rob looked over at me again, bonded by our mutual admiration and loss of a brother and best friend.

"Can you forgive me?" I bit my lip while I tried to gauge his response.

"I told you, nothing to forgive. There's no sense talking about what might have been. It's done, Dustin. I don't harbor any ill will toward you for something that happened almost twenty years ago. Jeff wouldn't want us to dwell on it, y'know."

I did know. Jeff was the biggest jokester, live-in-the-moment guy I'd ever met. "Still, it would mean a lot if you'd just accept my apology. You might not need it, but I do."

Rob stuck his hand across the table. "Done. I'll accept your apology under one condition."

"What's that?" I asked as I shook his hand.

"That you'll accept mine."

My brow furrowed but I didn't have time to ask what he meant. Cassie and Harmony returned to the table, followed by the waitress. By the time I'd signed the credit card slip and pocketed my receipt, the moment had shifted.

I stood, putting my arm around Harmony, and following Rob and Cassie to the door.

"Anyone up for a nightcap?" Cassie asked.

"I have to get back to feed the raccoons," Harmony said.

"I hope you're not letting all those wild animals run around the house." Rob smiled as he held open the door. "Your landlord might have a problem with that."

"Yeah, because that place is in such pristine condition." Cassie linked her arm through Harmony's as they made their way to the truck.

"So are we good?" Rob asked.

"Yeah." I nodded. "We're good."

"I'm glad." Rob gave me a half-hug-half-clap-on-the-back kind of thing, solidifying our agreement that the two of us were back on good terms.

"Hey, I meant to tell you"—I glanced back at him on my way to the truck—"you did good with that baseball field. Jeff would have loved that."

Rob grinned, the same kind of dopey grin his brother and I used to make fun of him for so long ago. "Thanks. That means a lot."

"See ya around then?" I'd reached the truck before Harmony and managed to open her door for her this time.

"Yeah, see ya around, bro." Rob lifted a hand in the air, giving a casual wave before he disappeared around a parked car.

"How did it go?" Harmony asked as she ducked under my arm and slid into the truck.

I leaned into the open doorway. "It went well. Really well."

"Good." She linked her fingers together behind my neck, pulling my lips down toward hers. "I told you not to worry."

I let my forehead rest against hers. "You were right."

She kissed me, a sweet, light peck of her lips to mine. "I think we should celebrate."

There was nothing I'd love more than celebrating with

Harmony. "I thought you had to get home to feed the raccoons?" I asked, already hot for her. One innocent kiss, and she had me eager for more.

"A little white lie. I just wanted you all to myself tonight. Liam's staying over at a friend's again." She batted her eyelashes at me, all innocent-like.

"You tease." My finger ran along her shoulder, under the strap of her sun dress. "I ought to go tell Rob and Cassie that you lied. Take 'em up on that offer for a nightcap after all."

She reached up, untying the straps then holding the top of her dress up with one hand. "Or you could take me home and have your way with me."

My blood heated as she taunted me, letting one side of her top dip lower. I reached down, adjusting myself for a very uncomfortable ride back to her place. "Watch your feet, babe."

Then I closed the door, eager to get her home and underneath me—a place I was getting way too used to having her.

33

HARMONY

"*C*an I get a touch more coffee, Harmony?" Frank tapped the handle of his coffee mug, drawing my attention away from the front window.

Now that Dustin and the boys were back at work on the studio build out, I was dying to get over there and see the progress they'd made.

"You bet." I reached for the carafe. Not quite enough to fill up his cup. Dang it. "Let me go find some more for you in the back."

"All right." He turned his attention back to his newspaper.

As I passed Ryder on the way to my cubby, he shook his head. "Why don't you ask Cassie to show you how to make coffee today?"

"Would you be quiet?" I set the carafe down on the counter while I reached for the jar of instant coffee I'd smuggled inside. "We had a deal."

"Yeah, Julianne loved those bath bombs." He waved a spatula at me. "You should sell those."

"Already do." I felt around in the back of my cubby. I could have sworn I'd brought the jar in from the car. Two of them. At the rate we went through coffee around here, I'd been stocking up as fast as I used them. "You know what else I'm selling now? Mud packs. I bet your girlfriend would really go for those."

"I'll check it out." Ryder slid his earbuds back in.

I crouched down to peer inside my cubby, desperate to find the magic crystals that would allow me to avoid the monster machine.

"Looking for these?" Cassie stepped around the corner, my two jars of instant coffee crystals in hand.

"What? No. I was just looking for...um...a hair band." My hand went to my hair which unfortunately was already held back in a ponytail.

"Harmony, why didn't you tell me you were having such a hard time with the coffee machine?" she asked.

My shoulders slumped. She knew. It was no use pretending any longer. "I'm sorry. I wanted to. I didn't want to admit I couldn't figure out how to master that horrible machine."

Cassie laughed as she set the jars down on the counter. "It's complicated, that's for sure. But I don't mind showing you again. And again after that if it doesn't sink in. You should know that."

"I know. I do. I'm just tired of being so bad at everything."

She put her hand on my shoulder. "You're not bad at everything. In fact, I'd say you're pretty good at a lot of stuff. I tried one of those mud packs on Robbie's knee last night and he said it really helped. Think you can make me some more of those?"

"I'd love to." I'd been harvesting mud a couple times a week from Dustin's property. Once the studio space was finished I'd have more room to expand my operation. As it was, I'd taken over almost half of the kitchen at home and was eager to get everything into one place.

"All right. Let's take this one step at a time." Cassie proceeded to walk me through the many steps of how to make a pot of coffee in the giant machine. I even took illustrated notes on my order pad.

Bound and determined to succeed, I followed her directions. As the first drops hit the empty carafe, I squealed and clapped my hands together.

"Today she makes coffee, tomorrow she'll rule the world." Frank raised his mug in a toast.

"Slow down. I don't want to get ahead of myself." I laughed as I wiped down the counter in front of him.

"He's right." Cassie put a hand on my shoulder and squeezed. "It won't be long before you're out of here and running your own business."

Happiness swelled up from deep inside, expanding through my entire body until I couldn't contain it. "I can't wait."

"You're going to be fabulous as an entrepreneur," Cassie said.

"You and Robbie have been so supportive. It'll be nice to have a place of my own." I snagged the half-full carafe of fresh-brewed coffee and refilled Frank's mug. "Once I get the business going, hopefully Liam and I can find a house, too."

"Plenty of places close to town if you're looking," Frank said.

"Oh, we'd need somewhere with some land, I think." I bit my lip, wondering exactly what we'd do with the menagerie of animals Liam and I had managed to collect so far.

"You still got that skunk and those raccoons out at your place?" Frank lifted the mug to his lips and took a sip.

"How's the coffee?" I held my breath while I waited for him to answer.

"Better than ever." He winked.

"Good. And yes, we managed to get Crackle and Pop up to the wildlife center, but it sounds like Snap might be with us for a while. His foot got injured while he was stuck in the engine of the truck and they can't keep him at the wildlife center indefinitely so we brought him back home." The little raccoon had gotten so attached to Liam, I didn't know how they'd manage to separate when the time came. At least he'd still have Petunia, Magoo, and the lovebirds to keep him company.

"You've got a good heart, Harmony." Frank took a few dollars out and set them on the counter.

"Where are you headed so early? We can usually count on you to stick around until the lunch crowd starts to arrive." I made change for him while he got up to go.

"Got a lunch date today." He nodded. "Keep the change."

"Thanks. And have fun on your date." I grinned as he gave me a little wave before he exited the front door. Dustin might not appreciate the fact his mom was obviously being romanced by Mr. Blevins, but I still thought it was cute. They deserved to find happiness together.

Speaking of happiness—I glanced around the café— now would be the time to make a mad dash across the street and check on the progress.

"I'm going to run over," I yelled toward the kitchen.

"Okay. I'll meet you there in a few," Cassie yelled back.

Eager to see what they'd managed to accomplish, I hung my apron on a hook behind the counter and headed across the street. As I pushed through the front door, the buzz of a saw greeted me. I inched up the steps, smiling as I remembered the first time Dustin and I previewed the space.

Finally, at the top of the stairs, I turned. Natural light filled the room. Since Dustin had removed one of the walls, sunlight spilled across the original hardwood floors. Gorgeous. Yes, a layer of sawdust and drywall dust coated everything. Yes, wires dipped from the ceiling, waiting for the electrician to put in a few more outlets. But I could see past all that. And what I saw took my breath away.

"Hey!" Dustin's voice carried over the buzz of the saw. "Hey, cut it."

The noise stopped, replaced by the blaring of a boom box in the corner. Dustin walked over and flipped the switch, leaving us in silence. "So, what do you think?" he asked.

"What's that?" I lifted my chin in the direction of the ancient boom box.

"What? I like to kick it old-school. You can't get bass like that on an MP3 player." He reached me and slid an arm around my waist.

My gaze drifted around the space. "It's stunning. Absolutely gorgeous."

"We had to change the design a little. There was a pipe in that wall over there so we shifted the half-wall to accommodate."

Dustin continued to talk about minor adjustments while I pictured myself in the space. I could actually see it: the tiny bottles of essential oils lining the shelves, the homemade mud packs and bath bombs wrapped in cellophane and tied with teal ribbons...all of it.

"So hopefully only another couple of days and we'll be ready to paint." Dustin took off his work gloves and tucked them into his back pocket. "Anything you want us to change before it's too late?"

"It's absolutely perfect." I couldn't keep the ear-to-ear grin from my face if I tried. To think that someone had gone to this kind of effort for me...it ripped my breath from my lungs. "Thanks."

"You're welcome." Dustin drew me into a hug, despite Rodney and Liam being nearby.

I let him. It still surprised me how naturally we seemed to fit. My shoulder slid perfectly under his arm. I was going to miss this.

"Did you bring over any cookies, Mom?" Liam shuffled over, eyeing the way Dustin had his arm draped over my shoulder.

I ducked out from under Dustin and rubbed my hands together. We'd been trying to keep a low profile around the boys, especially after their big blow up. "I was in such a hurry to get a peek, I forgot."

"I remembered." Cassie entered the space, three box lunches stacked in her arms. "Turkey and Swiss on wheat okay?"

Before she had a chance to set them down, the boys had each grabbed a box. She handed the last one to Dustin. "It's looking great in here."

"I can't believe what a difference you've made." I couldn't help but put my hand on Dustin's arm when I talked to him.

"Liam and Rodney did a lot of it. I've still got a bum shoulder, you know." He smirked. His shoulder hadn't seemed to be bothering him much during the nights we spent together.

"I can't believe you're going to be leaving me soon."

Cassie took my hand in hers. "Now that you've finally learned how to make coffee, you're moving on."

"Wait, she finally learned how to make a real pot of coffee?" Dustin's eyebrows shot up.

"I did. Even drew myself a diagram so I wouldn't forget." I gave him my best version of a "yeah, I'm a badass" grin.

"See? There's nothing you can't do." He shrugged.

I wanted to cover his scruffy face in big, wet, sloppy kisses but Cassie tugged on my arm.

"Show me the rest of the space?"

I led her around, pointing out the different areas of the shop. "Dustin said only a few more days and I'll be able to paint and move in."

"I'm so excited for you. It's all coming together, isn't it?" Cassie's smile could have warmed the heart of even an ice queen.

I smiled back, not quite a hundred-percent.

"What's wrong?" she asked.

"Nothing." I shook my head, trying to dislodge any worry. Having the space was just one more physical reminder that my time with Dustin was coming to an end. An end I didn't want to happen. "Did you see the massage rooms?"

Cassie shook her head, so I pointed to the back of the space. "Right back here. Follow me."

The space might be mine, but Dustin never would be. We were from two different places. He loved the spotlight while I craved peace and quiet. He craved the rush of adrenaline, the cheer of a crowd, while I adored running my hand through gobs of mud and figuring out the perfect way to relax after a hard day of work.

He might look at home in Swallow Springs, but his

home base was a thousand miles away. It might be time I started reminding myself of that. The longer we kept this going, the harder it was going to be when it came time for him to go.

34

DUSTIN

The phone rang, clanging through the trailer, the noise bouncing off the walls of the small space. I reached for it on the nightstand, my first thought that it might be Mom or even Harmony needing help.

"Hello?"

"Damn, do you ever owe me big time now." Mav, my agent. What the hell? The digital clock lit up one-thirty in the morning.

"Do you know what time it is?" I squinted at the bright red numbers before letting my eyes drift closed again. "Are you drunk?"

"Maybe a little."

Great, when did those tables turn? It used to be Mav would talk me down, sober me up, and bust my ass for being a dick. Now all of a sudden he was the one calling me in the middle of the night?

"So you're just in the mood for a heart to heart, or what?" I nestled my head back on the pillow, not willing to sacrifice sleep to hear the latest about his drinking buddies.

"I've got one word for you, D-man." Hell, he must be drunk. D-man?

"What's that?"

"Redemption."

"Why don't you call me in the morning after you've had a chance to sleep off the massive hangover you're bound to have?"

"For you, buddy. Redemption. For you."

"What?" I brushed the fuzziness of sleep away. What the hell was he talking about?

"How would you like a chance to redeem yourself on national television? Show everyone you're not the crackpot they saw back in May when you botched that burnout? Huh?"

"Well, yeah." Of course I wanted another shot at showing the world I actually knew how to ride a bike. I'd thought of nothing else since I'd tucked tail and drove out of California. "That would be great, but—"

"But nothing. I just had drinks with the executive producer of the show. She said they're willing to give you another appearance."

"That's great. When? Just say the word and I'll be there."

"Next Thursday night. Best night of the week. Do you love me or what?"

Thursday, Thursday, something was happening next Thursday. I rubbed a hand across my forehead, trying to retrieve the information. "Hang on a sec." I put him on speaker while I pulled up my calendar on my phone. Oh shit. Harmony's grand opening. "Thursday's no good for me. Can we do another night?"

He laughed. "Good one."

When I didn't say anything he let out another laugh, this one a little louder. "What do you mean Thursday's no good?

You think they're asking if you can fit them in? This is your shot. Redemption."

"I can't." I pinched the pulse points on my temple with my thumb and middle finger, anticipating a monster headache. "I just can't make that night work. I'm sorry."

"Do you have any idea what I had to go through to get this for you? I drank Cosmos. With cherries. I'm not a Cosmo drinker, D-man."

"I said I was sorry." I couldn't ditch Harmony on her grand opening, not even if it meant a chance at redeeming my own career. She'd never forgive me if I wasn't there, and the truth was, I wanted to be there. I had to. The past several weeks had shown me there was nowhere else I'd rather be than by her side, especially on such an important night. "Are you sure they don't have any other spots?"

"I don't know. I'll have to ask my new bestie when we get together to paint our nails next week." He groaned, the sound sawing along my nerve endings like a dull knife.

"I'm really sorry."

"You're sorry. Yeah, that's great. Tell that to the next major talk show host who has you on his show. Oh wait, there won't be any because you're going to go down as the dumbest client in history. Tell you what. Think about it. Call me in a day or two. All that fresh air must be getting to you because I know there's no way in hell that a Maverick Bengston client would turn this down."

The phone went dead.

Dammit. What had I done?

THE NEXT DAY I showed up at the studio, paint supplies in hand. Liam and Rodney helped me unload then we spread the canvas drop cloths I'd picked up at the hardware store over the floor.

"Need any help getting started?" I asked.

"Nah, we got it." Rodney held one end of the drop cloth while Liam took the other. The two of them were getting along better than ever. I had high hopes that they might even start up a real friendship by the end of the summer. I'd seen them laughing over something together on Rodney's phone and Liam had taken to bringing in extra sweets from the café a few times a week to share.

Maybe I had done something right this summer. My heart squeezed in my chest as I thought about the late night phone call. I hadn't been able to sleep after Mav hung up on me, so I'd sneaked into the house and started the coffee, then spent some quiet time on the front porch, trying to sort out what I wanted out of this life.

Now that Rob and I were on good terms, I wasn't as eager to get out of town. I had some money saved up— enough to give me a fresh start somewhere away from Hollywood. The boys and I had made good progress clearing the track. Maybe I could even set up shop around here and train a whole new generation of riders. My time in the spotlight was probably coming to an end anyway. Although, I really didn't want to go out on a flop. I needed to find a way to redeem myself before I called it quits. Mav was right about that.

As Liam and Rodney started cutting in and rolling the soft white paint on the walls, I moved over to turn on some tunes. Nothing like a little head-banging music to get me in the painting spirit. The boom box sputtered. Twenty years old, at least. I gave it a good bang with my fist and it came to life. *Kickstart My Heart* blared as I grabbed a paintbrush and joined Liam and Rodney. With Harmony's grand opening less than two weeks away, I wanted to get everything done so she'd have plenty of time to set things up exactly how she wanted them.

Having the three of us working, in sync for a change, we'd made good progress by the time we took a break for lunch. By dinnertime, the whole main area was done. I'd told Harmony not to come over until we had the whole space painted. I wanted her to be surprised and see it all at once.

"Let's call it quits for tonight guys." I poured the leftover paint back in the pail before hammering the lid in place. We still had at least one full day of painting left.

Rodney groaned as he stretched. He'd been cutting in around the edges most of the day, my least favorite job. "How long until we finish do you think?"

"Hey, can you turn off the tunes?" I pointed to the boom box in the corner. Rodney sauntered over, taking his time. The music stopped. "We can probably get most of it down tomorrow. That leaves Friday for touch-ups. Why, you have somewhere else to be?"

Rodney leaned over, trying to reach his toes. "No, my back's killing me, though. Hey, Liam, you want to go swimming when we get back to my grandma's place?"

Liam climbed down off the ladder he'd been using. "Sure. Just let me check with my mom." Then he pulled out his phone to send off a text.

I selfishly hoped Harmony would say yes. That would give us some alone time while the boys were swimming and cooling off.

"Mom said it's okay. Dustin, can I catch a ride back with you?"

"You bet. Tell your mom to come over, too. We can grill out tonight. I'll make enough for everyone."

We sealed up our brushes and tools so they'd be ready to go the next day. The boys walked out ahead of me, but I paused in the doorway, letting my gaze move around the room. Harmony was going to love it here. She'd already been through to clear the energy out. At least that's what she said she'd been doing. Looked to me like she'd just walked around with a bunch of burning weeds in her hand, trailing smoke behind her. But hey, if it made her happy, it was fine with me.

I'd never wanted so much for someone else before. But I wanted her to have this space. She and Liam needed it and everything it represented to create the future she deserved. And somehow, someway, I was going to figure out how I could fit into the frame, too.

35

HARMONY

*B*y the time Petunia and I arrived at Dustin's mom's place, the boys had taken off for the swimming hole just up the road. Mrs. Jarrett was out on a dinner date with Frank, and Scarlett was still at work at the Cut 'n Curl. That left Dustin and me with the whole place to ourselves.

I unclipped Petunia's leash when we got out of the truck. She didn't stray far from me anymore—not since she'd almost been run over by Magoo in the emu's outdoor pen. The smell of steak on the grill greeted my nose, making my stomach gurgle in anticipation. As I rounded the back of the house, I caught a glimpse of Dustin standing in front of the grill.

He had his back to me and a metal spatula in his hand. I waited while he gyrated his hips to some heavy metal floating out of his phone speaker. Stifling a laugh, I tiptoed closer.

His hips moved side to side and he held the spatula in front of him like a mic. My brain flashed forward, immediately conjuring up a vision of Dustin grilling burgers at our own place while Magoo, Petunia, and Snap frolicked around his feet.

I wrapped my arms around my middle as I painted a mental picture of a possible future together. Liam would be next to him, learning how to use the grill, and I'd come out of the house with a baby on my hip. Dustin's baby.

I sucked in a lungful of air like I'd been holding my breath. Is that what I wanted? Mulling the idea over, warmth filled my core. After the experience with Liam's dad, I hadn't let myself imagine a future with anyone. My sole responsibility in this world was taking care of my son. But somehow in the last several weeks, my focus had blurred. Liam was still my top priority, but Dustin had shown me there was room for me to take my own wants and needs into consideration as well. I just needed to figure out what exactly I wanted, and more importantly, what I needed and if that included Dustin Jarrett.

The vision slowly split into hundreds of pieces and drifted away. Shaking my head clear, I stepped onto the patio. Petunia ran ahead. Her nose brushed Dustin's leg, and he jumped. He turned around, catching sight of me.

I applauded. "Nice job. I hope your grilling skills are better than your dance moves."

A faint pink tinted his cheeks then his lips curved up into a gorgeous smile. "Oh, you haven't seen my best moves yet."

"Oh yeah?" I took a few steps toward him.

"Yep. Baby, I've got moves you haven't even dreamed of." He set the spatula down on the side of the grill.

"Is that right?" I couldn't help but giggle as he danced his way around me in a wide circle.

He moved in, catching me around the waist from behind and pulling me up against him. "That's right."

Delicious anticipation raced through me. No matter how many times Dustin and I got together, it always felt as exciting as the first. I kept waiting for the anticipation, for the tingles of awareness, for the crazy uptick in my pulse to subside. But every time I saw him, it seemed like my reaction got more intense.

"So what are you making?" I asked.

"Steak."

"Mmm. I can't remember the last time I had a grilled steak fresh off the grill."

"Baked potatoes."

"With all the fixings?"

"Yep." He leaned down, the scruff on his chin scratching my neck.

I pressed my back into him, letting the safety and security created by his arms surround me. I knew better than to let myself come to rely on this. But maybe, just maybe, this time it would be different. I'd spent my whole life protecting myself and Liam from getting too close to someone, from having our hearts broken by putting our faith in a man who had no intention of coming through for us. But Dustin hadn't given me any reason to doubt him. Every time he made a promise he came through. He wouldn't have suggested we take things a step further if he didn't mean it. Maybe it was time to let down my guard, let go of my fear, let someone in.

"The boys won't be back for a bit." His kisses landed on my neck, making my heart beat faster.

"Oh yeah?" I turned around in his arms.

"Yeah." He pressed his forehead to mine.

I ran a finger over his chest, letting the moment settle around me. The steak sizzled on the grill, a warm summer breeze wrapped around us, carrying the scent of fresh cut grass. I wanted to string the moment out forever, lose myself in the warmth created by the way Dustin's body pressed against mine.

"You okay, Harmony?" he whispered against my ear.

"Yeah. Just trying to imprint this all on my mind."

"And how's that going?" He reached up to tuck my hair behind my ear then leaned down and kissed along my neck.

"You're distracting me." I laughed as I brought my hands between us and gave him a slight push on the chest.

"You don't need to imprint it on your mind. I'm not going anywhere. We can do this whenever we want." He reached for me, pulling me against him.

My heart fluttered, like the wings of a fragile baby bird nervous to take that first flight. "What are you saying?"

He met my gaze. "I'm saying I've thought about it, and I want to be a part of your life. Whatever that looks like, however you'll have me."

I couldn't catch my breath, it stuttered and sputtered. Emotions I'd been holding at bay crashed over me, making me want to laugh and cry at the same time. Trying to get a handle on myself before he could see what a hot mess I was, I turned away. "I don't know, Dustin."

"It's okay, you don't have to know right now." His palm caressed my back, making slow circles on my shoulder blade. Even his touch grounded me, centered me.

"What you're asking, it's a lot." Wrapping my arms around my middle, I let myself imagine what it would be like to be able to count on someone. For me and Liam. Someone I could rely on for a change. Someone who was committed to making us a priority. I didn't need a man in my life—I'd proven that to myself time and again over the past several years. But that didn't mean I didn't want one.

"No rush. You take your time, okay?" He put both

hands on my shoulders and spun me around. "I know we didn't go looking for this—whatever this is between us. But now that we've got it, I don't want to let it go. We can take it slow."

"I'd like that." His smile matched mine before he lowered his head to take my mouth with his.

"Damn." He broke the kiss. "I've got to flip the steaks."

While Dustin checked on the meat, the boys came in. They must have finally made peace. Liam laughed at something Rodney said as they joined us on the patio.

"How was the water?" Dustin asked.

"Refreshing." Liam grinned. He'd changed so much since summer started. Working with his hands and engaging in physical labor had changed his physique. The muscles in his arms had become more defined, and he'd lost the last bit of baby fat on his cheeks. My baby was growing up. He could use a role model like Dustin in his life— someone to help him navigate the ups and downs of becoming a man.

"Refreshing, meaning it was cold enough to cause some major shrinkage." Rodney snapped his T-shirt at Liam and the two of them started chasing each other around the yard.

"Watch it," Dustin warned as the boys nearly crashed into him. "Sorry about that, I'm still working with Rodney on appropriate social skills."

I waved it off. "He's fine. It's just nice to see the two of them getting along."

"I think they bonded a bit over clearing the track. You know, I told Liam I'd ask you one more time. Any chance I can show him a few things on a bike?"

I jerked my head to look at Dustin. He'd captured his bottom lip with his front teeth, like he was nervously waiting for a response. My first inclination was to chastise him for even asking. He knew how I felt about having Liam on a bike.

"I'd start him off super slow, on a baby bike. Not much bigger than a lawn mower engine." Dustin glanced over to where the boys horsed around on the grass. "He almost knows as much about bikes as I do, at least from reading about them. When you hear him talk about it—"

I silenced him with a quick kiss. "Okay. But please, please, please, be careful."

He squeezed my hands. "Of course. He's going to be so excited. Can I tell him?"

"Sure." From the sparkle in his eye, I couldn't tell who would be more thrilled—Liam or Dustin.

Dustin cupped his hands around his mouth. "Hey, get over here. Wash up before dinner, then I've got something to tell you." While he waited for the boys, he took the steaks off the grill.

"Can I grab anything from inside?"

"Sure. Potatoes are keeping warm in the oven. Salad and everything else is already on the table." He shut the cover of the grill and followed me into the screened porch. "I was wondering, can I come over later?"

"You sure? You put in a whole day today and you said you'll be painting again all day tomorrow? Aren't you tired?"

"Never too tired to spend a little time with you." He lifted his eyebrows and blew me a kiss.

My heart bubbled on the edge of bursting. I couldn't remember a time I'd felt so light, so happy. "All right then. You've got a standing invite."

Dustin sliced up the steak and the four of us sat down at the table. The boys passed salad, bacon bits, and sour cream between them. Almost like they liked each other. Almost like a family.

"So what did you want to tell us?" Rodney asked.

"Oh, yeah. I almost forgot." Dustin gave me a half grin. "Liam, your mom said I could start teaching you how to ride."

"What?" Liam shot up from his chair, almost knocking it over backward. "Are you serious?"

"Liam! Careful." I knew he'd be excited, but I wasn't prepared for this level of intensity.

"Sorry, Mom." He hung his head, giving me a sheepish grin, before sitting back down. "You really mean it?"

I nodded, my mouth full of the miraculous steak Dustin had created on the grill. "Mmm hmm."

"But you've got to listen and you've got to be careful." Dustin pointed his fork at my son. "No showboating."

"Like you did on the Late Show, Uncle Dustin?" Rodney smiled as he lifted a bite of beans to his mouth.

Dustin narrowed his eyes at his nephew, but a grin teased across his lips. "You smartass. Your mouth is going to be your downfall you know."

"Thanks, Mom." Liam smiled at me across the table. "I'll be careful, I promise."

"I know." And I knew Dustin would keep him safe. I'd finally learned to trust, to let go a little, to put my faith in someone who deserved it. I breathed out a sigh of relief. It was nice to know I was no longer all on my own.

36

DUSTIN

I walked Harmony and Liam to her truck, already eager for the night ahead. Liam might have gotten used to the idea of me and his mom being a little more than friends, although we didn't want to throw it in his face. I gave Harmony a peck on the cheek and thumped my palm on the driver side door.

"Y'all have a good night."

"Thanks again for dinner." Harmony gave me a smile, one that held a promise of what would come later.

"You're welcome. Hey, Liam, we're starting at nine tomorrow, okay?" The sooner we got the painting done, the sooner we could get the furniture and displays set up. Harmony had already ordered everything and been storing it in the empty office space below the studio. I was eager to get it all done so she could see it.

"Yes, sir." Liam raised his hand in an attempt at a salute. "Think we might have time to take out a bike when we're done tomorrow?"

I lifted my shoulders as I looked to Harmony.

"If you want to have a lesson after painting tomorrow, I

can take a turn at making dinner at my place." A slight smile teased the edges of her lips.

I hadn't been invited for dinner at their place yet. Something new, maybe something to mark the start of a new dynamic between us. "I'd really like that."

"It's a date then." She winked at me.

"A date?" Liam grunted in disgust.

"Yes, a date." Harmony gave him a playful swat on the leg. "Dustin's going to be sticking around for a while, and you're going to just have to get used to us seeing each other."

"Fine. But can you not kiss my mom around me?" His face squished up like he'd just swallowed a jar of pickle juice.

I couldn't help but let out a laugh. "I'll try. We'll ease into it, okay, bud?"

Liam shook his head. "Whatever."

"You'll come around." I lowered my voice, then leaned closer to Harmony. "One day at a time, right?"

"That's right." She turned her head, laying a chaste kiss on my lips.

I wanted to press for more, taste her tongue, claim this minor victory in the battle to make her mine. But I was too aware of Liam sitting just a few feet away. "I'll see you later?"

She nodded. "Thanks again for dinner."

"You're welcome. Drive safe."

As she pulled away, I stood next to the drive, my heart full and happy. I was where I needed to be.

THREE HOURS later my heart was even fuller and happier, along with the rest of me. Harmony and I laid on the dock. She nestled into me, using my chest for a pillow. The scent of her hair surrounded me, along with the sound of the katydids as a light breeze blew across the pond. The stars twinkled up above, making me realize how small and insignificant our little corner of Missouri was in the grand scheme of things.

I ran a finger along her arm, totally fulfilled in every way with this woman in my arms. She shivered and I pulled her closer.

"What are you thinking about?" she asked.

"You. Me. Us."

She propped herself up on an elbow, a lazy smile gracing her lips. A sense of pride washed over me. I'd put that smile on her face.

"What about us?"

I kissed her forehead. "Just how happy I am here with you."

"You don't think you'll miss California?"

My chest rose and fell, thinking about saying goodbye to the limelight. "I'm sure I will a little. But it's not an even trade."

"What do you mean?"

"I mean, I'm giving up being alone, getting a few claps for an awesome ride. And I'm gaining my family back—my mom, Scarlett, Rodney..."

"I just don't want you to ever regret it. This needs to be your decision. I don't want you giving all of that up for someone else, whether it's your mom or sister or Rodney or me."

"Oh, baby. I would never regret it." I ran my hand down her back. "I love you, Harmony."

Her head snapped up, her gaze meeting mine. "What?"

As I said it again, I realized how much I meant it. "I love you."

"But—"

I silenced her protest with a kiss, taking her mouth with mine. Her hands roamed over my chest as my tongue swept the inside of her mouth, and I lost myself to her. I'd never felt love like this before and the sheer depth of the emotion overwhelmed me. But I knew it was true. Staying in Swallow Springs wasn't going to be so much as me making a decision, as it was me following what my heart demanded.

She pulled away first, her gaze meeting mine. "Are you sure about this?"

"What, that I love you?"

"That, and all of this. Staying here, giving up California." Worry creased her brow.

I kissed away her concern. "I've never been so sure about anything in my life. Are you sure you want me? I guess I just assumed—"

She pulled me close, cementing her lips to mine. When we broke for air, she gave me a smile. "Yes, I want you. All of you."

"So when can we make this official? Stop meeting on the dock and risking splinters in my ass?"

She giggled. "I'm trying to set a good example for Liam. I'd say we still have a ways to go before I'm going to be comfortable having you stay over at the house."

"Well then, we're going to need to add a futon or something to your office at the studio. Because I'm getting too old for this."

"I think that can be arranged."

As she leaned over me, my phone vibrated in my pocket. I ignored it. Nothing could be important enough to tear my attention away from this moment.

But then Harmony's phone rang. "Oh shoot, what if it's Liam?"

"Go ahead, answer it."

Whoever was on the other end wiped the smile off her face faster than I could have asked what was wrong.

"Oh no." Harmony pressed a hand to her chest. "Was anyone hurt?"

I propped myself up on my elbows, watching her face for any sign of what was happening on the other end of that phone line.

"I'll be there right away." She lowered the phone, her gaze never leaving mine. "There's a fire."

"What? Where?"

"The studio." She glanced down at the phone she held in her hand. "It's gone."

I scrambled out from under her, already throwing my clothes back on. "What's gone? What do you mean?"

"The building." Harmony pulled her dress on over her head. "It's up in flames."

I reached down, grabbing the blanket. "Let's go. We'll go see what happened, okay?"

She nodded, letting me lead her back up the dock. My heart pounded in my chest, like rumbles of thunder. There had to be a mistake. We were just there this afternoon. Someone was wrong. It was a sick joke. It had to be.

37

HARMONY

*T*he smell of smoke assaulted our noses as we got closer to town. Off in the distance an orange cloud rose above the buildings. My heart shrank, smaller and smaller until it felt like all the life had been squeezed right out of it. Dustin clasped my fingers in his on the seat next to me. I'd never been so wracked with anxiety, so afraid of what we'd find when we reached the studio.

The drive seemed to take forever. When we finally got to the main road, a barricade prevented us from getting any closer. Dustin rolled down his window to chat with the fireman standing nearby.

"What happened?"

I leaned close to him, waiting for a response.

"Whole building went up in flames."

"Which one?" Dustin asked. "Is it the bookstore?" The used bookstore sat in the building right next door to mine. Maybe they'd been wrong. Maybe it was the bookstore that caught fire, not my beautiful new studio.

The man shook his head. "Nah. The old accounting office next door."

Dustin squeezed my hand tighter. "They say what caused it?"

"Haven't been able to get close enough to find out yet. Right now we just need to get the fire contained so it doesn't spread. We ought to know more once we've had a chance to get in there and take a look at what's left."

What's left. Those two words split my heart in two like a crowbar, prying it apart. I pulled my hand away from Dustin and doubled over, the pain too much to take.

"Harmony, hey, it's going to be okay. We'll figure this out." Dustin's hand caressed my back, smoothed my hair.

I felt his hand moving, but it brought no comfort. Everything I'd worked for, all of my savings—it was gone.

A knock sounded on my window. I glanced up to see Cassie. She motioned for me to roll it down. Dustin must have pressed the button because the pane of glass slowly lowered. The air grew even thicker with smoke.

"Hey, Robbie and I are going to head to the VFW to wait it out. They said it's not safe to stick around here. Want to come with us?" She pointed to where Robbie stood on the curb.

"What do you say?" Dustin rested his palm on my cheek.

I nodded. It didn't matter where I was—the result would be the same. My dreams were gone, turned to ash. But how?

"We'll meet you over there," Dustin said. Then he raised the windows and put his arm across the seat behind me. After he'd turned the truck around, we followed the main road to the edge of town and pulled into the tiny VFW building parking lot.

My knees practically buckled underneath me as I got out of the truck. Before I hit the ground, Dustin was there, his arm wrapping around me, giving me support.

"We're going to get through this, I promise." He kissed my temple, my hair, my cheek.

Robbie met us at the door. "I'm so sorry, Harmony. Hopefully they'll be able to tell us what happened."

I nodded, letting Dustin lead me into the dim interior of the main room. Cassie slumped into a corner booth. I slid in across from her while Dustin and Robbie stayed at the bar.

Cassie reached for my hand. "It's going to be okay."

"But it's not. The whole building could be gone. All of my savings went into the renovations and the inventory."

She squeezed my hand. "We'll figure it out."

Dustin and Robbie joined us at the table. Robbie set down four glasses and Dustin filled them from a pitcher of beer.

"I can't believe it," Robbie said.

"What happened?" Dustin handed me a mug of beer.

"I don't know. Cassie was wrapping things up at the café, and I stopped by to help. We were going to head to a late movie." Robbie blew out a breath. "Then I saw a flicker of something in the window across the street. I ignored it at first. Damn, if I'd called 9-1-1 sooner…"

Cassie put her hand on his arm. "Thirty seconds wouldn't have made much of a difference."

"I'm sick about it." Robbie shook his head as he stared into his beer. "All the work you put into that place. Both of you."

"It's going to be okay." Cassie sat up straight. I wanted her enthusiasm to jump across the table, to infect me with perkiness and a Pollyanna attitude, too. "Whatever happens, we'll figure it out. There are plenty of other places you can set up shop downtown. And you'll have the insurance money."

I bit my lip and let my head tilt back. Dammit.

"You did have an insurance policy on the inventory, didn't you?" Cassie moved her hand from Robbie's arm and laid her palm flat on the table. "Oh God, Harmony, please say you got that policy finalized this week."

All eyes settled on me. My jaw clenched tight. I tried to choke out a few words but my mouth had gone so dry.

"Harmony?" Dustin put his arm around my shoulders. "You okay?"

"No," I finally managed. "I'm not okay." My shoulders lifted and fell. I couldn't stop the tears if I wanted to. I buried my face in my hands and squelched a sob.

"Honey, I told you to get that insurance policy before you went and ordered all that stuff." Cassie's hand landed on my arm.

"Can we focus on something else right now?" Dustin said, his voice low, almost like a protective growl. "It doesn't matter what was or wasn't done. Right now we just need to figure out how to move forward."

"I'm sorry. You're right." Cassie sighed.

I looked up, my vision blurred by the stupid tears welling up in my eyes. "I was going to do it first thing Monday morning. They needed a chunk up front and I had to wait for my paycheck."

Cassie frowned. "You could have asked for an advance. You know I would have helped you out."

I clasped my hands together, so tight my knuckles went from white to pink. "I didn't want an advance. You and Robbie have already done so much. I just wanted..." I took in a deep breath, trying to force the words past the tightness in my chest. "I just wanted to be able to do it on my own."

Dustin pulled my head down to lean on his shoulder. In that moment I needed the support so I let him. At least I wasn't going through this alone. That was the only bright spot. I tried to focus on that. I had Dustin, someone to lean on. I'd have to figure the rest out. If it meant working at the Lovebird until I'd saved up again, then that's what I'd do.

"It's going to be okay, Harmony." Dustin pressed his lips to my temple. "We're going to get through this together."

In that moment I wanted to believe him. I had to.

38

DUSTIN

*W*e stayed at the VFW for hours. They usually closed down at two, but the bartender said he'd let us stick around until the fire was out, and we could go back to the Lovebird. Finally, around six, Cassie got a call.

The four of us headed back over. I was afraid of what we'd find. Harmony hadn't said much while we waited for news, mainly just sat next to me, her head on my shoulder, her gaze focused on a spot on the laminate table. I'd tried to offer comfort the best way I knew how, but my experience in that department was severely limited. I wished I could take away her pain.

I parked in the lot next to the Lovebird. The fire trucks were still blocking the front of the building across the street, so we hadn't been able to get a good look at what was left. Harmony got out of the truck. Her jaw set while a look of sheer determination settled over her face.

We walked across the lot, my arm around her, ready to catch her if she collapsed when she got her first look at the building she'd poured her heart and soul into. She was trying to be so strong. I kept telling her she didn't need to be, to let me help her through this.

"Y'all have to stop right here." A fireman in full gear stopped us from going farther. "It's not safe to get any closer."

"I thought the fire was out?" I asked.

"It is, but the building's not safe. Whole thing could collapse at any moment."

"Can we just take a look? Harmony was going to open her studio on the second floor next week. Is there anything left?" My arm tightened around her and Cassie linked her arm with Harmony's—another show of moral support.

"You can move up to the edge of that truck"—he pointed to a fire truck a few feet in front of us—"but don't go past that, just in case."

"Thanks. You ready for this?" I asked Harmony.

She nodded against my shoulder.

The three of us inched forward, Robbie behind us. When we reached the edge of the fire truck we could see what remained of the building. Not much. The brick was charred, darkened from the flames. The stench of burned wood hung heavy in the air. Shattered glass from the windows covered the ground.

Harmony shuddered next to me. I pulled her closer, trying to shield her from seeing the worst of it. The entire roof had burned away, leaving the second story open to the night sky above. Anything she had in that space would have been burned or melted. From where we stood on the ground, I doubted if anything would be salvageable.

"What do you want to do?" I whispered against her ear.

"Can you take me home?" She turned to face me. Her eyes held a world of sadness. I'd have given anything in that moment to put the sparkle and shine back in her smile.

"Yeah. Let's go." We turned away, heading back to the truck.

Cassie caught up to us in the parking lot. "Hey, Harmony, why don't you take the weekend off work? Give yourself some time to think about things."

She looked up at Cassie and I wanted to hug her close. "I can't. If I'm going to rebuild, I'm going to have to save up again."

Cassie looked at me over the top of Harmony's head. "Will you stay with her?"

"I don't need someone to babysit me. I'll be fine." Harmony wrenched away from my side. "You think this is the worst thing that's ever happened to me?" She gestured around the parking lot. "I've been down before and managed to get back up. This won't be any different. I just need to come up with a plan. Now, Dustin, can you take me home?"

I nodded, not used to seeing her struggle to maintain such a positive outlook.

"And I'll be in for the afternoon shift if that's okay?" she asked Cassie.

Cassie nodded. "Whatever you want to do, hon."

Harmony wiped at her eyes. "Thanks. I'll see you later on this afternoon."

I shrugged at Cassie then followed Harmony to the truck, wishing I had some inkling of an idea on how to make things better for her. I'd never felt so helpless, so completely at a loss for what to do. But we were in this together. Somehow, I'd figure out a way to get that smile back on her face.

A HALF HOUR later Harmony trudged across her porch. Pulling an all-nighter seemed to have caught up to both of us. Exhaustion tugged at the edges of my vision, wanting to pull my eyes shut. Even the wicker chair on the porch looked like a viable spot to take a nap for a few hours.

"You want me to stay with you?" I asked.

She turned the key in the lock. "I think I just want to be alone for a little while. Is that okay?"

"Yeah, that's fine. I'm here for you, though. If you want me to stay, I will. If you'd rather be alone, that's fine too. Whatever you need, okay?" I pulled her in for a hug, trying to bolster her up with strength.

Her arms wrapped loosely around my waist. "Thanks for being there for me last night. I really appreciate it. I'm not sure how I would have made it through without you."

"I told you, I love you."

She leaned back, looking up at me. "I love you, too. You're the only good thing I've got left to show for my time spent in Swallow Springs."

"Hey, we'll get you back up and running, I promise. I've got some money set aside, and—"

"No." She shook her head. "I'm not taking your money."

"I'll loan it to you. Or be a silent investor. Either way, I believe in you and what you can do."

"Thanks. I just need a little time, okay?"

"Yeah, okay. I'll call you later?"

She nodded, nestling her cheek against my chest again. I wanted to wrap her up, shield her from the hurt and loss she must be feeling. But I also wanted to respect her wishes. This thing between us was so new. If it were up to me, I'd stay with her for as long as she'd let me. We'd come up with a plan together. Anything to put the spark back in her eyes.

"Call me if you need anything, okay?"

She pulled away. "I will. I've got to figure out how to tell Liam." Her voice wavered. "You and the boys spent so much time on that place. What a waste."

"Hey, it kept them out of trouble, didn't it?" I nudged her chin up. "And away from the pig farm."

Finally, a smile. It flashed by so fast I almost missed it, but it was a step in the right direction.

"I suppose."

"We'll get through this. Together." I gave her hand a final squeeze then turned to make my way back to the truck. I wasn't sure how to make things better in the short term. All I could think about that second was closing my eyes and getting some shut eye. But I'd spend the afternoon researching alternate locations for her. Whether she wanted my help or not, she was going to get it. I'd finally found the woman I'd been missing in my life and I wasn't going to let her try to navigate this on her own.

39

HARMONY

I closed the door behind Dustin. He'd been such a sweetheart to stay with me all night long. I felt a little sorry for running him off like that but I'd never had someone to share my hurt with before. I wasn't sure how to handle having him near. My usual MO at a time like this was to retreat, tuck myself away until I could think straight and come up with a plan. He would have stayed if I'd asked. But no matter how he tried, he couldn't hide the weariness in his eyes. He needed to sleep just as much as I did. It was best that we took some time to get some rest. Later on this afternoon I'd be ready to process.

Liam's door was closed. I turned the knob, careful to open the door without causing a squeak. My son had his head on the pillow with the sheets tangled around his legs. He might look like a man when he was awake, but in sleep he reminded me so much of the little boy I still saw in my mind. He'd be heartbroken about the fire. I brushed my hand over his forehead, sweeping the hair out of his face.

I'd need to be strong for him. To set an example that no matter what life threw at you, you had to keep on keeping on. He hadn't had a fair shot at things, growing up without a dad. I didn't want to get too far ahead of myself, but Dustin made me wish for things. He could be the one. The one to stand by my side. The one to be a father to my son. If I let myself go there, he could be the one I'd been missing all my life.

I'd always handled things on my own. It had been so long since I'd let anyone in. My heart told me it was time. After a nap, I'd give him a call and see if he wanted to swing by. It was hard to realize I didn't have to do it all on my own any more. My stomach did a flip-flop at the idea that I'd have someone in my corner this time. Someone to face the future with—good or bad. If nothing else came out of my time in Swallow Springs...if I never got my studio and never had a chance to move beyond waitress at the Lovebird café, at least I had Dustin.

My head had barely hit the pillow before my eyes closed. As I drifted off to sleep I hoped I'd dream of Dustin and the future we'd create together.

Dustin

A KNOCK on the trailer door woke me. I didn't have any idea how long I'd been passed out. Hell, last night had been draining on so many levels. For all I knew, I'd slept through a few days, not just a few hours.

"Coming." I pulled the shirt on that I'd worn yesterday. The stench of smoke encased me. I needed a shower and a pot of coffee. Maybe then I'd feel a little more human.

The sheriff stood on my steps. "Hey, Dustin. Got a minute?"

"Yeah. Come on in." I held the door open for him to enter the trailer.

He walked past me, settling into the small booth in the kitchen area. "Rough night last night, huh?"

"Yeah, you could say that."

"Well, I've got some good news." He took off his hat and set it down on the table between us.

"Oh, yeah? Good news would definitely be welcome right now." I clasped my hands together, wishing I had a mug of hot, steaming coffee between them.

"The fire marshal figured out the cause of the fire."

"Really?" I leaned forward. "Bad wiring?" That was my best guess. Although we'd had an electrician go over the wiring in Harmony's space, no telling how long it had been since the connected buildings had been checked.

"Bad boom box." He held up a melted piece of black plastic. "They said this radio y'all had been using in the space was left on last night. Know anything about that?"

The walls of my chest squeezed together, draining all the air from my lungs. No. That couldn't be. Rodney had turned it off, like I'd asked him to. "You sure about that?"

"Yep. The fire sparked from that outlet then spread in the wall before it got going. Damn shame."

"But, how could that have started a fire?" It had been fine. I'd used that radio for years and never had a problem with it. *Please don't let that be true.*

"Must have been a short in the wiring of the radio. Was it yours?"

Mine. Yes, it was mine. My boom box caused the fire. It may as well have been me that burned down the hopes and dreams of the woman I loved. I swallowed back the darkness threatening to overtake me. "Yeah, it was mine."

"Tough break." The sheriff stood. "I guess I'll head over to tell Ms. Rogers."

"Harmony doesn't know yet?"

"No. I wanted to check with you first." He put his hat back on his head, almost brushing the ceiling of the tight space.

"Thanks for stopping by." The manners my mom had instilled in me in didn't fail me now. I watched as he walked across the yard and climbed into his patrol car.

He lifted his hand in a wave before pulling around and heading down the drive. What the hell was I supposed to do now? He was on his way to Harmony's. To tell her I was the reason her studio went up in a wall of flames. She was going to hate me.

I sat down on the edge of the kitchen bench and cradled my hands in my head. It was my fault. I'd been a fool for thinking I could come back here and make a fresh name for myself. Every time I tried to do anything good in Swallow Springs, it turned around to bite me in the ass. And now I'd ruined Harmony's dreams.

She'd never be able to forgive me. Hell, I'd never be able to forgive myself. The need to flee, to get away, overwhelmed me. I couldn't bear to see the disappointment in Harmony's eyes when she realized I was the cause of her loss. But where to go?

I paced back and forth, down the center of the trailer, the conversation with Mav ringing in my ears. If I left today, I could be back in LA in just a couple of days, plenty of time to check over my bike and get in some practice runs before a performance on the late night show. I might not be able to salvage Harmony's dreams, but maybe I could salvage my pride by not going out on a failed stunt.

With my heart broken into a million pieces, I started packing up my stuff. I figured I had about an hour before Harmony showed up, ready to strangle me for the part I played in the fire. I couldn't face her. I couldn't face anyone once they knew what I'd done. Cassie, Robbie, my mom, Rodney, Scarlett, Liam...they'd never look at me the same. And Harmony...it was her I'd hurt most of all. A wave of shame crashed over me. Leaving would be best. I could send a check to the city, asking them to pre-pay rent on her choice of locations for the next year. She might not take help from me, but maybe she'd take it from the city. Jake would help me. He could have them say it was a grant or something.

Satisfied I'd find a way to make it up to Harmony, even if she didn't know it, I stowed everything I needed to in the trailer so I could get underway. What was I going to tell Mom, though? And Scarlett and Rodney? I'd figure something out. Once they learned the truth about what I'd done, they'd understand. I'd tried to face the past and beat down my demons. I should have known they'd never let me go.

40

HARMONY

I wrestled with the giant coffee machine, so not in the mood for dealing with the monster this afternoon. Seemed like my alarm had gone off before I'd barely managed a few hours of sleep. Even though Cassie told me to take the weekend off, that wasn't my style. So here I was, back at the Lovebird, where a glance across the street could send me into an emotional tailspin. At least Liam hadn't seen it yet. I broke the news about the studio before I left. He wanted to race over to Dustin's right away, but I made him wait. Dustin had spent all night by my side, the poor man deserved to catch up on his sleep.

So I'd left Liam to deal with the animals and made my way into work. The street was open again but the barricade across the front of the building remained. The fire trucks were long gone, leaving the smell of smoke still hanging in the air. I ached to find out if anything was left, but I'd been told no one could enter the building until the fire marshal had declared it safe.

"Sorry about your new business." Frank set his paper

down and slid onto a stool at the counter. "They figure out what caused it yet?"

I wiped at my eyes, then grabbed an empty mug and set it down in front of him. "No. I haven't heard yet."

"Just the coffee today." He patted his stomach. "I'm watching my weight now."

The goofy look on his face brought out a hint of a smile. "Any particular reason why?"

He blushed, a faint shade of pink showing under the white whiskers on his cheeks. "No, nothing special. Just want to get healthier."

"You should try one of my kale smoothies then." I hadn't given up on converting the residents of Swallow Springs to the dark side—where they'd learn to love leafy green vegetables, even if they hadn't been drowned in butter or slathered with ranch dressing.

"Let's not get too crazy." Frank lifted the mug of coffee to his lips. "I sure am glad you figured out how to work that coffee pot."

"Yeah, me, too." One more reason it wouldn't completely suck to be stuck waiting tables. At least I wouldn't have to sneak around with my instant coffee crystals anymore.

"I was starting to think I might have to head to Crawford for my morning cup."

"Oh, don't let Cassie hear you say that." I wagged my finger at him in warning. "She'll run you out of here herself."

Frank winked. "Let's let that be our little secret. What do you say?"

"Sure." I could never rat out Frank, not even if he wasn't willing to admit he wanted to trim up his middle for a certain older woman who happened to live with the man I loved. Thinking about Dustin put a smile on my face. The way he'd stayed with me last night showed me he was the one for me. I wrapped my arms around my middle, giving myself a hug as I thought about how it would feel to see him later on tonight. Being around him was the only thing that seemed to make the hard news a little more bearable.

The bell on the door jangled and Sheriff Sampson entered. Oh hell, what had Liam done now? My chest constricted, squeezing all of the air out of my lungs as I waited for him to approach the counter.

"Hey, Harmony." He took his hat off and nodded my direction.

"Looking for some coffee this afternoon?" I asked, trying to make my voice come out normal.

"Sure. I could use a cup." He sat down next to Frank who raised his mug toward the sheriff.

"They figure out who set that fire last night?" Frank asked.

"Well"— the sheriff cleared his throat—"that's what I came in to talk about."

"Oh?" My fingers slipped on the handle of the carafe but I somehow managed to grab it before it crashed to the floor. "You found out what caused the fire?"

"Was it vandals?" Frank asked. "If you ask me, y'all need to be more diligent about keeping an eye on the vacant buildings on the square here."

I couldn't look away from the sheriff. Frank rambled on about break-ins and graffiti while I stared at Sheriff Sampson's badge, willing him to say something.

He waited until Frank took a breath, opening up a break in the conversation. "Wasn't vandals, Frank."

"No? Then what was it?"

"A short. Someone left a radio going all night. It was an older unit, probably had a defect in the wires. The fire started there, then spread." The sheriff took the mug I'd filled and lifted it to his lips while I tried to process this latest bit of news.

"A radio?" I asked.

"Yeah, some ancient boom box. Dustin said it was his. I stopped by his place first to check."

"Dustin?" His radio? That ancient huge boom box with the double cassette deck caused this? "Are you sure it was the radio?"

"Sure as I can be. The fire marshal traced the origin back to that outlet. Whole radio fried, then melted. It's the only explanation." He took another sip of coffee, then stood and pulled a few bills out of his wallet.

"Oh, coffee's on the house."

"Thanks." He slid his hat back on top of his head. "I'll let you know if we learn anything else. But as far as I'm concerned, there's no reason to suspect foul play. Y'all have a nice day now."

I nodded, but inside I was a bundle of what-ifs and hows. What did he mean there was no reason to suspect foul play? If Dustin's boom box caused the fire...my brain struggled to make sense of the news the sheriff had shared. It was an accident. I knew that for a fact. But a little tiny part of me felt betrayed. How could Dustin have left it running? Why wouldn't he have turned it off when he finished painting yesterday?

"You okay?" Cassie came out from the kitchen.

"Yeah." I slid the coffee carafe back in place. "I think I need to go see Dustin. Do you mind if I clock out a little early today?"

"Of course. I would have been fine if you hadn't come in at all. Whatever you need." She put her hand on my shoulder, drawing my attention back to her.

"Thanks. I need to see Dustin. I've got to talk to him about this."

She nodded. "Are you all right to drive out there?"

"Of course." I untied my apron and hung it on the hook. "I'll be in tomorrow morning." There's no way I would run out on her on a Sunday morning, especially not when that was the best day of the week for tips.

"Good luck, Harmony." Frank lifted his hand in a wave.

I gave a half-hearted wave back, unsure why I suddenly felt the need to rush to Dustin. He knew, but he hadn't tried to call. I checked my phone on the way to the truck just in case. Nothing. What was he thinking? Based on how he'd handled the make-up with Robbie, I could only imagine. He put on a big show. Pretended things didn't get to him, that he was as tough on the inside as he was on the outside. But I knew that was a façade.

If he thought he'd caused me to lose everything, he'd be heartbroken. I couldn't bear to lose the studio and Dustin. As I climbed into the truck I sent up a silent request. Please let him be home when I get there.

I tried to call but it went straight to voicemail. My heart sunk in my chest, settling somewhere around my gut. I needed to get to him, needed to let him know this wasn't his fault.

41

DUSTIN

*I*t had been five days, four hours, thirty-nine minutes and fourteen, no fifteen, no sixteen seconds since I hooked up the trailer and burned rubber out of Swallow Springs. Harmony had called dozens of times but I couldn't face her yet, not even over the phone. She knew by now I was the reason her studio burned down. I was the reason her dreams had turned to ash.

She should be gearing up for her grand opening, but instead she was probably pouring old Frank another cup of coffee at the Lovebird Café. And it was all my fault.

I should have known better than to give Swallow Springs another chance. The town had chewed me up and spit me out once already. Why did I think it would be any different now? I'd lost a lot way back when Jeff had that accident. I thought my heart had been torn in two. But now, losing Harmony, I realized that was just a practice run for the sheer devastation I was going through now.

Mom called. Scarlett, too. But even though they told me everything I knew in my brain to be true—that it was an accident, that it wasn't my fault, that Harmony wouldn't hold it against me—I still couldn't bring myself to reach out to her. The fire was a warning. If I stuck around, there was no telling how far I'd drag her down with me. She deserved better.

"Ready?" Mav appeared at my side. "You're on in five. This is your chance, Dustin. Show them what you've got."

I pulled the visor down on my helmet. Mav was only doing his job. But with no one else around but myself to be pissed at, he made an easy target. I climbed on the bike, straddling the seat between my thighs. It felt good to be back on my bike. The doc had checked me out yesterday and given me the go ahead. I was all cleared for whatever asinine stunt my agent wanted to set up for me. I could start work on the movie now, too. Hopefully that would keep my mind off of everything I'd left behind in Missouri.

I gave the bike some gas, ready to move into position. The stunt they'd set up for me was one I'd done dozens of times, a simple jump over a few vehicles. They were having a food truck festival in Culver City so they'd made arrangements for me to jump over six taco trucks. Didn't matter to me what the hell they'd have me do. My heart wasn't in it anymore. I'd left it in the hands of a girl with a unicorn on her toenail and stars in her eyes.

One of the staff motioned for me to head outside. The studio doors opened and for a moment I was blinded by the light. I let my eyesight adjust before I rolled the bike closer to the ramp.

"Dustin! Hey, over here!"

I swore that sounded like someone I knew. But with hundreds of people crowding the area beyond the metal barricades, my ears were probably playing tricks on me. I glanced over, expecting to see a sea of strangers. But instead, I saw Robbie. Robbie Jordan? What the hell was he doing here?

I lifted my visor, sure that I'd seen someone who looked like Robbie, probably a whacked trick my brain was playing on me. But there he was, waving like a crazy mofo. And right next to him stood my mom. And Scarlett. And Rodney. What the hell?

"You ready?" One of the junior producers stepped closer, blocking the view of my family.

"Hey, can you hold on a sec?" I flipped the kickstand down with my foot and climbed off the bike.

"Sir, no, we can't wait a sec. You're on in three minutes."

"Yeah, okay." I waved him off, making a beeline for my mom.

She reached for me over the barricade. "Dustin Lambert Jarrett, what in the world are you doing? Are you trying to give your mother a heart attack?"

I took her hand. "No. Mom, I'm sorry. I had to get away."

"That's what you keep saying. You know what I think about that?" She squeezed my hand and blew a big fat raspberry at me.

I swiveled my head to look at Scarlett. "Is she okay? Are the dizzy spells getting worse?" There had to be some explanation. I'd never seen my mother stick her tongue out at anyone, much less blow a bad raspberry.

Scarlett shook her head. "There were no dizzy spells, you dope. Mom faked them to try to get you to stay in Missouri."

"What?" I turned back to my mom. "Are you kidding me?"

The staffer tapped me on the shoulder. "Um, sir, we

need you to get on your motorcycle now. You're going to miss your segment."

I put my palm up. "Just a minute."

"Yes, I faked the dizzy spells, but only because I wanted to keep you close." Mom reached for my other hand, holding both of mine between hers. "You've got to come home now."

"Is Harmony okay?" My heart dropped into my boots. If something had happened to her and I wasn't there, I'd never be able to forgive myself.

"No, she's not okay, you dumbass." Robbie finally spoke. "You ran out on her, just like you ran out on me all those years ago."

"This is different, Rob. With all due respect, Jeffy died. And I convinced myself it was my fault. I was just a kid. I know now that it was an accident, a mistake. But with Harmony...hell, it was my radio that caused the fire. My fault it got left on."

Rob shook his head. "You don't get it."

"I'm the one who left the radio on, Uncle Dustin." Rodney hung his head. "You asked me to turn it off and I turned it down instead. I'm the one who caused the fire."

"No. You listen to me. You didn't do anything wrong, Rodney." Like hell I'd have my nephew spend the next twenty years blaming himself for something that he couldn't possibly have prevented. "I should have thrown that piece of crap away a long time ago."

"Would you listen to yourself?" Rob poked a finger into my chest. I dropped my mom's hands and backed away. "You can't tell Rodney it wasn't his fault and shoulder the blame for this whole thing."

"Is Harmony okay?" I didn't want to ask, but I had to

know. I'd been dying inside, not being able to reach out to her. But I knew if I did it would just make it worse.

"She loves you." Scarlett stepped closer. "You need to come back. If not for you, then come back for her."

"She's better off without me." As much as it pained me to say it, I knew it was true. "I killed her dreams."

"Sir, if you don't get on that motorcycle right now, we're going to have to skip your segment." The staffer jabbed me in the arm.

"Don't do it, Dustin." Mom pleaded with me. "You don't have anything to prove to anyone except yourself. If you get hurt again, my heart couldn't take it."

Scarlett wrapped her arm around mom's shoulders and I let my gaze drift over them all, one at a time. Robbie looked like his head was about to spin around and steam would start pouring out of his ears. Rodney hung his arms over the barricade, his gaze on the ground. Mom and Scarlett stood huddled together, fear in their eyes.

What was I doing? I thought my redemption needed to take place on a public stage. Turned out the only one needing to witness my redemption was me. And the place I needed to find it was a thousand miles away, not on the back lot of a television studio.

"Sir." The staffer's finger poked me in the shoulder, firmer this time. "You've got twenty seconds."

At that moment, Mav burst through the doors. "Dustin, what's going on?" He smiled, obviously unsure how to spin the current situation.

"I've gotta go." I pulled the helmet off my head and handed it to him.

"What are you doing?" he asked, his jaw clenched. "This is your chance. Redemption, buddy."

I clapped a hand on his shoulder. "You're right. I do need to redeem myself."

Then I hopped the barricade and found myself surrounded by the people who cared enough about me to travel a thousand miles to bring me home.

"Let's get out of here."

42

HARMONY

I glanced at the clock on the wall. The minute hand jumped and for a moment it actually appeared to be going backward. Time had dragged since Dustin left town. I knew why he'd gone. But I also knew that he had to be the one to come back to me on his own. He'd run away from his ghosts and demons years ago. Even though he'd faced them by coming back to Swallow Springs this summer, he still hadn't completely forgiven himself for what he believed he'd done all those years ago.

A week ago I'd been preparing to open my own space. To finally have the studio I'd dreamed about. To have the opportunity to share it with someone who'd taught me what true love looked like. Now I was doing good to drag myself out of bed each day. I had to put on a strong front for Liam. He was devastated enough that Dustin had left without even saying goodbye. How could I explain to my son that his superhero was only human? That sometimes kryptonite existed within ourselves and it would take time for Dustin to work his way through the blame, even though he was the one who'd mistakenly claimed it?

"Hey, have you got a minute?" Cassie leaned through the window from the kitchen to the dining area. "There's something I want you to take a look at out back."

"Yeah, just a sec." I refilled Frank's mug before following her through the kitchen. She ought to know better than anyone that I had nothing special pulling at my attention. "What's up?"

She pushed through the door leading into the back parking lot. "Somebody has something to show you."

I stepped out into the late morning sun, shielding my eyes with my hand.

"Surprise!" A chorus of voices yelled, causing me to toss the carafe of coffee into the air. My heart ricocheted in my chest as my eyes tried to take it all in.

"Oh, shit." Dustin jumped in front of me as coffee splattered all over him, dotting his white shirt with brown splotches.

My hands went to my mouth. "Oh my gosh. I'm so sorry. What are you doing here? What's going on?" I reached for him, trying to wipe the coffee from his face. It dripped down his hair.

"Something about this reminds me of the day we met." He stood there, a gorgeous grin on his face. "I'm the one who's sorry. I'm the one who needs to be apologizing to you."

"I understand why you left." I glanced around. Dozens of people formed a semi-circle around us. "Can we talk? In private?"

He turned to the crowd. "Give us a sec, okay?" Then he led me back into the kitchen where Ryder stood at the grill, bebopping to the music playing through his headphones.

"He can't hear us." I whirled around, my back pressing against the wall. "What are you doing here?"

He stepped in front of me, crowding my space. "I'm so incredibly sorry about what happened."

I brushed his cheek with my hand. "I know. It's not your—"

"Shh." He put a finger to my lips. "I need to say this before I lose my nerve, okay?"

I nodded.

He took his finger from my lips and ran it along my cheek. "I've missed you so much."

Tears welled in the corners of my eyes. I willed them not to fall. He needed to do this.

"I was wrong to leave. When Sheriff Sampson stopped by and told me the fire was caused by my stupid radio...I didn't want you to hate me. I wouldn't have been able to take it."

I ran my hand over his arm, waiting for him to go on.

"You're the first person in my life who's made me want to be a better man. The way you breathe life into everything and everyone who crosses your path. Damn, Harmony, I couldn't bear to be the reason some of that shine slipped away. Does that make sense?"

"You're not—"

"Wait. I'm not done." He offered an apologetic smile.

My heart swelled. We were going to get past this, I could tell by the way he touched me, by the way he said my name. I just needed him to confirm it. He had to hear himself say it out loud.

"I love you so much. I thought it would be better for you if I left. But it didn't work out that way. I left my heart here when I drove away. You ripped it right out of my chest. I had to come back. I'll understand if you hate me."

I shook my head, unable to continue to listen to him beat himself up like that. "Stop. Just stop, will you?"

He met my gaze. Hurt shone in his eyes. I wanted to ease his pain, erase everything that had happened in the past week and fill the empty void with love and kisses.

"I don't hate you. Dustin, I love you." He looked down but I nudged his chin up, not letting him look away. "We're in this together. It's not your fault this happened. I'm not going to let you take that blame. It was a stupid accident, that's all. Just like what happened with Jeffy."

He glanced down for a sec then met my gaze again. "I just thought it would be easier for you if I left."

"Easier how? You said you wanted to give us a shot. Has that changed?" For a second I waited, my hope suspended between us.

"No, of course not."

I let out my breath. We were going to be okay. "Good. So no more flaking on me. Next time you get weirded out we talk about it."

He nodded. "Got it."

My heart swelled. The worst was over. "Then it's a good thing you came back because I'm going to need some help with stuff."

"Oh really?" His lips curved into a tentative smile.

"Yep. I've decided to put the studio on hold. Maybe it was a sign from the universe, but I think I'm going to focus my efforts on those mud packs I've been making."

"You don't say?" Now his smile covered his entire face.

"Yeah. I got a huge order from a place out in Beverly Hills."

He lifted his eyebrows and nodded.

"Wait." I put my hand under his chin so he couldn't avoid my eyes. "Did you have something to do with that?"

He shrugged. "I just shared some samples with a couple of places. Your mud packs speak for themselves. They asked me where they could get more so I gave them your number."

"Are you sure about that?"

"I promise. You've got a talent for healing. I could tell from the moment I met you, and you dribbled that smelly oil all over my hand."

"Lavender." I rolled my eyes.

"Will you come back outside?" He laced his fingers with mine, pulling me toward the door. "I really want to show you something."

We exited back into the lot where our friends and family still milled around. Dustin's truck sat in the middle, the back full of that gorgeous black mud.

"What's going on?" I felt the power shift, from me to him. This was his show, his moment.

"I expect you'll be hearing from some other places in the next week or so. Figured you could use some raw material to get your business going."

"You brought me mud?" I wrapped my arms around him, pulling him into a tight hug.

"Love in the form of mud," he joked. "I figured you can set up in one of the outbuildings on my property until you decide where you want to make your permanent home. And if you want to stay"—he shrugged—"I've got a few acres set aside that would be perfect for a little place for you and Liam."

"You want to sell me some land?"

"It's big enough to build a place of your own. With plenty of room for Magoo, and Petunia, and even that raccoon that you and I know you're never going to give up." He leaned closer, whispering. "And maybe I could move in sometime if you'll have me."

I shook my head. "I told you, I've got to set a good example for Liam. I won't live with someone unless it's—"

The sight of Dustin dropping to one knee made the words die on my lips.

"Harmony Rogers, will you marry me?" He held out a small robin-egg-blue box.

I glanced around our circle of friends. There was Scarlett, her arm wrapped around Rodney's back. Mrs. Jarrett stood next to Frank, their hands joined between them. Robbie and Cassie stood to the side, holding each other close. And Liam. He crouched down, a smile on his face, waiting for me to answer. I lifted my eyebrows, a silent question. He nodded, his smile growing even bigger.

"You think I didn't already run this by the man of the house?" Dustin asked. He put his arm out, motioning Liam to come closer. "Liam already gave his approval. I just need a yes from you, sweetheart."

"Yes." How could I say anything but yes? Yes to accepting Dustin's proposal. Yes to his offer to build the business of my dreams together. Yes to everything.

He slid the ring on my finger and I looked down, expecting to see a diamond. This man really did know me. There, sparkling on my ring finger, was a pear-shaped emerald.

"You remembered." I wrapped my arms around his neck and pulled him in for a kiss.

"Of course I remembered. You said green was your favorite color. Now, can we go home? I need to take a shower and wash off all this coffee you managed to spill all over me."

"Yes. Maybe if you're nice to me I'll even scrub your back for you, get into all those places you can't reach on your own."

He groaned, sending a sliver of desire coursing through me. "Don't make promises you don't intend to keep."

"Oh, I'll keep it all right. Now what are you waiting for? We've got some mud to drop off, don't we?"

He turned to Scarlett and said a few words before taking my hand and pulling me toward the truck.

"What was that all about?" I asked as I slid into the passenger seat.

"I asked her if she'd be willing to keep Liam overnight. He and Rodney can have a sleepover and stay up all night playing video games."

"Oh yeah?"

"Yeah. That means you and I can have a sleepover too."

"And stay up all night doing what exactly?"

He leaned over the center console and captured my mouth in a kiss. "I'm sure we'll figure something out."

My heart could have burst with happiness, it was so full of love and gratefulness. As Dustin pulled out of the parking lot and onto the road, I took a deep breath of the fresh Missouri air. I'd been looking for purpose my entire life. And now I'd found it.

Mired in enough mud and enough love to carry me forward no matter what the future held.

Love and mud.

I'd never been happier.

EPILOGUE

Scarlett

"You two are more sugary sweet than a truckload of cotton candy." I swatted at Dustin's arm as I passed. Harmony stood in front of him at the kitchen counter, her backside nestled into his front, mixing up another batch of mud facial packs. I was happy for my brother that he and Harmony had found each other. But it still hurt a little that Dustin, self-confirmed eternal single stud nugget would find his happily-ever-after before me.

"You're just jealous." Dustin dipped his hand into the bowl and flung a finger full of mud at me.

"You'd better cut that out. If Mom finds mud on her kitchen floor she might take a wooden spoon to your bum." He had no idea how close his statement cut to the truth. I *was* jealous.

Dustin grinned. "I'd just tell her you did it."

"You wouldn't dare."

He shrugged, scooped up another finger of mud, and flipped it my direction.

I ducked. The mud smacked against the white refrigerator door then oozed down the front, landing in a puddle on the hardwood floor.

"Dustin, you'd better watch it. I'm liable to side with Scarlett on this one." Harmony lifted her hands from the large bowl in front of her. Dark, wet mud covered her fingers. "What do you say, Scarlett? Can we take him?"

Dustin darted toward the sliding glass door to the porch with me hot on his heels. Petunia scurried after us. She never could stay out of the action. Harmony brought up the rear, the big bowl of mud on her hip.

"Cut him off by the garden," Harmony yelled.

I veered toward Mom's raised garden bed. Dustin wouldn't dare step foot in there. Harmony went the other way. We had him cornered.

Dustin crouched low, looking like a pro wrestler waiting for his opponent's next move. His gaze darted back and forth between me and Harmony.

"You ready to go clean up the mess you made in the kitchen?" I asked, drawing his attention.

"Not even close."

Harmony scooped up a whole handful of mud and sent it sailing. It smacked into his cheek, a huge brown glob.

I hunched over, laughing at the sight of my big brother with a face full of mud.

"What was that for?" He stalked toward Harmony, the smile on his face belying the way he clenched and unclenched his fingers. It was on and Harmony stood in his direct line of fire.

"Us gals have to stick together." Harmony shrugged, lobbing another handful of mud his way.

He reached her, slinging an arm around her waist and dipping her into a low, deep kiss. The bowl Harmony had been holding tipped over and rolled away as she lifted her arms to wrap around Dustin's neck.

I caught my breath as the two of them caught each other. Not in the mood to watch two very much in love, horny, muddy peeps go at it in my mom's backyard, I picked up the bowl and headed back into the house.

If my moody, ornery older brother could find someone that made his hard heart soften again, maybe, just maybe, it wasn't too late for me.

Want a little bit more of Dustin & Harmony?

Click on the link below to snag an exclusive bonus scene and sign up for Dylann's newsletter!

Mud Pies & Family Ties Bonus Scene
(www.dylanncrush.com/mudpiesbonus)

Next up at the Lovebird Café...

Hot Fudge & a Heartthrob

We only have one thing in common...we're both excellent liars.

Scarlett

When Theo Wilder stops in at the Lovebird Café, looking for an experienced guide to show him around the deserted caves surrounding Swallow Springs, I seize the opportunity to get down and dirty with the heartthrob scientist. Rumor has it there's hidden treasure on our home-stead and I've been itching for a way to claim it. He doesn't need to know I have an ulterior motive or two...

Theo

Scarlett Jarrett doesn't seem like a typical cave enthusi-ast. But if I want to move up the ranks I need to find an edge and my best bet is letting the sassy, southern local help me get acquainted with the area. So what if I don't tell her exactly what might happen if I find what I'm after?

When Mother Nature fails to cooperate, we find ourselves short on luck and running out of time. We'll need to come clean with each other if we want to see the light of day. And in the process we might just find more than we're looking for.

Grab a copy of Hot Fudge & a Heartthrob today and get ready to laugh, cry, and fall in love with Scarlett, Dustin, and the rest of the folks at the Lovebird Café.

Keep reading for a sneak peek at Chapter One...

HOT FUDGE & A HEARTTHROB
CHAPTER 1

Theo

What doesn't kill us makes us stronger. I repeated the mantra for the hundredth time that morning as I faced down my current mortal enemy, also known as the front door of the Bat Conservationist Alliance. Granted, the door itself wasn't working against me, but behind the frosted glass, I was sure a torrent of hellfire and brimstone waited in the form of my self-righteous co-workers.

In no rush to sacrifice myself, I studied the thick black letters. In my past year of working at the Alliance, I'd never spent so much time standing in front of this door. If I had, I probably would have noticed how crooked the "V" in Conservationist was. Fighting the urge to peel the offensive adhesive letter off the glass and re-attach it, I took in a deep breath and wrapped my fingers around the handle. Before I could give a push, the door opened and I stumbled inside.

The sound of paper party horns assaulted my ears as a gruff hand clapped me on my shoulder. "Glad you're back." My dad, who also happened to be my current boss and the director of the Alliance, offered a somewhat apologetic smile.

A cascading rumble of deep laughter surrounded me. My co-workers had gone all out. If roles had been reversed and one of them was returning after a particularly embarrassing on-the-job ordeal, I probably would have done the same.

I shrugged off Dad's grasp and lifted my head to look around. Someone had suspended paper bats from the drop ceiling over my corner cubicle. A sign sat propped against my ancient desktop monitor: *Welcome back, Lunky.*

"Lunky?" I turned around, wondering who'd come up with my new moniker.

"Yeah, we thought it was fitting." Lewis, one of my co-workers, stepped forward. "Spelunker...Lunky. Get it, big guy?"

Shaking my head, I pulled my chair out from my desk. "Real clever."

"Come on, there's work to be done." Dad waved his hand in the air, causing my co-workers to scatter. Then he leaned closer, lowering his voice. "They're just having a little fun with you."

I nodded. "Yeah, I know."

"If you're serious about turning this into a career, you're going to have to get back down there and show them you can handle it. You're a Wilder for heaven's sake."

A Wilder. No shit. I'd been living in the shadow of Papa Wilder and Big Brother Wilder all my life. I'd even moved to Canada and played pro football in an effort to escape the incessant calling of carrying on the family name. Even though I tried to outrun my surname, I would always be a Wilder. I was done trying to avoid it. Even if I did have to start from the bottom and work my way up to earn my dad's approval.

I slid my laptop out of my bag and set it on my desk.

"How's the ankle?" Dad asked.

"Fine. Should be just like new in a few weeks." My ankle would heal—according to the doc it was just a sprain—but my pride might take quite a bit longer to knit itself back together.

"That's good. We missed you around here."

"I bet." The sarcasm leeched out before I could stop it.

"It's true. You're one of our most valuable employees." Dad rested his arms on the half-wall surrounding my cubicle.

"You sure you don't mean I *was* one of your most valuable?" I tried to joke. The injury to my ankle, and the huge hit to my ego, were the tip of the iceberg. My real struggle in getting my head back in the game had nothing to do with either.

Dad clapped me on the shoulder again. "You'll get your confidence back. This cause is in your blood."

In my blood. Like I'd ever be able to forget it. Dad was the one who'd started the Alliance over thirty years ago. "Thanks."

"Let me know if you need anything as you get settled."

"Will do." I waited for him to turn and head back to his office before I faced my computer. As it whirred to life I cast a glance over the notes I'd left on my desk. I hadn't been to the office in the past two weeks. As the Director of Communications and Outreach for the Alliance, I was used to spending a lot more time sitting at a desk than in the field where the "real" scientists worked.

Most of my co-workers, including my brother, had

earned their jobs at the Alliance by scouring caves and mines for the more than thirteen-hundred species of bats we worked to protect. Even though I had enough degrees to qualify me as one of them on paper, I didn't have anywhere near the same amount of time in the field—a fact I'd hoped to rectify when I volunteered to join them on an investigative trip to one of the caves we monitored in eastern Tennessee.

I knew coming back to the life I'd tried to leave behind wouldn't be a walk in the park, at least not until I battled back my inner demons. But I'd been enjoying myself up until the point where I'd had to shimmy through a tunnel to get to the back of a cavern. Though I hadn't played football in what felt like forever, I still had the build of a linebacker and somehow managed to wedge myself into the tunnel, cutting half of the group off from the other.

Thankfully I'd only suffered a sprained ankle when they'd finally tied a rope around my feet and managed to yank me back out the way I'd crawled in. After spending twelve hours stuck in a tube of cold, damp rocks, I knew I was in for at least a few weeks of ribbing. The paper bats and cardboard sign were just the beginning.

"So, how've you been?" Lewis's hair popped up over the wall that separated our desks, followed by the rest of his head. No matter how he tried to tame it, his hair always stood up on end like he'd just been spit out by a tornado. "Get caught up on your reading during your time away?"

I leaned back against my chair. "It's not like I was sitting around on my ass all day."

After they'd hauled me out of the tunnel and the local doc patched me up, I'd spent the next week driving myself around the back roads of southern Tennessee, visiting local libraries, conservation groups, and even Boy Scout troops in an effort to educate the public about the plight of the area's endangered bats.

Lewis grinned. "Good thing you didn't get too scratched up. Your dad needs your pretty face to bring in those donations and keep us afloat."

"Screw you." Lewis was always giving me a rough time about my desk job while he and the other guys worked in the field. One of these days I'd figure out a way to get back at him, although it would probably be a while before I was ready to wiggle through the caverns of eastern Tennessee.

"Hey, we all pitched in and got you something." He handed me a paper gift bag with a piece of tissue paper sticking out of it.

I reached in and pulled out a T-shirt. "Bat lovers let it all hang out?" A drawing of an upside down bat hung off the word 'out'.

"Yeah. Figured you could add it to your collection."

"Thanks." I spent my life in jeans and crazy ass T-shirts. Although, I had to be careful about which ones I chose to wear when I spoke at the schools on my route.

"Where you heading next?" Lewis asked.

"I'm not sure yet." I'd promised to finalize my travel schedule before the end of the week. Now that summer had turned to fall, kids were back in school and it was time to make the rounds and educate them about bats, especially how important it is not to disturb them during hibernation. I enjoyed talking to the kids but was ready to take on a bigger role, assuming I could handle it. Thanks to getting myself stuck in the cavern, I'd probably set myself back another few years.

"The team's heading to Arkansas next week to pitch in on a field study." Lewis gestured toward the paperwork on my desk. "I suppose you'll be tied up with school visits or you'd want to come along."

I held back a laugh. "Good one."

"I ever tell you about my first site visit?" He pushed his thick glasses back up onto his nose.

"Only about a million times. You trying to make me feel better about making an ass out of myself?" I groaned as I crossed my arms over my chest.

"I'm just saying, we all have our little fuck ups. You'll get past it. Your dad's just making you pay your dues right now. He'll probably have you leading your own team by next summer."

"We'll see about that." Lewis didn't know anything about my dad. If he did, he'd know that any accomplishment I ever made would always fall short compared to the efforts of my older brother. It didn't help that I had a natural knack for sabotaging myself in my efforts to impress him, either. "For now I've got to figure out how many days I need to take my dog and pony show on the road and cover all of the elementary schools in my region."

"Let me know if you need help planning your route."

Rolling my eyes, I turned my attention back to my computer. Asking for Lewis's help was the last thing I'd do. If I wanted to move up within the organization, I needed to figure out a way to get more traction for our group. That meant more eyes on our projects, and more opportunities to inform and educate the public on our mission.

I scrolled through the emails that had accumulated in my inbox. An alert I'd set up months ago caught my attention—one way I kept a close eye on any bit of regional news involving bats. As I clicked on the link, my pulse notched up. Seeing anything bat-related outside of a scientific journal was cause for concern, especially when it revolved around an endangered species like the Myotis sodalis, or the Indiana bat, as it was commonly known.

Based on the research the Alliance had been doing for the past several years, the number of Indiana bats was on the decline, especially in Missouri. Due to disturbances by development and people destroying their natural habitat, the colonies couldn't find space to live. The website popped up and music blared from my speakers. I slammed the cover of the computer down, but not before I caught the attention of everyone in the small office.

"Sorry about that."

"What'cha got there?" Lewis peered over my shoulder.

"Nothing. Just checking email."

"You want to grab a bite for lunch?" Lewis was a creature of habit and didn't stray from his typical tuna on wheat from the sandwich shop on the corner.

"Nah. I need to run an errand." I pushed back from my desk. "I'll be back in a bit."

Once I slid into the front seat of my truck, I pulled the email alert up on my phone. The screen filled with a video focusing on the narrow mouth of a cave. While I watched, a long line of bats began to stream from the opening. The camera flashed to a kid's face and I checked the tag at the bottom of the video. Filmed outside of Swallow Springs, Missouri, and just posted yesterday. It was hard to tell because of the grainy quality, but those could be Indiana bats and there were a ton of them.

Maybe it would be best to keep it to myself for a bit. I'd be heading to Missouri over the next couple of weeks when I made my rounds and could check it out before putting the rest of the team on high alert. Finding a new colony of Indiana bats might finally catch the eye of my dad.

As a tagalong on my dad's lifelong conservationist

efforts, I'd been all over Missouri, Kansas and the majority of the Midwest in his quest to save endangered species. But in all of my travels, I'd never heard of Swallow Springs. I opened a new window and searched for the name of the town. Not far from Nevada, Missouri, it sat in the southwest third of the state, an area well known for its limestone caves.

If I could discover a new colony of Indiana bats it might be worth the risk of finally facing my own bullshit. I could find someone local who knew the caves to take me in. The agency had been struggling for funding. A find like this might renew interest in their goals. It wouldn't hurt to drive over and take a look. I'd just schedule my route around the schools in that part of Missouri. The worst that could happen is that I'd waste a little time.

But if I found a new site for the endangered bats? It might just finally catapult me into my dad's inner circle…a place I'd been trying to get to for years.

Did you enjoy the first chapter? Snag your copy of Hot Fudge & a Heartthrob today!

Thanks for picking up this copy of *Mud Pies & Family Ties*! If you'd like to go back to where the series begins, grab your FREE copy of *Lemon Tarts & Stolen Hearts,* the prequel novella for the Lovebird Café series!

For a FREE copy of *Lemon Tarts & Stolen Hearts*, click here! (www.dylanncrush.com/signup)

ABOUT THE AUTHOR

USA Today bestselling author Dylann Crush writes sizzling contemporary romance that will make you laugh, cry, and fall in love. A romantic at heart, she loves her heroines spunky and her heroes super sexy. When she's not dreaming up steamy storylines, she can be found sipping a margarita and searching for the best Tex-Mex food in Minnesota.

Although she grew up in Texas, she currently lives in a suburb of Minneapolis/St. Paul with her unflappable husband, three energetic kids, a clumsy Great Dane, a lovable rescue mutt, and two very chill cats. She loves to connect with readers, other authors, and fans of tequila. You can find her at www.dylanncrush.com.

ACKNOWLEDGMENTS

Writing is such a solitary venture. I spend days, weeks, months typing away without knowing how my book will be received or if it will resonate with readers. So THANK YOU to all of the readers who have reached out to let me know they enjoyed one of my books or who have left a review. It makes a huge difference!

To my fellow authors who encourage me to keep going, even when the words don't want to come...especially the Romance Chicks (Christina Hovland, Jody Holford & Renee Ann Miller) and my Romance Happy Hour bestie, Dawn Luedecke.

And finally, to my family who continues to support this crazy dream of mine. Love you more. XOXO

ALSO BY DYLANN CRUSH

Holiday, Texas Series

All-American Cowboy

Cowboy Christmas Jubilee

Cowboy Charming

Lovebird Café Series

Lemon Tarts & Stolen Hearts

Sweet Tea & Second Chances

Mud Pies & Family Ties

Hot Fudge & a Heartthrob

Tying the Knot in Texas Series

The Cowboy Says I Do

Her Kind of Cowboy

Crazy About a Cowboy

Standalones

All I Wanna Do Is You

Getting Lucky In Love

Made in the USA
Columbia, SC
30 March 2025